FIELD ANOMALY

KAREN GRANT

RAVENOUS CRANE PUBLISHING • LOS ANGELES

FIELD ANOMALY

Author: Karen Grant
Cover and Book Design: Marty Safir, Double M Graphics

Published by
Ravenous Crane Publishing
9101 Louise Avenue
Northridge CA 91325

ISBN 978-0-9960791-0-5

9 8 7 6 5 4 3 2 1

To my family,
the center of my universe

FIELD ANOMALY

ALAINA'S NOTE TO READER:

The past is not a dead thing; it lives in the Record for anyone who can read it. A master reader can see inside the hearts and minds of the people she reads. I am a master reader of the Record. That's how I'm able to tell you the true story of Bethanne Amundson and the events that led to my family's disappearance.

ALAINA AMUNDSON

1

CATALYST

PART ONE: BETHANNE

Tuesday, May 22, Midnight. Central Daylight Time

Bethanne left the lights off as she ascended the stairs in the shadowless dark. She usually relaxed at night, able at last to release the strict hold on her energies, a hold that defined her waking life. Her house was safe. She had chosen this particular house because the man who built it 75 years before had been an electrician and had aligned each socket to allow a plug to enter only one way. Now, though, something was going on with the electricity—she could feel it—so she just shut off all the lights once her children had gone to bed.

As she was passing her daughter's bedroom, Claire's voice disrupted the silence. "Mom? You going to bed now?"

"Yes, honey. How about you? Ready to call it a day?"

Claire watched her mother's silhouette soften the doorway as she entered. "I don't know," she answered. "I guess so. There's nothing else to do; my eyes are too tired to read anymore."

"So you're just laying here?"

"Yeah, just thinking about things."

"Anything I can do?" Bethanne asked. She sat down, her hand searching out Claire's.

Claire's fingers folded into her mother's. "No. I don't even know what I was thinking about really. I guess everything. Why do you stay up so late all the time?"

Bethanne longed to tell her daughter; she longed to tell anyone. "I like nighttime, I guess," she replied, the thinnest veil of truth she could offer. "I'm going to bed now, though." She squeezed Claire's hand and let go. Leaning over, she kissed her cheek and stood up. "Try to get to sleep," she said. "Do the relaxation exercise, ok?"

Claire smiled. Meditation was her mother's answer to everything. "Sure, Mom," she said. "G'night."

Bethanne heard the smile in Claire's answer and smiled too. "Goodnight, baby. I love you."

"I love you too, Mom."

Claire watched her mother's dark form disappear. She felt herself let go of the turmoil in her head. Claire let herself imagine the beach she'd once visited on a family trip to the Gulf coast. The water was turquoise and the sand was as soft and white as flour. The imagined sound of the tranquil surf soothed her toward sleep.

Bethanne continued down the hallway. *She's not a child anymore.* Claire, now 16, would be a junior in the fall. Unbelievable. She passed Scott's door, pausing to hear his steady breathing. Scott, too, was growing up fast. Though he'd just turned 14, he was already as tall as she. Soon he would reach his dad's height and then some. David would like that.

Bethanne entered the upstairs bathroom and felt for her toothbrush. She brushed her teeth in the dark, her face in the mirror an illusionist's trick conjured by the full moon rising above the window frame. Here was the truth, frozen in the desperate eyes of her own ghostly reflection. *Why me?*

She bent over the sink to spit, breaking the spell, then picked up her hairbrush and pulled it through her russet colored hair as she walked into her bedroom. *I need another haircut.* She placed the brush on her dresser and lit the rose candle before turning to face the small altar adorning the east wall of her bedroom. She was scared. Soon even Iowa City wouldn't be safe. She knew too much. She sat cross-legged on the rag rug that humbled the hardwood floor of her room; her grandmother and great-aunts had made it for her mother, and Bethanne got it when her mother died. The spiral of rags grounded her, gave sense to her place in the universe.

She began to breathe consciously, removing all the day's stresses, focusing on each breath drawn and released. She watched her day backwards, observing herself back out of her room, unbrush her hair and teeth, stop by Scott's room, and so on, seeking perspective on her comings and goings, her emotions, her perceptions. Years ago, when she first began using this exercise, she would attach herself to every passing thought, enslaving herself to each one until, eventually, she would nod off before her backwards reverie had reached the evening meal. But now she was no longer the slave; she was the master, easily guiding herself back to her first morning thought, her waking moment, thereby clearing the way for whatever would appear from the other side once she went to bed and fell asleep. Something always appeared.

PART TWO: JACK

3:15 a.m. Eastern Daylight Time

Jack Stevenson hurried up John St. heading for Nassau and Fulton Center. He was alone as far as he could tell. New York City was lit up from the street level to the top floors of the Trade Center more than 1000 feet above him, thus obscuring the night's full moon. Hints of darkness between the blaze of neon and storefront could have tipped him off to threats uninhibited by the cameras, but Jack was preoccupied. *God damn it. Why did I stay so long at the damned office? Stupid; pathetic. For what?* It didn't even matter because everyone else on the crew was still there. They'd probably be there when the sun came up. And when the final proposal was signed, Jack's name wouldn't be on it because he wasn't there. He'd been at Colsun's for ten years, but loyalty meant nothing these days. In fact, if you stayed anywhere for more than a couple years, you were a loser. And now he'd get maybe, what, four hours sleep before the party. He could've stayed and caught a train home at 7:00. *Damn Tess and her Breakfast Birthdays.* As if his coming home for Alek's birthday would make them a family again. Jack wasn't even sure which birthday this was. *Eleven? Twelve?*

When was the last time he'd even seen Alek? Alek stayed in his room. Hell, they all stayed in their rooms with their computers and vids and realtimes and whatever else they had to facilitate communication with everyone they didn't actually live with. Jack felt harassed and guilty at the same time. He knew he hadn't tried. As he turned another corner and continued walking, something in the atmosphere shifted; something wasn't right. He stopped. *What the hell? What am hell am I doing on Dutch? Perfect.*

Lance was waiting. He didn't know that's what he was doing, but when Jack appeared, fuming his way down the street, Lance knew. He'd been hanging out with his muse playing CG music that stimulated a high energy response. Comgen's initial computer generated music was ancient history, and Koenig's compositions from the early 1970s were unremembered. Personal binaural brainwave tech had been introduced—inadequately—by iDozer in 2000 something, also unremembered. The muse was the next step. If used correctly, it promised you could dial a mood just like Rick Deckard, but most people didn't buy into it. The dispossessed, however, had discovered an unintended function, and that became it's most frequent use. Certain settings gave you some serious bang for your buck. These settings were subsequently blocked and any attempt to access them was illegal. Lance's setting was illegal.

Jack's eyes narrowed when he saw Lance. This guy did not look good; he was wearing a skin tight, shiny gold shirt that hugged his skeletal torso until it met his shiny silver stretch pants tucked into black boots. His tinfoil Zorro mask completed the ensemble. He whipped around the sidewalk like lightning accumulating amperage, looking for a place to strike. *No, not good at all.*

"Hey," Lance shouted, going rigid.

Jack looked over his shoulder gauging distances. He took a few steps back toward the corner.

"Hey, I said. Whatsa matter; can't you talk?" Lance vibrated toward him.

"I can talk," Jack remarked.

"Cool. Good for you. Whatcha doin' here?"

"Excuse me," Jack said. He attempted to move away from Lance.

Lance, however, wasn't finished yet. Not by a long shot.

"I asked you a question," he snarled, moving to block Jack. "What are you doing here?" he asked, menacing each syllable. "This is my street."

"What do you mean your street? Your name's Dutch?" Jack looked into Lance's eyes. Lance was standing still, but his eyes were whirling. *Good move, Jack. This guy is nuts.* "Look," Jack explained, "I'm just trying to get home; I took a wrong turn. I'm sorry I disturbed you. You just go back to what you were doing, and I'll be on my way." He backed up a few more steps. "Catch you later."

"I'll catch you now," grinned Lance. He lunged toward Jack, leaping onto his back and pulling him down to the sidewalk. Lance was strong, primed by his tech combo that continued to play as he gripped Jack's perfect hair in his silver-gloved hands and repeatedly slammed his head into the sidewalk keeping time. Jack's life ended before the song did. Lance didn't notice.

When the song was over, Lance got up and looked at his vid. 3:30. He was spent and trembling. What now? He needed to relax. He dialed the desired mood into his muse and closed his eyes to better hear the first tones insinuate themselves into his psyche. *Nice.* He strolled away toward the light.

INTERLUDE

2:30 a.m. CDT

Bethanne woke up and looked at the clock. 2:30. *Great.* She felt a strong disturbance in the field. *I wonder what happened?* She lit the candle on her bedside table and let its dim halo inspire the passionless blue moonlight. She walked soundlessly out of her room and down the hall until she stood once again at Claire's open doorway. She remembered when Claire was just a baby, weeks old, still sleeping with she and David. One night, the baby woke up crying, inconsolable. Bethanne changed her, fed her, bounced her; nothing worked. David walked around with her too, but she kept crying until he left the room and started down the hallway in their old Garfield Place apartment in Brooklyn. The baby stopped crying abruptly and fell asleep on David's shoulder. When, a month later, the baby woke in the same distress, Bethanne was too exhausted to get up and David wasn't home to help. She reached over and pulled down the shade to extinguish the moonlight and maybe her headache along with it. Claire quieted immediately. So, it was moonlight. Weird. Bethanne never bothered to test the effects of the full moon on her second child; she just shielded them both from it while they slept. She kept track of the moon's cycle after that and gradually widened her interest to include the constellations and then astronomy and then astrology. She acquired more esoteric knowledge, realizing almost immediately that she had a gift.

It is beginning. This chilling realization pulled her out of her reverie and back into real time. *What am I going to do?* She steadied her breathing and calmed herself. With an indulgent smile, she pushed away from the doorframe. Did she think by standing in front of Claire's bedroom door she could keep her daughter safe? She could stop time? She went back to bed and blew out the candle. *Let it come.*

PART THREE: JEFF

12:30 a.m. Pacific Daylight Time

Jeff glanced at the corner of the screen. *Half past midnight already? 3:30 New York.* Might as well go to bed; he was tired, and even Delamater would be sleeping at 3:30. He went out onto the back deck. "Linux," he called. "Hey, Linux; time for bed!" *Great.* "Ok, man, I'm closing the door. You'll be out here 'till morning!" Jeff made exaggerated steps back across the deck toward the sliding glass doors into his living room. Nothing.

Jeff lived on a dirt road near the loop at the bottom of Wolfback Ridge Road on the backside of Sausalito. His multi-level wood house was surrounded by the tall trees that eventually led to the giant redwoods of Muir Woods. His best friend, Morgan Davis, had a place at the end of Laurel Lane on the other side of the ridge that afforded him a view of the town and bay, but Jeff preferred the isolation of his place. He could go weeks without seeing anyone if he wanted to. Anyone but his dog, that is. "Linux! I'm serious. Get in here right now!" Still nothing. *Must've dug another hole.* He took the flashlight off its hook on the rail and began his examination of the fenced perimeter. *There.* At the southwest corner of the yard, Jeff found the hole Linux had dug. He sighed and picked up the shoes he'd left outside the door and sat down on the steps to put them on.

Morgan had given him Linux, a yellow lab, as a puppy three

years ago. Jeff had never owned a pet, even as a child, so he had been unprepared for the affection he felt as soon as he held the throbbing pup. Now Jeff's love for the dog was full-blown and deep. *Hope it's a possum and not a skunk this time.* He grimaced remembering the hydrogen peroxide bath he'd had to administer after Linux's last tunnel to freedom. After securing the gate behind him, he aimed his flashlight up the only trail into the forested hillside behind his house and began his search.

Suddenly, from far up the hillside, Linux barked. A low-pitched whistle immediately followed. Every primal hair on Jeff's body responded. In quick succession, he heard two more whistles. *Not a skunk, a mountain lion.* Jeff tore up the incline, shouting, following the crashing direction of the chase. A panicked yelp preceded a guttural snarl. Jeff cried out as he stumbled away from the path and toward the last sound. Now all he could hear were the impossibly low *ahs* interrupted by the chilling hisses of a large cat mumbling above its prey. Jeff pictured Linux, his neck grasped in the lion's jaws, and felt impassioned fury burst from his chest into his limbs. He grabbed a thick stick and charged forward.

He finally saw the lion under a tree about fifty feet away. It looked up at him, its yellow-green eyes alert and challenging. Opening its jaws, the cat let Linux drop to lay unmoving at its feet. Jeff and the cat stood facing each other in silent consideration. Abruptly, Jeff shook his head and aimed the flashlight directly into the cat's face. He let loose a fierce howl and rushed toward it, his stick raised. The cat leapt with flawless grace into the nearest tree and glided high into the dense branches as Jeff stopped helpless beneath.

Linux is dead. Jeff moved toward his dog and dropped to his knees, placing his hand on Linux's inert body. He knew the cat was watching and that he was vulnerable kneeling as he was over his dog, but he didn't care. He lowered his head briefly onto Linux's chest and let the short, blond fur bristle his cheek.

Moments later, he reached a sufficient internal resolve and stood up. He looked down at his beloved dog. *Linux—you were a great friend.* "You can't have him, you piece of shit," he yelled toward the cat, hoisting his dead companion across his shoulders. He knew the cat wouldn't follow him; mountain lions tire quickly and if challenged, they do not defend their territory. *Chicken shit, really.* Jeff trudged away, grateful for the weight of his dog, his penance for an inadequate fence.

He found the trail and began his journey back home, his flashlight off now that the full moon had risen. Something about the cat bothered him. It was more than the simple fact that it should have been content with all the deer, its natural prey, out here. It was more than the terrible fact that it had killed his beloved friend. It was something about the way the cat had looked at him. Though Jeff had never encountered a predator face-to-face in the wild before, the look the cat gave him was familiar, which made no sense at all.

Jeff placed Linux on the porch, got a blanket from the footlocker under the stairs and covered the dog's body. Without another glance, he walked straight to his room, undressed, and took a long shower. *The world is shit.* He finished and toweled off before climbing naked into bed. He hit the universal remote that put all the tech in the house to sleep. He'd call Morgan tomorrow, but for now he just wanted to be unconscious, and he didn't want to use his muse if he could help it. Ironically, though he had created many of the tech marvels used in everyday life, Jeff wanted to live without relying on them. He concentrated on his breathing as the yoga teacher at Berkeley had taught him years ago and gradually he relaxed into a light sleep that would keep his mind off Linux for the next four hours.

2

DAYLIGHT

Still Tuesday, 6:30 a.m. CDT

Bethanne woke to the frantic chirping of the newly hatched chickadees in the large elm outside her bedroom window. She lay still. They were perfect; their demands sparkling the early morning air like dewdrops. She lifted the cotton sheet and let it billow the cool morning air onto her slender body as it complied reluctantly to gravity. *Time to get up.* In the bathroom, she re-encountered her reflection as she brushed her teeth, marveling how sunlight always rallied her to the day's tasks erasing the fears of the night. She took a brisk shower and dressed in her uniform—jeans and a collared shirt—the perfect camouflage. She did not wear make-up. She finished and walked back into her room, picking up the brush where she'd left it the night before. *Really, really need a haircut.* She sat again on the rug and let her eyes rest on the objects she had chosen for her altar: her grandmother's thimble; the Ukrainian Easter egg she'd painted years ago; the Mammillaria herrerae, a small cactus she'd fallen in love with when she'd first seen its bright pink flowers beside a highway in Arizona; and the geode she'd cut in half herself at the rock shop in Florissant, Colorado. *Mineral, plant, animal; all you need for metaphor.* She closed her eyes and went back to the tide pool she'd found on Pismo Beach with Scott when he was just four years old. While they waited for a large group of tourists to ascend the steep stairs hugging the cliff face, she and Scott watched an innocuous puddle of seawater come to life. Here was a small, black fish darting from pebble to pebble; there, a tiny crab scooting a pebble up a rock. Suddenly, she and Scott were transported into this silent, miniature world while the magnificent surf crashed unnoticed on the rocks just yards away. Bethanne always found her faith in this place. As she breathed in and out, the scene faded and geometric images appeared before her mind's eye. They made no sense, but as she passively watched them coalesce and disappear, her head cleared. As soon as each cell in her body breathed a rich breath, when she felt buoyed and full of life, she remembered her dream: she would ask her physiology professor a question.

The teacher, Dr. Theodore Marks, had become increasingly dissatisfied with this course. He was bothered by a conflict between the prevailing thought of the day and what he was seeing phenomenologically; it didn't make sense. His nature, however, did not allow him to confront the hierarchies of his field; he was considering an early retirement instead. Bethanne needed to ask her question this morning, a week before finals; the last day of regular classes. He could consider her question now and still present the final.

Bethanne took one or two courses every semester while she worked at the south circulation desk in the main library at the University of Iowa. She kept a mild profile in a relatively easy job that allowed her to meet almost everyone at the school. She made sure that she earned a B in each class she took. She was a nice lady; easy to overlook. She seemed normal. Bethanne, however, was not normal, and every day she stayed under the radar was testament to the powerful grip she held on her electromagnetic presence.

Done. She opened her eyes and stood up stretching her arms

overhead. *Let the day begin!* She walked out of her room and called out to her children on her way down the hall. "Up and at 'em! Rise and shine!" The sound of her own mother's voice played in undertones with hers. Same words, decades later. She went straight to the kitchen and took some fresh strawberries out of the refrigerator and set out the granola. Soon Scott would appear for breakfast followed by an unenthusiastic Claire who, relentlessly, resented having to get up every single morning—even now at the end of the school year. Bethanne was excited about her day. Dr. Marks had important work to do; he needed to get started.

"Hey, Mom," Scott said cheerfully.

"Hi, honey. How'd you sleep?"

"Okay. Are you working today?"

"I am indeed. I have a class this morning and library 'til 7," Bethanne answered. "Oh, I just remembered, I told Donna I'd go out to dinner with her after work. It's Claire's turn to make dinner anyway, so you guys are on your own."

"Cool." Scott put a few strawberries on top of his granola before pouring milk into the bowl. "Do we have any mulberries?"

"If you'll recall," Bethanne smiled, "You and Steve ate most of them before you got back here."

Scott looked up and grinned. "Yeah, sorry about that." He and Steve had been picking mulberries from the same small stand of trees since they were little. As the years passed, fewer and fewer berries survived the trip home.

Claire surveyed the room before entering; she saw that Scott was almost finished eating. "I'm going to be so glad when this week's over. I hate getting up in the morning," she complained collapsing into her chair.

"Only four more days, Claire," Scott reminded her. "You can do it!"

"I know I *can* do it; I just don't *want* to do it."

"Well, you don't have a choice," Bethanne remarked. Claire's complaining annoyed Bethanne. This girl had no idea how easy her life was. How do you teach that? "Now, get busy with breakfast; the bus will be here soon."

The two siblings finished breakfast and cleared the table while Bethanne put the last items into their lunch bags. Though they all left for school at the same time, they parted company at the bus stop; Bethanne could walk to school because they lived on East Jefferson, only a few blocks from the university library. Bethanne had time to enjoy the spring morning and still arrive by 9:00 for Dr. Marks' class.

3

FENCING

Still Tuesday, 8:00 a.m. PDT

Jeff was startled awake by the emptiness of his house. *Damn.* He closed his eyes and took a few deep breaths choking back the lump lodged in his throat. *God damn it.* He regained control, scrabbled his sheets with his feet until he was free and got out of bed. He checked his vidcom. *I'm burying the dog after breakfast. Screw you, Delamater.* He brushed his teeth and went into the kitchen. He pressed the link for breakfast and chose a smoothie then tapped the touchscreen point for Morgan.

"What do you want?" Morgan answered on the first ring.

"What do you want?" Jeff replied, the rote response of a conversational formula dating back to high school.

"Hey, you don't sound so good," Morgan observed.

"I'm not. A mountain lion got Linux last night; he's dead."

Morgan didn't respond. *Oh, man.* The silence stretched out giving meaning to Jeff's loss. Finally, Morgan said, "I'm sorry, man. You must feel like shit."

"I do."

"Did you find the lion?"

"Yeah, but it got up a tree. I didn't have anything to kill it with anyway. I'm not sure I would have—it's not like this isn't its territory."

"True, but you'd think with all the black-tail over there, it would leave dogs alone."

"Guess not. Anyway, I've got to bury Linux and fix the fence. You want to help?"

"Sure," Morgan said. "You need anything from Waterstreet?"

"No, I've got tons of shit on hand for digging graves... Sorry. Um, thanks anyway."

"No problem, man. I'll just grab some breakfast and head over."

"Cool." Jeff hung up and saw that Delamater had called again. *What a pain in the ass.* Jeff walked to the counter and picked up the smoothie the kitchenbot had prepared and returned to his main monitor. *Might as well get this over with.*

"Did you have a nice sleep?" Delamater inquired from the screen. Paul Delamater was excessively handsome. With a brilliant smile adorning his perfectly balanced face, his green eyes sparkling with intelligence and humor, he was used to people wishing to be close to him. Jeff had to fight off the impulse toward camaraderie.

"What's that supposed to mean?"

"Nothing." Delamater's smile disappeared. "I've been trying to reach you for the last half hour."

"Wow. A half hour." Jeff checked his record. *A repetition set at 60-second intervals. No wonder it felt like a long wait for Delamater.* "What can I do for you?"

"There's been a murder. Looks random. Guy's head beat to a pulp on Dutch near John St. 3:30 this morning. Murderer walked away."

"Okay. That sucks. What's it got to do with me?"

"The tech didn't identify the perp. Come on, Jeff. You know your tech is supposed to keep this from happening. The perp's still at large. So what happened?"

"How the hell should I know? I'll run it through and see what comes up."

"Yeah, you do that. And after you figure out what happened, figure out how to fix it."

"So did you get the id of the guy yet?"

"Yeah, half an hour ago. It took us six hours for a possid because he was disguised and he'd jacked up his implant. The cameras around John St. caught it all and we got some stuff from the victim's implant, but then the perp, name of Lance Bolton, disappeared."

"Shit."

"Right. I need this fixed, Jeff."

"Delamater, hold on. I haven't even toyed with a new refinement. This could take some time … and money."

"Yeah, yeah. I know the drill. I ask for it, you make it, I overpay for it, you stay anonymous, and I get credit for saving the world. It works every time. We can do this, Jeff."

"I know. All for a good cause." Jeff cut the link. He finished the last few swallows of the smoothie and set it aside for the kitchenbot. Delamater pissed him off. Both Delamater, the east coast police commissioner, and Derek Burns, the west coast commissioner, were trying to eliminate crime in America, but Delamater wanted all the credit. Which was fine except he also wanted to crush Derek Burns. Jeff didn't get it. The tech he had developed was used on both coasts; in fact, his tech was used the world over, which had made both he and Paul Delamater very wealthy men. Still, the goal was to eliminate crime wasn't it? So why the competition? *Whatever.* Delamater had hired him, so as long as he got paid, he didn't need to understand every single nuance of his boss's mind. He was reassured by the fact that Paul Delamater's basic philosophy was simple: one crime is one crime too many. Delamater believed he would rid the whole world of criminals by being able to see every movement of every person every minute of every day and then, by iding everyone who lived in the world, he would know who he was watching... starting with the United States.

Furthermore, Delamater was a consummate salesman in an open market. The average American citizen was more than ready to give up freedom for safety, and that fact, coupled with everybody's insatiable desire to be famous—or at least recognizable on screen—made Jeff's increasingly intrusive tech easy to embrace. Yet, the citizens had drawn the line at drones. Domestic drone surveillance had been one step too far. Didn't really matter though. It had soon become clear that it wasn't the eyes that failed, it was the identifying tech, and drones wouldn't solve the iding problem; neither would satellites. What Delamater needed was universal iding, and that's what the implants were for.

Morgan stood in the doorway watching his best friend at his monitor. Jeff, his tall, muscular frame hunched over the vidscreen, looked outdistanced by his own thoughts charging up neural pathways no one else even had. Morgan placed his hand on the door's id panel. He and Jeff had been friends for a long time. Jeff was only ten when he joined the ninth grade class; it had been a big deal—covered by the local news. Size wise, he was about average for his age but that was small for ninth grade. His pre-adolescent body coupled by his massive intellect made Jeff the victim of almost every clique at school. Even the nerds shunned him. Physically, Morgan was his exact opposite. He was tall and athletic, destined to be a hero on this year's basketball team even though he was just a freshman. Morgan was also every girl's secret or not-so-secret crush, the archetype of health and beauty with his milk chocolaty skin and closely cropped fro. But as popular as Morgan quickly became, he always included Jeff. By junior year, they'd go to parties together and watch the other kids get wasted, laughing at the ensuing mayhem, but always staying sober themselves. Jeff had grasped early on the intricate balances of the chemical and electrical systems of the brain—no way was he going to mess with that. Morgan had his own reasons. Cliché, really. His dad had chosen his addictions over everything else in his life. When Morgan was old enough to figure it out, he promised his mother he would never do that. He kept his promise.

The door clicked open as soon as Morgan touched it, recognizing him as the only person besides Jeff allowed inside the house. Morgan stepped into the room and grinned briefly; he was always amused by the contradiction between the condition of Jeff's room at school—parts of half-completed tech, open books laying everywhere, dirty clothes carpeting the floor—and his house now: over four thousand square feet of meticulous order. Morgan recalled his mother's household harangues. "This bed's not going to make itself." Well, now it did; housebots made the beds and kitchenbots prepared the food. Every household that had had a vacuum cleaner and a dishwasher at the turn of the century now had the requisite bots.

"Hey," Morgan murmured, sobering instantly as he walked toward Jeff whose eyes ricocheted back to the screen as soon as they'd met Morgan's.

"Yeah, hey." The lump reappeared in Jeff's throat. He blinked to get rid of the excess moisture in his eyes before pushing back his chair. *Later, Delamater.* He got up and glanced sideways at Morgan as he walked around him toward the back porch. "Let's take care of Linux first, then we can tackle the fence."

"Sure," Morgan replied. *I'm with you, buddy.* Morgan glanced down at the blanketed mound on the porch then followed Jeff's eyes out to the fence. It was a strong fence. The cedar posts were only ten feet apart and Jeff had used 12-gauge, high quality wire. "So, what's the plan?" Morgan asked.

"I want Linux out under the white mulberry over there," Jeff pointed. "Then, I want to extend the depth of the fence wire to the bottom of the posts another foot. That damn dog could really dig a hole. We'll need to dig a trench under the entire perimeter of the fence." Jeff looked back at Morgan. "No problem, right?"

Morgan didn't question Jeff's need to fix a fence for a dog he no longer had. "Yeah, no problem. What else would I be doing on a beautiful day in May?"

"Nothing that would actually justify your existence," Jeff retorted.

Morgan glanced sideways at him and Jeff shot him a rueful smile. It was going to be a long morning.

4

BIRTHDAY

Still Tuesday, 9:00 a.m. EDT

Tess Stevenson woke up alone. Again. *Jack, you asshole.* Her bedbot reminded her that it was *Alek's Breakfast Birthday* this morning. She hoped the kitchenbots had remembered, though of course they had. When she finished dressing and styling, she entered the kitchen and found the breakfast table piled high with strawberry crepes, eggs, Taylor's ham, and orange juice. She tapped the screen's recorder, and the camera followed her progress down the hallway as she sang *Happy Birthday* to Alek. The camera blinked off to allow Tess to wake Alek, remind him of the day, and let him know that his dad was once again a no-show. When the camera switched back on, Alek pretended to be asleep. He slowly opened his eyes and smiled. "Hi, Mom," he said. "How are you this morning?"

"Oh, I'm wonderful, darling," Tess enthused. "Happy Birthday! Come to breakfast."

"Gee, Mom, my birthday breakfast? That's awesome." Alek got up and followed his mother out to the burdened table. "This is amazing! All my favorite food!"

"I know, dear. What else—it's your Birthday Breakfast!"

"This is going to be the best birthday ever," Alek said, his eyes widening with gratitude. "I'm going to go get Matt." Matt's room was down the hall from Alek's. Matt was almost seventeen and always angry. Alek had no idea if Matt would play along with the birthday charade or not. "Matt, hey; it's my birthday today and the tapes are rolling."

Matt looked like he hadn't gone to bed at all. His eyes, red and blurred, met Alek's and stayed there. "You're joking, right?" he asked. "When is she going to stop this bullshit?"

"Just come on," Alek needled. "I did it for you when *you* turned 12."

Matt despised both his parents. These ridiculous family films were just one more piece of evidence that their whole lives were fake. *Total BS.*

Alek moved further into the room. "Matt, come on. I just want to eat breakfast; it looks incredible. Mom's nuts. We both know it. If you don't come out, we won't eat. Can't we just do it and get it over with?"

Matt looked up at his brother's pleading face. *Shit.* "Okay. Is Dad already out there?"

Alek looked down at the floor.

"Oh, man. Tell me he's home!" Matt shouted. "He didn't come home for your birthday? I'm going to kill that mother—"

"Matt, don't. I don't even want him here, okay? Please, just be happy."

Matt looked at his little brother. It wasn't Alek's fault things were so effed up. Besides, he was hungry too. "Okay. I'm happy. Let's go."

They walked out of the room and smiled into the kitchen camera over Tess's shoulder. All of their friends and relatives—and the whole planet for that matter—would see the happy, well-adjusted family celebrating the youngest son's birthday together. Naturally,

Tess would insert Jack before posting it. These days, everyone enhanced their life postings to the vid, and then, they all collectively, tacitly agreed to ignore that fact. Memories of true events got blurred almost immediately as the transfigured versions became the only versions.

After breakfast, the boys went back into their rooms and Tess completed the posting. As she prepared to send it out, she noticed a small red circle pulsing in the lower right hand corner of the screen. She'd never seen that before. She tapped it. The screen cleared, then lit up with the chiseled face of a police officer behind a metal desk. His name, Sgt. Baker, marched across the bottom of the screen along with his precinct number. "Mrs. Stevenson, one moment please for Commissioner Delamater."

What's going on?

"Mrs. Stevenson," intoned the gorgeous man now onscreen. "I'm Paul Delamater, East Coast Commissioner. I'm sorry to bother you this morning, but I'm afraid I have some bad news."

She recognized Delamater's face, of course. Everyone knew him; he was a worldwide celebrity that New Yorkers proudly claimed as their own. And here he was, saying her name on her vidscreen. After the shock of recognition, Tess's thoughts returned to herself. *Ok, deep breath. Right. I look fine; in fact, I look better than fine. Thank you, Alek! Perfect day for a birthday.* She realized that Delamater expected something from her. She composed her face accordingly. "What's wrong?" Tess asked, looking appropriately alarmed.

"I hate to be the bearer of bad tidings, Mrs. Stevenson, and I hope someday soon I will never need to make a call like this again; however, in spite of all that I have done to make this great nation safe, your husband was found dead this morning on Dutch Street."

"What do you mean dead? How can he be dead?"

The moment became real.

"Ma'am?"

"I mean, how can he be dead? Are you sure it's him. What would he be doing out late at night? Nothing, that's what. You've made a mistake. Did you call his office? That's where he lives, not here."

"Mrs. Stevenson, I know you're upset, but you must realize we've made the proper id. That's irrefutable. We would like to talk to you down here at the station. As soon as you tapped us, we sent a car. It should arrive in less than three minutes. Please be ready."

Tess didn't like to leave the apartment—ever—but the chance to meet Delamater was enticing. "Will I be meeting with you?"

Delamater smiled his stock accommodating smile. "Well, no, I'm not available myself, but Sgt. Baker will be available to you from the moment you arrive."

Tess absorbed this information reluctantly. If she wasn't going to meet Delamater, why would she go?

"Well, thanks anyway, but I don't want to come down to the station. I've got things to do. What would I do there anyway? Why do you want me there?"

"Well, ma'am, usually the family wants to see the body of their loved one one last time before cremation. The family usually decides then what to do with the ashes."

"Really. Now we'll want to see him? I don't think so. And as far as I'm concerned, you can take care of the ashes."

"Fine, Mrs. Stevenson." Delamater instantly recalled the car with a tap on his screen before continuing. "We will extract his implant and deactivate it. His account is registered with Beaman and Smith, who will execute his will and update your implant immediately. This conversation will be logged and filed in current docs for 30 days. We will bill your account for cremation and removal of the ashes."

"I owe you? Aren't the streets supposed to be safe now? What if I go media on you?"

Perfect. He would be able to count on her if the time came to make his new tech public, but that time wasn't now. Regardless, it was clear that she didn't give a rat's ass for her husband. "Mrs. Stevenson, I'm sure you'll do whatever you feel is necessary. I'm sorry for your loss." He touched the screen again as he smiled his parting smile.

Tess flicked the touchpoint with disgust. *Nice work, Jack. Now Alek will remember his birthday as the day you died.* She shrugged and tapped the pharmacy point on the screen. By the time she walked back to her room, the secobarb was sitting next to a glass of fresh water. Since the boys were already in their rooms working on the last week of compuclasses before the summer break, she decided she'd tell them later. No use spoiling their whole day. Besides, it wasn't as if they'd notice Jack was gone.

Delamater shook his head when the screen went black. *Harsh. Well, maybe Jack Stevenson deserved it.* He sent the conversation file to his secretary, the first step in the regimented process that deleted a citizen from occupancy status. But Jack Stevenson wouldn't be forgotten; Delamater would use his death for the next stage of his surveillance plan that would finally rescue mankind from itself. Jack's death would have the added advantage of shutting up that crazy bitch civil rights lawyer, too. Lakia and her pathetic collection of anti-tech, right-to-privacy liberals were the ones responsible for killing the drone program and challenging the implant law. If his boy Jeff could fix the implant problem, the web would be impermeable and crime would be obsolete because no one would be able to get away with it.

A few hours later, Sgt. Baker confirmed acquisition of Lance's implant. Lance had reappeared, mask and all, to eat a hotdog from a street vendor; the cameranet sourced his id in less than a second. A lone officer had approached Lance, nodded a greeting, and focused his emp. The emp sent an electromagnetic pulse directly to Lance's central nervous system; it was set to paralyze his limbs. Lance fell and was cuffed by the policebots accompanying the officer. They threw him into the police car and, as soon as he was delivered to the station, his implant was removed. The techies would figure out how it had been disabled, and Delamater would inform Jeff because, no matter what Jeff developed next, he would need to deal with the implant issue.

5

QUESTION

Still Tuesday, 10:00 a.m. CDT

Bethanne was never the first to arrive in class. She never sat at the front or in the back of the room. She was careful to time her questions toward the end of the semester. Her first semester at Iowa was fraught with missteps; the worst was in her evolutionary biology class that year. Shortly after school began, she had asked her professor why the ideas of Darwin and not Kropotkin had flourished in the west when clearly Kropotkin's ideas of mutual aid as the contributing factor in species selection were as elegant as Darwin's survival of the fittest. It had been a long time since Serena Lambert had considered Kropotkin. She had stared down at Bethanne, opened her mouth to speak, and closed it again. Twice. Then she had dismissed the class while she packed up her things and left the stage. Lambert came back to teach the next day, but as the semester went on, she became more and more distracted. Bethanne worked hard to restore the professor's equilibrium, but she knew she could not interfere further with Lambert's freedom. The students began to complain about Lambert's lack of conviction in Darwin's theory, which was becoming more apparent with each passing day. Finally, the semester ended and Serena Lambert took a sabbatical. Bethanne was exhausted, but she had learned an important lesson—she had learned to wait. She had also learned to become invisible; Lambert had sought her out several times after Bethanne had asked her question, and she had had to play dumb— an error on the third step, Right Speech, of the eightfold path. It wasn't, however, a desire to be left alone or a lack of courage that gave rise to Bethanne's desire to trivialize her part in asking these seminal questions, it was an imperative. Bethanne had to remain anonymous to continue her work.

Dr. Theodore Marks entered the classroom at precisely 9:00. The computer recognized him and lit up the large screen behind the podium. "We have now examined all the organs of the body and how they work individually and as part of the physiology of the human being. As we begin this summary prior to the final, I will take questions by raised hands." Iowa City was one of the few universities left in the Midwest that used live professors and real books, which was why Marks had chosen to teach here rather than synch his lessons over computerized learning games for the so-called schools in the cities near either coast.

The students asked the questions Marks was expecting; questions they assumed would be on the final. He finally called on Bethanne. "Ms. Amundson," he said, glancing down at his class list to make sure he had it right. He always seemed to forget this woman's name.

"Thank you, Dr. Marks. I was looking at J. L. Bremer's historic films of early embryonic blood circulation and noticed that the blood seemed to be self-propelled before the heart was actually functioning. Bremer's notes reveal that he was impressed with the spiraling motion of the blood, but it seems he overlooked the fact that what he was seeing kind of ruined the whole pressure propulsion idea of the heart. Maybe I misinterpreted what I was seeing, so, I guess my question is, does blood have its own momentum separate from the heart or is it inert?"

Dr. Marks blinked a few times then closed his eyes. Bethanne closed her eyes, too, while she sent her energies out in a stream that washed over Dr. Marks as he stood still at the podium. The students were confused. What the hell was she talking about? Surely Dr. Marks wasn't seriously considering her question. Of course the heart was a pump. That was a fact of life.

Dr. Marks watched himself approach the doors he'd closed on the heart's role in the body. On neurocardiology. He recognized the concepts he had been willing to walk around to stay in the mainstream. He couldn't do it anymore. The ideas he had long held in abeyance began crowding toward the front like eager reporters shouting for face time. He gave each idea its turn with him and then, satisfied, it would recede. Dr. Marks was not agitated; he was at peace. Finally, a student behind Bethanne whispered, "Do you think we should just leave?"

Dr. Marks opened his eyes. He had no idea how much time had passed as he stood motionless in front of the room. He looked out at the expectant faces and realized that he couldn't answer Bethanne's question truthfully and still give the final exam at the end of the semester. *Now what?* "I'm sorry, Ms. Amundson. I will not pursue this question before the final; perhaps once the course is complete I will investigate … " As he said the words, he saw that they were true. "This review is concluded. The test is on Tuesday a week from today at 11:00 a.m. here in this room. Class dismissed."

Bethanne disappeared into the mass of students leaving the lecture hall. Her energies were contracted and bland. No one approached her. Her classmates, though intrigued by her enigmatic question at the end of class, were already making plans for the rest of the day as they exited the room and made their way down the hall.

As she walked toward the main library, one of the last in the country containing actual books, Bethanne stifled a yawn. Though she was heartened by her successful encounter with Dr. Marks, she was exhausted. As a rule, it didn't cost her much to focus her energies in such a small dose, but she could usually count on uninterrupted sleep the night before to sustain her. *What happened at 2:30 this morning?* Burge Hall was on her way; she stopped there, as usual, for lunch. She liked to eat alone after class because it gave her time to transition from student to librarian. She walked around the salad bar piling her choices on top of the spinach and mixed greens she'd laid as a base. When she'd completed her construction, she took the salad out to the tables dotting the lawn and sat at an unoccupied one. Had she been eating anything but a salad, she still might have strolled along the campus walkways because she didn't like sitting around much, but she'd chosen the salad on purpose to force herself to sit and recoup her energy.

After crunching through the first few bites, she realized that even the salad was too much work. She closed her eyes and let herself expand for a moment. Donna entered her mind; her friend was agitated about something. Somehow Bethanne had missed this when she'd mentioned her this morning at breakfast. Donna had been hired to work in the library, and Bethanne had been chosen to mentor her; they had quickly become best friends even though Donna was several years younger. Now, as Bethanne extended her attention out toward Donna, the only insight she could safely discern was that Donna hadn't slept well either. *Join the club.* Bethanne reoriented herself and ate a few more bites of the salad before walking her bowl to the conveyor. Time for work.

* * *

Still Tuesday, 2:00 p.m.

Bethanne stowed her purse in the locker under the circulation desk and as she straightened, she saw Donna appear with her customary cheerful smile. Donna's dark brown eyes, framed and enlarged by her raven colored hair, sparkled with humor. Though she had a compact, sexy build, her confident demeanor made her seem larger than she was. Her harsh internal criticism of herself would be confusing if it had been at all evident to the outside world—except for Bethanne. Bethanne worried about the cruel voices Donna listened to inside her head, the ones that overlooked all her good parts. *So Donna's a complex person; who isn't.* "Hi," Bethanne smiled back. "Where were you?"

"Ladies' room," Donna answered.

"Yeah. So, how are you? You look a little tired."

"I *am* tired. I woke up in the middle of the night completely freaked out about something; I don't know what it was. Nightmare, I guess."

"I had one, too. I woke up around 2:30."

"That's weird," Donna said. "That's when I woke up." Her eyes narrowed in mock suspicion. "What's that all about?"

"How should I know?" The back of Bethanne's neck was tingling, though. Donna was different today; she was attracting unseen attention.

"What is it?" Donna asked.

"Oh, nothing. So, do you remember your dream?"

"No, and no thank you," Donna laughed. "That's all I need—my memories haunt me plenty. I never remember my dreams."

Two students arrived at the desk laden with books. "Back to work," Bethanne said. *Thank God.* It wasn't just Donna who was changed. Something was afoot; she recalled her revelation in the middle of the night. Yes, something had been set in motion last night that would change everything, and Donna was somehow involved. "Disparate players summoned by numinous incantations ..." Bethanne had written this in a poem not long ago. She continued, "and they, becharmed, respond." *Not good.*

6

ANSWER

Still Tuesday, 12:00 noon PDT

Jeff and Morgan worked all morning. When Morgan left for a lunch date, Jeff showered and pulled on his sweats before sitting down at his computer. He saw the message from Delamater about the implant. *Right. Something incorruptible.* Jeff briefly wondered how Delamater would get any new tech past Congress, then realized that Delamater would never have asked him to figure it out if he didn't have a plan already in place. Delamater's genius for acquiring influence and power was uncanny— and unstoppable— and Congress had been a joke for years.

Jeff swung his chair around and confronted the empty room. *Damn mountain lion. Damn dog.* He got up and walked back into his bedroom. Opening his bureau, he grabbed a tee shirt, shaking out its folds before pulling it over his head. He wandered into the kitchen to pour himself a glass of water. Returning to the computer, he held his hands over the keyboard until his thoughts animated his fingers, automatically parsing the images that flashed across the vidscreen from one set of arcane diagrams and equations to another. Surprisingly, the use of voice-activated computers wasn't universal; the tech community continued to type as a means of recording original ideas, most likely as a privacy holdover from the crowded rooms in which this kind of work had begun. The tendency to type fell in and out of popularity with the general populace.

Jeff had been at the forefront of the most advanced surveillance tech pinning the world's inhabitants to ever-closer scrutiny. Historically, mass use of surveillance in public places was jump-started by the destruction of the World Trade Center towers on September 11, 2001. Now, no place in the world existed that didn't have camera coverage from at least one angle, even if it was only from a satellite above. Jeff's job was to make cameras the ubiquitous eyewitnesses to every movement of every inhabitant and to accurately identify every inhabitant—especially criminals. His first system enabled all the cameras to communicate with each other; they could follow a criminal until he was apprehended. Of course, many techies could have accomplished this, but Jeff, who was only 14 and a high school senior at the time, was the first. Delamater hired him at once and exclusively.

Before Jeff's work with Delamater began, there was a public outcry when, in 2013, an intelligence analyst with a top-secret security clearance, Edward Snowden, revealed the extensive data gathering of the NSA. Now, though, only a few people complained about the cameras and Internet spying, and those who hadn't been able to adapt eventually left the big cities where surveillance was inescapable. The distracted citizens who stayed were largely oblivious to the erosion of freedoms and rights that accompanied each new technological advance. The switch from chips on I.D. cards to small wrist implants at birth seemed a logical one. The implants each had a unique electromagnetic identity that was recognized by all cameras everywhere, a failsafe if the biometrics failed. No wallets, no purses: freedom. When the disruption of an implant's normal transmission occurred, the system would immediately contact the nearest police station while it coupled implant data with the nearest camera's record of what had happened. Consequently, murders were rare. Only three people knew it was Jeff who had created the ultimate cloud architecture that unified all the systems. And hardly anyone else grasped that every privately owned computer, handheld or otherwise, conversed indiscriminately with the cameras and satellites that instantly shared everything with the authorities—with Delamater. Delamater was considered a hero.

Yet now another murder. *Shit.* Always a way around each new tech. And this time it was really something so simple—a tweak of an implant and a mask. Jeff already had the crime scene data, so he began manipulating and expanding the source intel asking for answers the system didn't know it had. Then he just backed away and let his mind go slack; let it be a receptor only. The victim knew—he absolutely knew—that Lance was trouble. Sure, most of the danger was perceived in the visible spectrum, but there was something else, too. Jeff saw the answer he was looking for; it appeared as if by magic. All of his best creations came this same way; Jeff didn't question it. This new idea, though, was huge— maybe the final surveillance tech he'd ever need to create. *Ha. The egg of Columbus; too obvious.* He pushed himself out of his chair and went to the back porch. The sun hadn't moved much since Morgan left. The wound in the grassy lawn where they'd buried Linux made the whole yard look vulnerable. He shook his head and forced his eyes up to take in the beauty of the forest beyond.

Jeff lived outside the grid he had created. He enjoyed his freedom and anonymity, his ability to move around without anyone knowing what he was doing, and he'd extended that privilege to Morgan. Jeff needed to stay anonymous, was happy to stay anonymous, because of his work for Delamater. He knew he was fortunate, but he lacked the context in which to see that the freedom he enjoyed once belonged to everyone. He returned to his computer and, standing above it, struck the key that would hide all his work in his cyberspace safe. *Delamater is going to pay me a fortune for this.* Striding back to the porch, he opened the glass door and walked out. He sat down on the steps without Linux. He began to cry.

* * *

Still Tuesday, 2:00 p.m.

A short time later, Jeff was back at the computer. He just needed to get a couple things down. He didn't struggle much with the project because he knew from the beginning that the initial steps would merely augment his previous work. The answer lay within the electromagnetic field generated by each human being. The EMF had to be as individual, as identifiable, as fingerprints or DNA, right? He was sure it was, but he would need to test it out in the relative quiet of his sparsely populated neighborhood. After compensating for all ambient noise, Jeff composed a program allowing him to employ holographic optical micromagnetometers to isolate the electromagnetic force, the bioenergy field signature, of each of his neighbors. His thoughts gave a quick bow to Cohen for his initial measurements of MEG and Zimmerman for creating SQUID. Without their work, this wouldn't even be an option. *There it is.* He decided to focus on the holographic torus generated by the heart's EMF as that was stronger than the field generated by the brain. This torus would hold the most identifiable and predictive picture, so he designed tech to perceive the EMF signature from a distance. Choosing a star as the onscreen icon for each person, Jeff moved out into his neighborhood analyzing the attributes of each neighbor's torus, carefully cross-checking it with the information already in the system from each implant. Easy. *So, what's the spectrum of electromagnetic vibe within acceptable variances? What's normal?* The data indicated that the variance in magnitude between each person's torus wasn't that significant, but he allowed the star's size to indicate onscreen the relative strength of field generated. Ever refining and testing, Jeff coordinated the tech to id each person. Of course, other tech existed using the human body to id itself—fingerprints, iris-scanning, face-recognition, DNA, implants—you name it, but all of it required proximity and corporeality, which nullified any predictive capacity it might possess. If this system worked, and it looked like it was working, it would be the bridge over every river. Jeff sent his tech over to the east side of the mountain into Sausalito and leaned back in his chair, closing his eyes. He knew enough about psychology to recognize his fatigue for what it was: depression. *Fine.*

* * *

Still Tuesday 3:00 p.m.

Jeff woke up an hour later to Morgan's smiling face. "Hey." Morgan handed Jeff a cup of iced coffee. "Working hard?"

"Sometimes. What are you doing here?"

"Something about a fence. Don't you remember? It's 3:00."

"Shit. I forgot all about it." *Linux.* Jeff paused to take a swallow of the coffee. He held the cup still while he looked through the glass doors into the back yard.

Morgan interrupted his reverie. "We don't have to, man. Whatever you want to do."

Jeff refocused and faced Morgan. "I don't want to. I don't have a damn dog anymore, so what's the point."

Morgan digested this and decided to venture into Jeff's personal space. Jeff had become isolated from practically every other living being—human or otherwise; it deserved noting. "Um, I know you're torn up about Linux, but you know, at least he got you out of your head sometimes. Linux kept you real, man. Got you out of that chair. Maybe you should get another dog."

Jeff looked away. *Replace Linux?* He shot Morgan an evil look. "I'm fine. I'm more than fine. I've got work to do—major work." He didn't look at Morgan as he went on. "So, I guess you made the trip for nothing." He added, "Catch you later," grinning ironically to himself before returning to his work.

Morgan had already said more than he'd intended. *Good work, Morgan. Why can't you just keep your mouth shut? Now it'll be days until he calls.* Morgan shrugged. "Ok, Jeff. Have it your way. You know where to find me." He strode out the door without looking back.

Good riddance. Jeff took another sip of his coffee and set it down. His program was advancing rapidly through the process as it accumulated the data Jeff had sent it searching for. Now, just a few hours since onset, everyone in Sausalito was identified. Jeff watched the system's progress into southern California. *Beautiful. Let's see what we can see.*

Jeff scanned the data, placing the map overlay at his cut-off, the northern border town of Smith River, California. He scrolled south to test his program's capacity to id everyone. *Wait a second.* The ancillary data wasn't making sense. Occasionally, the system had picked up an anomaly in the field—a reading that showed a person with a stronger EMF than the norm. Jeff picked a few of them out and ran a comparison. He discovered that the stronger charges weren't tied to observable environmental factors. Wouldn't it be logical for environmental influences to play a big part on the EMFs? Yet as he surveyed the field, he saw that that wasn't the case. He expanded outward again to look at the established norm. He was surprised to find that people living in barrios and ghettos were as likely to have normal EMFs as middle-class people living in the suburbs or the ultra rich living in their opulent beach communities. It made no difference where they lived. So that was weird, but weirder yet was that the anomalies in the field had ids that showed them in all walks of life too; no great difference existed between the chip bios of the anomalies and those of the normal spectrum EMFs. *Why not?* To aggravate him further, Jeff recognized a trend showing that subsidiary people with whom the anomalies were engaged also tended to have elevated EMFs, yet the anomalies themselves hadn't perceptively exploited their potential influence. *What's that all about?*

Of course, the program was elegant. Performing exactly as Jeff had designed it, the entire population of the United States would be identified. Jeff, however, hadn't expected his analysis of the data to reveal anything esoteric. Never before had Jeff strayed from the narrow purpose of his new tech; if its original purpose was diverted later, it wasn't his problem—it simply didn't matter. But something was going on here, a mystery, and for some reason, the loss of Linux maybe, Jeff was not only receptive to it, he immediately decided to transform the tech's purpose. After giving the program a few demands, Jeff went to the kitchen for a sandwich. When he returned to the screen, he noticed the scan had stopped over a suburb of Los Angeles in the San Fernando Valley. A star occluded a community on the northwest edge of the valley. Northridge. It rang a bell. Oh, yeah. A big earthquake back in the 1990s. *What the hell?*

7

FIRST FIRE

Still Tuesday, 7:00 p.m. CDT

Bethanne and Donna were tired, but they were hungry, too. Donna, proud owner of one of the few cars regularly used in Iowa City, drove west on Melrose turning toward Sushi Popo, their favorite restaurant. During dinner, they didn't talk as much as Bethanne had wanted to, but Donna was out of sorts; preoccupied. About an hour later, she dropped Bethanne off at home.

Walking through the kitchen door, Bethanne found Scott cleaning up the dishes alone. "Hi, honey. Where's Claire?"

"She said she has to study for a test so she went up to her room and left me here with the dishes."

"Hm. What did you guys have?"

"Claire made sautéed crap, and I was so hungry I ate it."

"I'm sure you thanked her for it, too?"

"Sure, Mom. How was your dinner?"

"Well, it was delicious. I should have thought to bring some home for you."

"It's no big deal. You'll be cooking tomorrow night, right?"

Bethanne laughed. "Yes, Scott. I'll be cooking tomorrow night.

Do you want chicken parmesan?"

"More than anything in the world."

Bethanne grinned, "You've got it. Now go upstairs and get your homework done." She called a greeting up to Claire before settling down at the kitchen table to study a bit for her biology final.

Later, when she poked her head into Claire's bedroom, she found her daughter on her bed reading a Harry Potter book. "Again?" Bethanne asked.

"Yeah; I can't help myself," Claire grinned. "I just love these books. They remind me of when I was little and Dad was reading the first one to me."

"He loved that. Remember how you'd have to nudge him when he started to nod off?"

"Uh-huh. He'd start trailing off and making up words."

They laughed. "How was your day, baby?"

"Mostly okay," Claire paused, assessing her mother's mood. She decided to continue. "But the most bizarre thing happened after school."

"Really? What?"

"Well, I was just starting to walk home with Stacy and I suddenly got so scared—I mean really, really scared. It felt like the whole world was going to end. I guess I kind of spaced out or something because I even dropped my bag. Stacy must think I'm nuts."

Bethanne looked at her hands; they were balled into nervous fists. *No. Not yet. She isn't old enough yet.* She would not let Claire become a target.

"Mom? Are you okay?" Claire asked.

"I'm fine. I'm a little concerned about you, though. So, what happened next?"

"Nothing. The feeling just kind of passed. It's not like it went away exactly, it's more like it just became, I don't know, like normal or something, you know: meant to be. What do you think it was, Mom?"

"I'm not sure. The brain is a complicated thing; who knows what triggers it sometimes."

"Maybe it's the same as Harry Potter. I mean, that's exactly how it felt. Like how Harry feels when Voldemort thinks about him. Of course, I'm not exactly Harry Potter. I mean, I know that none of that is real."

Bethanne sat still; a potent look lingered between them. Bethanne had hoped that Claire would be spared this, and if not spared, at least granted more time. It had been a long journey to this moment. Less than a month after David was gone, Bethanne got out of New York City. Manhattan was fast becoming the focus of the nightmare anyway. The crowds on the city's sidewalks were thinning as more people began working from home—telecommuting, purchasing online, watching movies; what did they need to go outside for? Technology kept pushing the isolation envelope, so when Bethanne found herself alone with two small children, it seemed logical to move back to the place of her birth—a real community. Yet, who moves to Iowa? When she graduated from high school, Bethanne rebelled against her mother's disapproval of the clamor and tech of big cities. Bethanne longed for all of it, and she couldn't wait to move to New York for college. She loved NYU, loved Washington Square, loved the Village—loved all of Manhattan. Meeting David was perfect. He'd been coming down the stairs of the lecture hall in C95 when their eyes met. Electricity—a blue line of charge almost visible—connected them. They both halted mid-stride. Later, the same electric flash would identify other people who were to become important in her life, but David was the first. With David, she'd simply stood still until he reached her. They faced each other, standing way inside the comfort zone. He'd said, "I must know you from somewhere." She could feel the smile of acceptance spread across her face as she looked into his eyes, the same blue she would see eight years later in her daughter's eyes. She'd said, "My name is Bethanne." David had cocked an eyebrow; this was not a big city name. "Bethanne—I love it. I'm David." They'd been inseparable after that, even though he was a junior who wanted to be a fireman of all things and she was a freshman who wanted to be a writer.

At that time, New York City was fast becoming one of the safest cities in the western world. Bethanne reluctantly recognized that its method of becoming so also justified her mother's distrust of technology. China and the rest of the East had been under the thumb of Big Brother for a long time; Manhattan bowed to him shortly after the 9/11 disaster. First there were cameras covering the streets, now this. No movement went unrecorded. And her mother's other fear, that a great lethargy would come from media's incursion, had also come to pass; had, in fact, progressed exponentially with the advent of virtual universes. Politically, U.S. citizens had been losing ground for a long time, but when the Supreme Court elected a candidate for President without an effective challenge by voters, the impotency of the populace was set. No government since had been able to set the country right, and technology had overrun any sense of community still existing. Would this have been possible without numbing the citizens of America? So entertained and debauched; *Brave New World* for real. As the media rapidly encroached on every aspect of life, Bethanne got rid of the television. She adopted the home rules her mother had had, the same ones that she had once rebelled against, the same ones she could feel her daughter resent now.

Claire, bald and beautiful, had been born in their apartment in Boerum Hill three years before the identification implants became mandatory in New York. Later, every teen's eighteenth birthday was celebrated with an implant that would place them on GPS, on IRS files, on police networks until they died. The implants were much heralded by the media. Bethanne had been sickened by a bank ad: *An ATM in your ARM.* It was all happening so fast. And though Scott, too, was born before the implants were required at birth, a new law had passed: students entering school were now required to have them.

Bethanne and David led a simple life in the city considering the complexities of their environment. David had started his career at Ladder 161 in Brooklyn, then Ladder 123. He became a lieutenant at Ladder 27, Cross Bronx Expressway, a little after Scott was born. He had the traditional three-day on, three-day off schedule, which worked perfectly. Bethanne, a writer for the *Daily Slope*, would plan her column during naptimes and complete it on one of the days David was home. Because they were fairly close to Prospect Park, the children got plenty of fresh air. Her children knew not only what trees and grass looked like, but also what they felt like and smelled like, and they weren't afraid to get dirty. In fact, Claire loved playing in the mud with her little brother whenever it was available. Every afternoon, Bethanne would tell a story she made up—she'd been making up stories since her own childhood—at naptime. On David's workdays, Bethanne made dinner; David made dinner on the days he was there. He read to the children at bedtime. It all worked, but it was suffused with the anxieties and fears broadcast in the culture every day.

Then, one night while Bethanne was fixing dinner, she heard David yell. He wasn't home, though; he was still at work. She shot out of her body and saw flames everywhere. David and two other firemen were searching the fourth floor of a building in East Tremont. Someone had said people were up there, above the fire. The flames and the heat grew too intense too fast; the three firemen jumped from a window to the ground. Bethanne watched in horror as David leaped out. Now she was standing next to his crumpled body. She watched someone check his pulse; it was weak. Soon others arrived and put him on a gurney that they loaded into an ambulance. But Bethanne wasn't paying attention to that. She was standing facing David, inside the comfort zone, as they had all those years before on the stairs of C95. "I love you," he said without using words.

"Oh, David. Please, please don't go. I can't do this alone. I don't want to do this without you."

"You won't have to. I'll be watching over you for a long, long time."

They embraced. Bethanne trusted him. He wouldn't leave her. And he never did.

Moments later, she was back in the kitchen stirring soup. She turned off the stove and stood over it wondering what to do next. She knew she was in some state of shock, but it was tempered by her encounter with David. She went into the children's room. Claire was sitting in her little rocking chair next to Scott's bed, pretending to read him a story. Bethanne knelt beside her and kissed the top of her head. Without looking up, Claire asked, "What's wrong, Mommy?"

"Oh, honey, I have some sad news."

"Is it about Daddy?"

Bethanne's breath shot out, blowing Claire's fine curls aside. "Yes, it's about Daddy."

"I know. He said he was leaving and that I wouldn't see him for a long, long time."

"That's right," Bethanne whispered. *Oh, Claire, you're wide open.*

"Daddy came to visit Scott and me. He said everything was going to be okay because you're a wonderful mommy and you'll know what to do. He said we'll be okay."

And Bethanne knew they'd be okay, too, eventually. She got through the phone call telling her to come to the hospital, she got through the funeral, the memorial service, the commemoration, all of it, sensing always that David was close by. Two weeks later, she was planning her escape to Iowa. Leaving was her only choice because the door into David's world didn't close after the night he died; the invisible world that had faded in her late childhood had reemerged. And everything that she could see in that other place, including David, was telling her to get out of New York City. She did. She moved back to Iowa because Iowa was behind the times. Much of the Midwest was behind the times—on purpose. And what Bethanne had once found loathsome was now a virtue.

The spirit world had faded for Claire, too, or so Bethanne had thought. They didn't talk about it, Bethanne because she wanted to keep Claire safe, and Claire because she sensed her mother's reluctance. But here it was. Claire was saying that Voldemort was thinking about her, and Bethanne had to take it seriously. Bethanne, still staring into Claire's eyes, recognized that she'd been protecting herself as much as she thought she'd been protecting Claire. Claire's gift was enormous, but undeveloped; she didn't know how to use it yet.

"Mom?"

"Yes?"

"We aren't safe here anymore, are we?"

Bethanne sighed. It was true. "Not really. We do have some time; how long, I don't know."

"But it doesn't look like we can hide anymore, does it?" Claire watched her mother closely. She watched Bethanne take a deep breath and close her eyes. She watched her breathe out and once again meet her eyes.

"No, we can't hide anymore. I just have to figure out what that means."

"I think I know, Mom. I think we need to help out. We need to stop Voldemort."

Secretly, Bethanne was delighted that her 16-year-old daughter loved the fantasy of the Harry Potter books, but this was no fantasy. "He's not Voldemort, sweet one. Voldemort's fiction. Our guy has been around since the beginning—since before the beginning. He's not fiction. He's intelligent and strong and ruthless. But, you're right; I have to stop him, but I'm not sure how yet. I don't even know what the next step should be."

"Did you already know about him before tonight? You've been acting kind of weird lately, but I didn't want to say anything."

"I'm sorry, honey," Bethanne whispered taking Claire's hand again in hers. Giving tone without volume to her voice, she went on. "I have been so preoccupied with protecting you and hiding myself, that I've lost touch. How much do you know?"

"Not much; mostly just feelings. I'm pissed off that I was blind-sided today by the not-Voldemart guy."

Bethanne smiled grimly. "Yeah, I know how you feel. Claire, honey, the truth is, he's so much smarter than we are. He's going to fool almost everyone; even we can be fooled—maybe especially us. So we're going to have to keep on our toes. Right now though, and I hate to say it, we should probably change the subject. I have no idea what kind of attention we might be attracting. I'm afraid we'll just have to see what presents itself because things are still mostly hidden from me; I have to set myself up perfectly to see with any clarity at all, which leaves us vulnerable. On the other hand, worrying about it is useless, so we've got to just let it go for the time being." Bethanne struggled toward normalcy for Claire's sake. "So, that's that then. Time for you to get to sleep. Scott says you have a test tomorrow."

Claire locked eyes with her mother. She wanted to make sure that her mom knew they wouldn't be the same together anymore. She saw her mother acknowledge it.

Bethanne gave Claire's hand a squeeze and got up. "Thanks for taking care of your brother tonight," she said.

"No problem. Of course, he loved my dinner," she added sarcastically, "but then that's his problem. Good night, Mom. Love you. See you in the morning."

"Love you, too, sweetheart" Bethanne said turning around at the door. "Good night."

Bethanne stopped by Scott's door and poked her head in. He

was under his covers, leaning over to turn off his bedside lamp. "Good night, honey. Sleep well," she said.

"I will. You sleep well too."

"I will," Bethanne lied before flicking off the hall light. She leaned against the wall for a moment wondering if she would ever sleep well again. Then, pushing herself off, she walked toward her own room. This much she knew for sure: no more questions for college professors; her work was on a whole new level. She wondered if she was up for it. She shook herself. If she didn't get started on her meditation, fear would paralyze her.

It was still early; the moon hadn't reached her bathroom window. She quickly brushed her hair and teeth barely glancing in the mirror. *Damn. I forgot to make a hair appointment.* She lit the candle and sank to the floor crossing her legs and smoothing the rug with her hands. She pictured herself kneeling before the tide pool. She widened her reach, clearing her mind of every thought. Each cell in her body filled with buoyancy and light as she watched the swirling geometry of color coalescing before her mind's eye. Slowly the color began to take on form turning itself into a picture of coming events. A bubble of fear threatened to burst the picture. She had never been this aware before and she felt unsure, unworthy. But a reassuring presence enfolded her and, with renewed courage, she allowed herself to go into the picture world she could just now observe.

She had been right; extraordinary forces had been mobilized.

The scene became clearer; she saw an old man sleeping beside his wife. Homemade bookshelves lined the walls of his small house. The couple slept close to each other, still deeply in love, still interested more in each other than anyone else. Bethanne recognized the loving wisdom emanating from the man. Right. Pictures flashed before her. She knew him! He'd been a teacher at NYU; a sub for a year while the tenured professor took a sabbatical to complete his book. This man loved teaching; he hadn't written a book. How had he been chosen for this year in the city? All the students loved him, though, and wished that he would stay. His second semester class was one you could take as a freshman, but the upperclassmen grabbed all the seats before the younger ones could register. He'd allowed her to audit the class. Bethanne saw now the enormous power of his soul, his heart forces emanating outward, holding his current students in his wise embrace. Yet how ordinary and dear he looked lying next to his wife. Bethanne watched them breathing in unison—together even as they were asleep and unaware.

Suddenly, the atmosphere changed. Something was wrong. A flood of darkness washed over the serene picture. It covered the small house with a malevolence so pure that Bethanne couldn't breathe. Her adrenalin pumped escape messages, but she was transfixed by what she was watching. The man didn't wake; Bethanne tried to scream, but she wasn't really there—she had no power. *How do I stop this? Stop! Please!* But she was too panicked to control even herself. She had to warn them. *Get out!* she screamed. Abruptly, she was ripped from the scene, back into her own body sitting before her altar on the spiraled rug. She collapsed on her side breathing raggedly and sobbing. *What was going to happen to them?*

8

ROAD TRIP

Morgan pressed the answer icon on his vid. *Jeff? He's not pissed off?* "What do you want?" Morgan asked instinctively.

"Road trip. Now," Jeff replied. He was agitated, and Morgan twisted to face the screen and focus on Jeff's face.

"What's up?" he asked.

"Long story; just put some shit together. We're going to L.A."

"When?"

"I want to be there in the morning, so we'll have to leave around 5:30."

"I'll be there," Morgan replied signing off. He rolled his eyes at the empty room. He knew there was no point trying to engage Jeff when he was like this. He'd been Jeff's business partner ever since college. When Jeff moved back to California to go to Berkeley, he'd asked Morgan to come with him. Morgan was being recruited by the bigs on the east coast, so when he talked to Berkeley, the school, overjoyed, responded by giving him a shared basketball and baseball scholarship. Meanwhile, Jeff was starting to make serious money working for Paul Delamater. By the time he graduated, Jeff realized he would need someone to manage his enormous wealth, someone he could trust. Morgan became Jeff's face to the world so that Jeff could stay invisible. Morgan decided to pack in the morning; he felt drained by some obscure force—like he'd been visiting a friend in the hospital. Morgan hadn't expected his protective feelings toward Jeff to endure into adulthood, but they had. Jeff was still emotionally immature, and dealing with that was part of Morgan's unwritten job description. The past two days had made it abundantly clear that this aspect of his job might be the one most exercised. He climbed into bed and the lights shut off.

At 5:00 the next morning, Morgan opened his closet. He chose black casual slacks and a black tee. He put an identical set of clothes in an overnight bag along with a perpetually packed toiletries kit. He had learned to travel in one color scheme, and black worked for everything.

Morgan threw his bag into the trunk of his Audi r8. Surely one of the most beautiful cars on the road, it excelled at maneuverability—and it was so very, very fast. With fewer cars on the road these days, traffic was always light and speed limits had been abolished. He spirited the r8 through the tight curves of Toyon to Platt to Monte Mar Drive to Wolfback Ridge, continuously steering around the luscious curves. He just never got tired of it.

A few minutes later, the two of them were on the 101 heading south. Jeff was busy with his laptop creating secure links to his base. Finally he closed the lid and looked over at Morgan. "Ok. So here's what's going on. I have to see this guy who's got this amazing EMF. Off the charts. And surrounding him are all these other people with elevated EMFs. I want to meet him, see if I can tell anything just by being in the room with him, you know?"

Morgan did not know. "What the hell are you talking about?

"My program is set to id everyone's EMF." He remembered this was new and added, "Electromagnetic field. Everyone's is different. Anyway, I let the computer go to work while I took a short nap last night and when I woke up, there's this guy. A total anomaly affecting the entire field around him."

Morgan was quiet.

"What?" asked Jeff?

"Why are you iding everyone's EMF, Jeff?"

"I'm doing it for Delamater. What do you think… it's just another one of his 'Let's protect everyone from everyone' projects I'm working on."

"Why? Aren't the implants enough?"

"What's your problem? And, no, the implants are not enough. First of all, not everyone has one—not by a long shot. And even though everyone on the east coast does, some guy just got killed in Manhattan and the killer got away because he tampered with his implant and wore a mask. Delamater is completely pissed off. So, anyway, I had to figure out some new tech that couldn't be subjugated."

"Right. Doesn't Delamater scare you? I mean, he's whack. Jeff? You see that, right?" Morgan's distrust of Delamater was epic. He did not for one second believe that Delamater was doing any of this for altruistic motives. Delamater wanted power. "Morgan, you're wrong." This was an argument they'd had many times—one Jeff knew he didn't spend enough time thinking about it, which was why he didn't spend *any* time thinking about it. "Whatever; screw you. I have to call him now."

Jeff returned to his computer and hit Delamater's icon. "I've got it," he stated when Delamater's face appeared onscreen.

"You've got it. What've you got?"

"The answer—maybe the ultimate answer."

"Okay, let's hear it."

"Not so fast, Delamater. I've still got lots of work to do. I've got to set it up and then I'll need time to research and test it. But it's big—huge. After this, you probably won't need me anymore."

"That seems unlikely, Jeff." Delamater smiled his intimate,

we-are-good-buddies smile at Jeff. "I'll always need you."

"No you won't. Look, this tech won't require hardware; no chips, no implants, nothing. It'll use something we're born with; something natural."

Abruptly, Delamater was gripped by a powerful desire, alien to his implacable sense of order. "Well, let's hear it." He had to know. He had to know details; he had to know everything Jeff knew. Everything. Now.

"I can't tell you yet," Jeff replied.

"No, Jeff. You need to tell me now," Delamater insisted, straining to breathe normally.

"No I don't," Jeff answered, off-put by Delamater's emotional struggle apparent onscreen. "I'll tell you as soon as I know more." He disconnected.

Delamater sat still for a moment then exploded off his chair sending it into the wall of windows behind him. "Doesn't he know I can destroy him?" he screamed. "I can bring things on him he can't even imagine! He'll—"

Sgt. Baker stood outside the door frozen in place.

* * *

Wednesday, May 23, 6:00 a.m. PDT

Jeff closed his computer again. *He knew Morgan was right about Delamater.* He glanced over at his friend who was in his road-trip mode, seat slanted back, one hand loosely holding the wheel while the other rested lightly on the gearshift knob. Morgan was purposefully ignoring him. *Right.* "Ok. Delamater's an asshole; is that what you want to hear?"

Morgan said nothing and continued to stare out the windshield.

"Fine. You're an asshole too. So, do you want to know where we're going?"

"Yes, boss." Morgan affected a negro slave version of his naturally deep, rich voice. He did not change expressions or look at Jeff when he spoke.

Jeff let a second or two go by before bursting into laughter. Morgan joined in, and the tension of the past two days whipped out the open windows. Of course, Morgan had some idea where they were going, and anyway, all he had to do was GPS the destination, but Jeff loved maps—another of his idiosyncrasies. His early devotion to them had sent him around the world before he was allowed to cross the street without holding his mother's hand. Jeff loved shortcuts and alternate routes, the kind you'd have to know about before asking GPS for directions.

"This guy I was telling you about, the one with the massive EMF, lives in Northridge, a town in the San Fernando Valley. I want to go the back way, though, so take the 154 to Santa Barbara and eventually we'll get on the 118; the school's south of that."

"What school?"

"This guy, Stuart Thompson, teaches at a private school. He'll be at work by the time we get down there."

"We're driving all the way to Northridge to see a schoolteacher?"

"Yup. He's the one with the massive torus."

"Taurus. Isn't that a zodiac sign? You're into horoscopes now? Who are you?"

"No, you idiot. A torus is a geometrical figure. Um. In this context, I think it has been called an aura."

"Oh, my man. We are on some scary fairy ground here; are you sure it's not horoscopes?"

"No, listen. It's all scientific as hell. The deal is that the electromagnetic force from any living body forms a field around it. And, well, it's individual. Everyone's field is unique—it varies in size and shape—a bunch of ways. Anyway, this guy's field is huge compared to most people. So, that in itself is compelling. But, like I said before, what really has me intrigued is that the people around him have elevated EMFs, too. The thing is, though, this guy screws up the norm over long periods of time. I examined several elevated EMFs scattered around in that region; no current overlap. Then I go into the records and find out these other anomalies all went to this same school. I have got to meet this guy."

"Hmm. Very interesting. But if he's got such big juice, why is he teaching school instead of running the world?"

"That's another thing I'm wondering about. Anyway, I guess we'll see when we get there." Jeff set his computer on the floorboard and took off his shoes. He told the seat to move back then put his feet up on the dash and looked out the side window as they passed the exit for Stanford. He remembered the arch rivalry between Berkeley and Stanford and smiled. It had all seemed so important then, even if you weren't into sports; the academic departments were, if anything, even more competitive. His school days seemed forever ago though really only ten years had passed since he'd received his doctorate in computer sciences. What a joke that had been. He'd known more than the teachers when he walked in the doors at 14. He wondered if this teacher in Northridge knew something he didn't.

Morgan, meanwhile, was happy for two reasons: one, Jeff knew that Delamater was an asshole, and two, his friend was finally outside the rigid lines of his own property. *When was the last time Jeff had even been on the other side of the ridge?* And the car's system had pulled up Hendrix's Greatest Hits. *Well she was walking through the clouds / With a circus mind that's running wild . . .*

* * *

Morgan drove as fast as the roads allowed. In places where the highways had been kept in repair, he pushed it over 100, flashing past small towns like Salinas and smaller towns like Soledad. In some places, though, the highways weren't as essential; people that still drove mostly used the local roads. So here and there, Morgan needed to proceed cautiously. They stopped for gas in Pismo Beach three hours after leaving Jeff's.

Pismo was still a funky beach town with lots of head shops and motorcycles. *How is that possible?* The rapacious growth of both coasts had somehow missed this place. Jeff was hungry for a breakfast burrito, but he was saving himself for a little hut on Milpas in Santa Barbara, so he grabbed a bag of chips from the rack in the station's mart and scanned the bag with a tiny wand he kept on his keychain. The purchase was recorded as if he'd scanned an implant. This wand, though, caused the cameras to blink. Jeff's tech was intricate and unavailable. He had created it to stay off the grid when he had to be in a public place, but he used it automatically, without thought; just part of his life.

After Santa Barbara and the burritos, the 101 and the PCH became the same highway for a while, hugging the vertical coastline for several miles. The ocean's rippled light was interrupted by the humps of the Channel Islands lit by the morning sun ... *Gold and rose, the colors of a dream I had ...* glowing in washes of hazy yellow at the horizon while the flickering water dazzled the sand and rocks along the shore, glazing the right side of their car. In Ventura, the r8 left the oceanside and entered farming country. This also seemed anachronistic, like Pismo, but its quaint rural appearance existed not for food but for flowers. Still, both Jeff and Morgan appreciated seeing the lusty colors springing from the green leafage and brown furrows of the backdrop. At a 4-way stop, Jeff noticed a red wheelbarrow sitting in a yard near an old barn. A couple of white chickens picked their feet up over the blades of grass. "So much depends ..." Jeff said in unison with Morgan. They both laughed. "We can remember the 4 line-poems. Dr. Granger would be so proud," Jeff smiled toward Morgan's nod of mocking agreement.

This was their last rural scene. Soon they were in Moorpark, once a small town now an outlying suburb of the conglomerate Los Angeles. Morgan sped along the uncrowded highway, exiting at Tampa Ave. A mile later, he was stopping in front of the driveway leading up to the school.

"Here we are, boss," Morgan joked again.

"Right. Ok, then. Just a second, I'm going to make sure Thompson is here." Jeff touched his screen. "Yeah, he's here."

"So, you going to get out or what?" Morgan asked when several seconds passed without Jeff moving.

"Sure. Um, you can just stay in the car if you want."

Morgan looked at him as if he'd lost his mind. "Ok. Are you kidding me? I had no intention of going in. Call me when you're done."

Jeff looked uncomfortable. "Why, are you going somewhere?"

Morgan looked more closely at Jeff. "No, man, I'm not going anywhere. I'll just park aways away so I don't look like a kiddie stalker." He paused watching Jeff's face. "So, see you later."

Jeff hesitated again, fidgeting and awkward. *What am I worried about? What's the worst that can happen?* He opened the car door and stepped out into the hot sun. *Oh, yeah. The San Fernando Valley; a bazillion degrees all summer long.* He bent down and looked in at Morgan, who was watching him intently. "Ok. See you when I'm done."

"Yeah, ok." Morgan shook his head. Jeff was getting weirder by the minute.

9

FIRST ENCOUNTER

Wednesday, 10:30 a.m. PDT

The school had three buildings, a grassy lawn, and an outdoor basketball court within sight as Jeff approached from the street. He saw lots of students sitting and laying on the grass talking or resting; others were eating at picnic tables placed beneath shade trees. When he got closer, he realized that teachers were sitting among the students apparently in easy conversation with them. Everyone was talking, not a vid or realtime in sight. *Okay. This is different. And where's all the tech to keep strangers like me from wandering onto campus?*

Jeff approached a table that was predominately teachers and cleared his throat to get their attention. "Excuse me. Hello. Um, my name is Jeff, um Spears—Jeff Spears. I'm looking for Stuart Thompson. Can you tell me where I might find him?"

"Hi, Mr. Spears," said a young woman, her red hair gathered in a ponytail. "I'm Julia. I think Stuart is in his classroom; is he expecting you?"

"No; actually I'm kind of here on a whim."

"Oh. Well, we can see if he has some time. I can show you there if you want."

"That'd be great." Jeff tried to calm down while Julia extricated herself from the table. *What am I afraid of?*

Julia led him into the second building and down a short hallway, its walls covered with beautiful artwork. Jeff slowed to look at it, noticing with amazement that each painting had a different signature. *Student work?* "Is this an art school?" he asked.

Julia smiled. Obviously, this was a question she'd been asked many times. "No, but we do have art requirements. We also manage to find a way to fit art into most of the academic lessons. We find students learn better if they have a way to express themselves individually; it makes the material matter more." She stopped in front of a door standing open on the left. "Here we are," she said.

She walked in and greeted the room's only occupant. "Hi, Stuart. Sorry to interrupt; do you have a moment? There's someone here to see you."

Stuart Thompson was standing in front of a map at the back of the room. He turned in response to the greeting, looking briefly at Julia, then meeting Jeff's gaze. An electric shock pinned Jeff to his place on the floor. The old man, his turquoise shirt tight across his overfull belly and his white hair jumbled around his head, was smiling genially, but his eyes pierced into Jeff's, exposing him as he stood defenseless next to Julia.

"This is Jeff Spears; he said he's here on a whim. Mr. Spears, this is Mr. Thompson."

Thompson smiled. "Thank you, Julia. I do have a moment."

"Okay, then, I'll just get back to my lunch. See you later." She nodded to each of them before closing the door behind her.

Jeff stayed rooted where Julia had left him. Thompson came toward him with his hand extended. "Nice to meet you, Mr. Spears. What can I do for you?"

Jeff jerked his hand into position and almost leaped back when Thompson's hand grasped his and shook it. Electricity zapped straight through him; he felt his hair stand on end. *Say something.* "Uh, um… good… um, nice to meet you, too," he managed to stammer.

"Are you all right?" Thompson asked. "You don't look so good."

Jeff disengaged his hand from Thompson's and took a deep breath, closing his eyes. He opened them to see Thompson's friendly eyes holding a look of concerned inquiry. *What the hell is wrong with me?* Jeff now saw that Mr. Thompson was only a harmless, old schoolteacher. *Okay.* "Nothing; I'm fine," he answered, re-establishing his self-control, "and please, call me Jeff. I was hoping to ask you a few questions about your school and your teaching. I've been doing some research and, well, do you have any time in the next day or two?"

Thompson appraised Jeff and came to a decision. "Jeff, I've got a little time before my next class. We could get started anyway. Will that work for you?" He led Jeff to a table at the front of the class and offered him a chair.

Before Jeff could say anything, Thompson continued. "Why don't you tell me why you've come to see *me* specifically."

Jeff had his story ready. "Right now, I'm investigating the effects teachers have on their students, both in the short term while the kids are taking classes and in the long term, after they've graduated and moved away," Jeff replied. *So far, all true.* "The government is paying me to do this research," he added. *Still true; kind of.* "Well, you've been teaching for a long time, and I thought you'd be able to shed some light for us on these—effects."

Thompson listened carefully. Too carefully for Jeff's taste. This whole endeavor was looking more and more like a fiasco. "Short-term effects are measured by grades, I suppose. But long-term effects, I don't know," Thompson answered. "Those would be impossible to measure with our current methods, wouldn't they?"

Jeff refocused on Thompson's eyes with alarm. *Does this guy know something?* "Um. Well, I think I might be onto something that could lead to real measurements. I'm just in the beginning phase, though. Just gathering data right now. Maybe we can start by talking about what you teach."

Thompson's brows lifted with along the corners of his mouth. He seemed amused. "I teach history, Jeff. Ancient history, modern history, forgotten history, the usual. No big deal really."

This was going nowhere. Jeff had to come up with a good question or just leave. "Do you find your job rewarding? I mean, like you say, teachers can never really know how their work turns out—it can't be measured. And your subject, history, um, kids aren't really even interested in history anymore, are they? I mean, whatever they need to know they can find out on the vid. They can watch re-enactments for almost everything that ever happened. Why even go to school?" *There.*

Thompson's gaze intensified as he measured Jeff. Jeff shrank back involuntarily. Always supremely confident, Jeff was faltering under Thompson's scrutiny. When the old man sat back to relax against his chair, Jeff knew he had passed some kind of test that he shouldn't have passed. He was grateful, but he felt guilty, like he'd gotten away with cheating.

"Let's see," Thompson began. "Students are naturally curious; it's just where they are—in their development, you know? Often they don't know what to be curious about, though. They can be led or misled, especially in today's culture. So, the one thing the teacher needs to do is to establish some kind of authority, some expertise that isn't available onscreen. The teacher has to know his field. In this way, the teacher earns a student's trust and respect. It isn't easy, though. Young people are suspicious of adults because adults have bungled everything up as far as these young people can see. Kids have BS detectors with powerful range and precision, and they use them on everyone."

"Ok," Jeff replied. "So, you're saying that once a teacher knows his subject, he's good to go."

"No, that's not what I'm saying. I said that knowledge was *a* requirement not *the* requirement. A teacher must do many things"

"Like what? I mean, have you done or said anything in particular, you know, some kind of special information that would, um, change a student and, you know, last—even after graduation— maybe a lifetime?" *There. That's the one I need to know. Come on, old man; give it up.*

Thompson looked down. He was disappointed; Jeff sensed it. Jeff watched as the old teacher made a new decision before looking up. He cocked his head sideways and grinned. "Tell me something, Jeff."

"Sure; what?"

"Do you know anyone who's an insatiable learner? What do you think is the motivation?"

Jeff prepared to let loose his easy laugh, the one that brushes aside all things personal, but it caught in his throat. It would be inappropriate. Thompson's authenticity, his genuine interest in him, disarmed him. Now it was Jeff's turn to look down and reconsider.

His mind's eye watched a scene from his youth coalesce. He'd been precocious—he was a genius, after all, and that had already been apparent for many years before he'd first become friends with Morgan. Morgan worked hard for his grades; he was smart, a top student, but he always took the most challenging courses and accepted nothing less than an A. Morgan was earnest in his pursuit of knowledge; he was grateful for the opportunity to learn at Worcester Academy. One of the few boarders who was also a full-scholarship student, he studied late into the night in the school library at Rader Hall. Jeff, on the other hand, had already hijacked the school's computers and spent his late nights at Rader conducting excursions into the school's computer files.

One evening, Morgan approached him. Jeff muted the screen showing the salaries of the lacrosse coaches, something Morgan would find interesting since he was on every single team that mattered. Jeff was only ten years old—too small to compete on any of the teams. "What do you want?" he barked.

"What do you want?" Morgan answered.

Silence. Then, "You came over here," Jeff retorted.

"Yeah, but you were looking at me."

"Was not."

"Were too," Morgan said. "Look, it's no problem. I'm just wondering if you wanted to ask me something or not."

"No."

"Well then, can I ask you something?"

Jeff examined Morgan. He seemed sincere not sinister. Maybe he was different than the other jocks. "Sure; why not?"

"Could you show me how to do the imaging for this calculus problem?"

"Eff you," Jeff said immediately. Anyone who was in calculus would know how to do it.

Morgan didn't move a muscle. His eyes locked onto Jeff's as if they'd reached out and grabbed hold. "No," he said quietly. "Eff you."

Jeff didn't move either, but he wasn't a fool. In any way. Yeah, this guy could take him without breaking a sweat, but that wasn't it. This guy was sincere. "Sorry," Jeff said. "Reflex."

Morgan straightened up and smiled without breaking contact, like an impromptu game of Killer—you blink, you die. "So, what's it going to be?"

"It won't take long at all," Jeff answered. "Have a seat."

Morgan sat down and they began working together. Once Morgan understood the process, they stopped working and an awkward silence cooled the air between them.

Morgan, a more sociable boy than Jeff by far, broke it. "I didn't have my own computer growing up."

"No way," Jeff exclaimed, earning a warning flash to be quiet from his screen.

"Way."

"Everyone has a computer."

"I didn't."

"Why not?" Jeff was incredulous.

"My mother didn't believe in them."

Jeff's laugh barked sharply and earned another warning from the screen, this time in yellow. "You can't not believe in computers. That's like not believing in tables and chairs."

"I know. Mom's a bit nuts. Well, maybe more than a bit. She thinks an evil force operates through them. I didn't learn anything about them until I came to school here. This year. I mean, she homeschooled me to keep me away from the things. Anyway, once I got accepted here, she had to let me use one. This place is a dream come true for her—the kind of place she always pictured me, except for the computers, of course. She says nothing matters more than education."

Jeff noticed the labeled files, color coded by subject stacked next to Morgan's backpack. He saw hardcopies of text-notes for world history. *Wow, this guy is serious.*

Morgan noticed Jeff's appraisal and said, "I've got to succeed. For her. I know she's worried about the devil in the computer, but she sent me here anyway. She probably prays every night for my safety." Morgan smiled, prompting Jeff to smile back.

"My mom prays for my safety, too, but for different reasons." Jeff swept his hands down past his small physique.

Morgan started laughing. Jeff joined in, prompting an audible hiss from the screen, which caused them to laugh even more. A moment later, a brittle woman, whose appearance would be the prototype for the robo-librarians to come, marched to the table and showed them the way to the door. "Out," she whispered hoarse and angry. Her outrage created a bond between the two boys that would have taken much longer to form without her.

When they left the library, they were still laughing. A gang from the varsity lacrosse team was lurking down the sidewalk. They'd decided that tonight would be a good time to teach Jeff, that smartass little know-it-all piece of shit, a lesson. But the kid was walking with Morgan, so when the two boys reached them, the other boys just said hey and looked awkward. *What the hell is Morgan doing with that freak?*

Once they'd passed them, Morgan turned to Jeff. "What do you think of those guys back there?"

"I think they had a change of plans once they saw you."

"Yeah, me too. Look, let's go over to Stoddard. You need to start spending some time in the basement. Martial arts, I think. That's something I can show you how to do." And so Jeff's training began, and the friendship's tentative bond became a permanent one.

Jeff returned from his reverie to find Thompson offering him a warm, knowing smile. "That's how it is, Jeff. Relationship is often the thing that takes us out of our own waters into fresh, untried terrain. Trust, an uncommon commodity these days, wouldn't you say?"

What the hell? Thompson's words ripped through Jeff's daze. *Who is this guy?*

"Jeff, wouldn't you say trust is a rarely used capacity these days?"

Jeff shook his head, clearing it so he could focus on the question. "How do you know what I was thinking?" *That's not what I meant to ask.*

"I don't," Thompson answered, sitting back again. "I'm just good at reading faces. I can always tell when a person is thinking about love. It always looks the same; it's unmistakable. Interest in someone, sharing what you know and caring what the other knows; that, along with trust, usually amounts to love. It begins in such fragility—by luck, one would think. If one thing is missing, it doesn't happen at all."

Jeff thought about it. What if he'd refused to help Morgan that night? His whole life had been influenced by that one chance event. *What if I hadn't been* in *the library that night? Or if Morgan had asked someone else for help?* Everything would be different. He would be different. He was who he was now because of Morgan.

Jeff shook his head once more. Every question led to a deeper one. His strange, charitable mood frightened his established rationality. He didn't like thinking this way; it wasn't predictable and didn't promise reasonable answers. But he did have an answer once he'd pulled back from the direction Thompson had turned him. This was clearly one of the ways the anomalies affected the people around them.

"So, you see, Jeff," Thompson continued, "Teachers must love their students, too. It's probably as important as the subjects they teach."

Jeff had heard enough. He stood up and offered his right hand to Thompson. "Well, I've taken up enough of your time. Thank you. You've been very helpful."

Thompson squinted at Jeff. *This kid is being used.* "Well, I'm not sure what I've said that's been so instructive, but I'm glad I could help."

For some reason, Jeff wanted to avoid Thompson's eyes. *What? I'm not doing anything wrong.* But he was, after all, hiding his real purpose. Not exactly a lie, per se, but, well, not the truth either. *Just get out.* "So," Jeff said pulling his hand away from Thompson's, "Thanks again."

"You're welcome, Jeff. And good luck with your research."

Jeff hastened out of the room just as a group of students entered for their next class. *Nice timing... saved by the bell... ha, ha.* He left the building just twenty minutes later *twenty minutes?* through the hallways now crowded with students and teachers. He was confused; his feelings complicating his already muddied thinking. He practically ran down the hill to the car.

Morgan saw Jeff loping toward the car, but he couldn't get a clear read. "So, how'd it go? Did you find out anything?" he asked as Jeff threw himself into the seat. "You were only in there half an hour; was the guy there or what?"

Jeff met Morgan's eyes and jerked his head around to face out the passenger window. *Right. I love Morgan. If something happened to him, my life would suck. Guys don't love guys—unless they* love *guys; right?* Jeff suffered awkwardly, terrified that Morgan would be able to read his mind. Yet they'd been friends forever; why shouldn't he care about him? *Thanks a lot, Mr. Thompson.* "Look, let's just get out of here; I'll tell you on the way back."

Morgan started the car and they drove off while Jeff sat motionless looking out his window. Jeff had felt so good in there with Mr. Thompson. He'd accessed a part of himself that he'd neglected for years. Except for his affection for Linux, Jeff had sealed off his emotional self. *Why?* It's not as if he had been deeply hurt by anything. Sure, both his parents had died when his dad's Cessna crashed up near Mammoth, but that was years ago, and he'd been out of college and living on his own. He'd dealt with it, right? As he thought about them, though, he realized he'd not really felt their deaths at all. What had happened to him? He hadn't been this numb growing up. *When did I turn this stuff off?* A sudden urge to turn on his computer stopped his inquiry. He zoomed in on a large star blazing across the screen. Jeff widened his view back out and saw the star glowing, surrounded by lesser lights, two of them moving away at about 40 miles an hour.

10

SECOND FIRE

Thursday, May 24, 12:30 a.m. PDT

Jeff startled himself, suddenly awake and disoriented. He looked at his screen. *12:30. Definitely not time to wake up.* He got up anyway and shuffled toward the sliding glass doors without turning on the lights. Gazing out past the small mound under the tree—*something's out there*—he stood perfectly still and waited. Yes, something was out there all right. He stepped closer to the glass finally pressing his face up against its smooth coolness. The moonlight reflected silver off the dewy grass, and the fence wires stretched like silver ribbon around the jeweled lawn. Something big was out there. Suddenly, the moonlight reflected on impossibly green eyes and the dark shadowed form that blackened its silhouette into the air behind it. *The cat. What the hell?* Here was his enemy, clear and simple. Evil incarnate. Except that its eyes were communicating a message Jeff didn't understand. "You are complicit," it seemed to be saying. "Without you, I wouldn't exist."

"I didn't kill Linux, you piece of shit!" Jeff screamed through the glass. "You did it. You killed him, you treacherous son of a bitch. Get out of here!"

The lion stared, unaffected by Jeff's outburst. If anything, the cat's unyielding gaze seemed even more demanding—willing Jeff to recognize the merger they'd created.

Jeff twisted himself off the glass and went for his rifle. *Too bad it doesn't have an implant.* Jeff halted mid-stride. *What? Where the hell did that come from?* Was he going to shoot the lion or what? What did an implant have to do with it? Jeff turned back around and went to the glass. The lion was gone. He stood for a moment looking out at the moonlit scene then turned once more away from the doors. He shoved the strange encounter out of his mind. *I need sleep.* He strode to his room, his night vision operating sufficiently to get him into bed without slowing. He looked at his screen one more time. *12:40.* Ten minutes. *Unreal.*

When he next awoke, it was 5:00 a.m. He turned on his vid to see what the computer had learned. A lot. The western states were mapped; every person west of the Missouri River had an EMF id. *So, now what? Call Delamater.*

Delamater had a short fuse on his good days; he was having a bad day. When he picked up Jeff, he was still screaming at Sgt. Baker. This, by itself, was not a good sign because Delamater preferred to communicate with his personnel onscreen. He'd already tried that this morning, and his written tirades—scathing, elongated and twisted—had not sapped his ire. He needed actual human contact so he could observe the results with all his senses. Jeff leaned back in his chair and put his feet up on his desk, waiting.

"Find out what happened. Now, you idiot." The veins in Delamater's neck arched like snakes throbbing and full. "Derek Burns will not talk to me like this. Why wasn't I informed? God damn it!"

Baker spun on his heel and lurched away. Delamater turned to his screen and took a deep breath. "Another murder. Two murders in fact. Quite a string of violence we're looking at, Jeff."

Jeff sat up. This was not supposed to happen. "Where?"

"Your beach." Delamater grimaced. "Burns thinks I know something about it." Derek Burns, the West Coast Commissioner, was Delamater's counterpart and archrival.

"Why? What happened? What does Burns have?"

"Not much. I don't think it was murder. It was an electrical accident—well, disaster is more like it. The house just burst, like electrical pressure—I know, it doesn't make sense—but it was like every socket, every wire just exploded all at once. The house and everything in it disintegrated.

"And someone was inside?"

"Yeah. Some old guy and his wife."

"Ok. So, why does Burns think you had anything to do with it."

"Well, it's interesting that you ask that, Jeff." Delamater's eyes shot a deadly glare through the screen. "Seems someone the tech couldn't see visited this guy yesterday morning—someone by the name of Jeff Spears."

Jeff leaned forward, squinting into the screen, returning Delamater's fierce look with one of disbelief. "What do you mean?"

"You tell me."

"When did it happen?"

"12:30 a.m. Pacific."

Jeff thought back. He'd been awake. That's when the cat came... looking at him like he was a criminal.

"The neighbors didn't see anything unusual, but the guy's coworkers remember a nice man, a Mr. Spears, visited with Mr. Thompson around 10:30 or so yesterday morning. Of course, Burns doesn't know it's you. But someone who can't be tracked—someone invisible—Burns figures the guy has to have significant tech. And, other than this friendly visitor, nothing out of the ordinary happened to Mr. Thompson yesterday."

Jeff immediately shifted into scientific mode. "Right, so Burns thinks this Jeff Spears did it? You sure he doesn't know me?"

"He doesn't know who the hell you are. But out of nowhere,

this guy who eludes cameras shows up at a school deep in Burns' territory, and later, in the middle of the night, a house explodes like a missile hit it. Who has this kind of tech, Jeff? That's why Burns called me."

"Do *you* think I had anything to do with it?" Jeff asked.

"Jeff. After all this time, you think I don't know you? You couldn't whack a bug that was stinging you. But something happened—these people were fried—and you were there that morning. Why?"

Jeff looked away again. Something was deeply wrong. Who had targeted the old man? He dropped back against his chair; his hands slackened their grip on its arms. He prodded his memory until he saw Delamater's face the last time they'd spoken. He'd been angry then, too. "So, when did you find out where I'd gone?"

"Jeff, I can always find out where you are." Delamater smiled and tilted his head. "However, I don't always know what you're doing. Sure you don't want an implant for yourself?"

Jeff smiled back, mimicking Delamater's head tilt. "No, thanks."

Delamater grew serious. "So, I think it's time you tell me what you're up to."

"I disagree. I have some more tests to do, but in the meantime, I think you may be on to something. I'm going to have to, um, disengage more completely. For the next day or so, you won't find me. I'll call you as soon as I have an application for this tech that seems appropriate, one that I can safeguard. For the record, what happened to Stuart Thompson is seriously messed up. And your ignorance of the whole thing tortures the limits of reality... sir. I'll see you later."

Jeff's face blinked off the screen. Delamater couldn't breathe. His heart filled his throat threatening to choke him. He poised himself, hands on the desktop, balls of his feet pressed to the floor, ready to leap off his chair. Suddenly, a dark, heavy blanket pressed him back down and a reassuring voice becalmed his mind. "This

is good, Paul. This is fine." Delamater surprised himself by reacting passively to the soothing, baritone words. Supremely calm.
Everything is going to work out perfectly.

* * *

Thursday, 6:00 a.m. PDT

It took exactly one hour. He'd already worked out a plan ahead
of time for just such an emergency, so Jeff compressed layer after
layer, byte after byte until all that his computer knew fit into a
device the size of his keychain wand. Then he shot the wand into
his arm. He methodically dismantled his house's tech until the
whole place was silent… and dark. *Amazing.* Without the cyber
chatter, the world could be heard. He stepped outside into the
warm, early summer day. The birdsong above him sounded new,
original, unaffected by time. Jeff walked down his driveway pulling
along his wheeled suitcase. He was invisible. His wand, as small
as a toothpick, magically bounced every aimed piece of tech away.

Morgan was ready at the corner of Alta and Wolfback. Jeff got
in the car. "Time to be Claude Rains," he said.

"What's that supposed to mean?"

"Invisible Man. The first. Anyway, I've got something that will
make you invisible."

"Won't people worry about the car driving itself?"

"Ha, ha. The car's been invisible since the moment we bought
it. Anyway, hold out your arm." Jeff shot the pin into Morgan's
extended arm. "Oh, right. This is going to hurt."

"What the hell is wrong with you?" Morgan cried, jerking his
arm away. He expected Jeff to respond, but after meeting his eyes,
Jeff turned to look out his window. "Fine. So, where to?" Morgan
decided to keep at a distance. Jeff was clearly in the middle of
something big. Not just emotionally immature, Jeff was an odd

duck; Morgan had known that since the beginning of their friendship when he'd found Jeff hacking into the school computers. Jeff
had been such a target, too, a magnet for the school thugs. Initially,
Morgan had felt sorry for him, the classic big, stupid athlete
befriending the brilliant but helpless nerd. Except Morgan wasn't
stupid and Jeff wasn't helpless.

Morgan could have been an arrogant despot with his size,
beauty and brains, but he wasn't. He was friendly and humble, and
once he'd established that Jeff was his best friend, Jeff was accepted.
Even the gangsters left Jeff alone. Morgan was honest, too. When
someone asked him a question, he'd tell things true—even when it
was painful for the other person to hear. If you didn't want to know
yourself, you didn't hang around Morgan. So, even though he was
enormously popular, he was also kind of alone. Jeff was the perfect
friend. No matter how earnestly Morgan spoke to Jeff, Jeff did his
own thing. They had equal power in their friendship; equal power,
equal respect. It had worked for almost fifteen years.

Morgan had been burned often enough to know how much
space Jeff needed, and whatever Jeff was facing now demanded
lots of space. This time, Morgan wouldn't initiate any conversa-
tions; Jeff would work himself out of his shell when he was ready.
On the other hand, something had broken loose; Morgan could
feel it. *Man, what I wouldn't give to have been a fly on the wall in
Northridge.*

"We're going to Colorado."

"Colorado."

"Right. We're going to Denver. There's another guy I have to
see.

"Ok. Another teacher?" Morgan asked as he directed the car
toward San Francisco and Interstate 80.

"Kind of, except this one's still alive."

"What do you mean?"

Jeff cleared his throat. "So, the old guy I visited… his house

blew up last night. Killed him and his wife. Seems a bit coinciden-
tal to me; you?"

"Oh, man. How did you find out—Delamater?"

"Yeah, Burns called him. Knows I was there, too. Well, knows
someone who didn't show up on the grid was there. Someone who
tricked the cameras. Someone named Jeff Spears."

"So, how'd the house blow up?"

"Delamater said that the electrical system just went nuts—all
on its own. I don't think anyone believes that. But Delamater says
he doesn't know what happened, and he looks like he's telling the
truth. I tapped into his conversation with Burns to crosscheck it
with what he told me. Checks out. He looked shocked as hell. It's
weird though."

Morgan smiled. *That's my boy.* "So you think Delamater had
something to do with it."

"I don't know what to think. Delamater doesn't know dick
about my new tech. He has no idea why I was meeting with this
guy. I don't know, man. It's all screwed up."

"So why are we in the car, Jeff?"

"I found this other guy in Boulder with a star even bigger than
Thompson's so I'm going to talk to him, see if I can figure things
out—"

"What star?"

"Oh, sorry; the onscreen icon for personal EMF. Anyway, I
can't let anything happen to the Colorado guy, so I've taken us so
far off the grid we don't even exist. And I cleaned my house—not
a trace of content left in any of the tech. You and me, buddy; we're
the only free human beings in the world."

This thought, however, brought neither of them joy. They
couldn't even look at each other. Jeff had been key in fashioning the
current world into existence, and they both knew it. Jeff needed
atonement, big time, but he was going to have to find it for himself.

11

ANOTHER DOG

Thursday, 7:00 a.m. CDT

Donna rolled onto her side allowing her eyes to drift out of focus; the tree in the back yard metamorphosed into a child's round crayon version of itself. She resented its green halo because she resented the summer altogether. She couldn't afford to travel even though she had accrued some vacation time. She had her own car, but she couldn't take it far. Hardly anyone did these days because the cost of gas was too high and the cost of a new car that didn't use much gas was even higher. No one flew—well, that wasn't true, of course. Some people flew, but she didn't know any of them. Only one airline, US Coastal Air, had big jets that flew between just four cities: San Francisco, New York City, Los Angeles and Washington D.C. The government still looked like it existed; it was good to keep up appearances. But everyone secretly knew that the media and police had replaced knowledgeable civil servants in the same way that television anchormen had replaced knowledgeable journalists back in the day.

The other bad part about summer was that Donna would not see Bethanne as much. The library reduced hours during the summer months, and Bethanne wanted to be with her kids while they were out of school. Donna had grown to rely on Bethanne's wise council. Sometimes, just the presence of her best friend was enough to get her centered. She rolled back and set her book down on the bedside table. Every Saturday morning she stayed in bed an extra hour to read. She was reading a hardcover copy of Russell Banks' *Angel on the Roof.* She loved short stories; had even written a few herself, though she'd never sent them to a publisher in spite of Bethanne's encouragement. *What is it about Bethanne?* A few years had passed since alcohol and depression had consumed all of Donna's time, yet she still relied on Bethanne to keep her sane. *Why?* Why was she still plagued by this sense of inadequacy? Why was she still so desperate for the approval of others?

Lady jumped up on the bed and stepped onto Donna's stomach. Donna closed her eyes and absentmindedly stroked Lady's thick, gray fur. *Thank God for cats.* Without her cats, Donna would be utterly alone. She remembered the conversation with Bethanne about cats that had changed her life. They'd been working together for just a week when Bethanne had asked her if she had any pets.

"Yes. Two cats. Lady and Style."

"I love cats, but I'm one of those strange people that like dogs just as much," Bethanne had said.

"I really can't take dogs at all," Donna had said. "They seem so much more vulnerable than cats; they're so needy, so dependent, so ridiculously loyal."

"And all those things are bad?" Bethanne wondered.

"Yes," Donna had answered without hesitation. "Besides, I don't like to be tied down."

"Oh, so you travel a lot."

"No, I..." Donna paused, embarrassed. She couldn't take care of a dog. She wondered, briefly, if Bethanne could smell her morning pick-me-up. No, vodka doesn't have an odor. "Well, I don't travel so much anymore; I guess I just prefer cats."

When she got home that night, she got out a fresh bottle of wine and replayed the conversation in her head. Why was it bothering her so much? *Bethanne asks too many questions. That's it.* But that wasn't it. She didn't ask too many questions; not at all. What was it then? *Oh, to hell with it.* She picked up the bottle and went outside to smoke and drink until she could pass out.

When she collapsed onto her bed in the wee hours of the morning, she drifted to the edge of sleep. *What about Max?* She gasped and sat bolt upright. *Oh, my God.* Suddenly, it all came back to her.

She was 15 years old. She was sound asleep. Like so many other nights for the past few years, her father was knocking lightly on her bedroom door. She always locked it, but eventually she would open it for him. This time she decided she wasn't going to. The knocking grew more persistent.

"Donna?" her dad hissed. "Donna; open this door right now."

Donna lay still holding her breath in bed. She pulled the covers over her head and remained silent.

"Donna, goddamn it! Let me in. I mean it."

Her heart promised to burst from her chest. She held herself rigid; in her head she was screaming. *Stop it. Stop it. Please. Please leave me alone.*

Her dad began pounding in rhythm to the syllables of his shouted words. "O-pen-this-door-right-now!"

Her mom was out with the girls again; her mom wouldn't save her—again. And her dad would probably kill her once he did get in. Then she heard Jack's voice.

"Hey, Dad. What the hell? Is something wrong?"

Tom swung on his son. "Jack, get back to bed. This is none of your business." But he didn't pursue entry; he turned away and staggered off toward his own room.

Jack stood outside his sister's door not knowing what to do. "Donna? Are you okay?"

Donna pulled the covers off her head. "Yeah. I'm fine." And she was fine, right? She turned on her light and picked up the book lying on her bedside table.

Jack shrugged and walked back across the hall to his own room. *This family sucks. I can't wait to get out of here.*

The next morning, Donna woke up, showered and dressed. She wondered what her father would be like, but then again, he would probably be just like he usually was when her mom and brother were around. She made her bed and went down to the kitchen. Her mother was sipping a cup of coffee, but she didn't look like she had been up long. She never got up early after being out with her friends. Her dad had already gone to work, and Jack was gone, too. Jack left early most mornings because the school jazz band—he played trumpet—practiced before class three days a week.

"Hi, honey," her mom mumbled. "How are you this morning?"

"I'm fine. How are you, Mom?"

"I'm a little tired; we stayed out pretty late last night."

No, duh. Maybe you should stay home more often.

"No Max?" Donna asked looking under the table where her German shepherd usually lay during meals.

"I haven't seen him this morning. He's probably making sure the postman doesn't get lost. Now eat your cereal and don't forget to take your vitamins. I'm going to go back to bed for awhile."

Donna finished her breakfast, rinsed out her bowl, and grabbed her backpack. She walked out the back door toward the garage where she'd left her bicycle leaning against the back wall. She rounded the corner and stopped dead. On the ground next to her bicycle was Max, his throat sliced, the blood black and thick around him.

Dad killed Max. He knew no one would come back here but her. He was telling her not to lock her door again. She went over to Max's body and patted his side for a moment. But she didn't cry. She stood up and went back into the house. Her mom wasn't in the kitchen anymore. Donna took down the flour tin filled with emergency money then went up to her room. She grabbed her duffle and filled it before walking back outside and down four doors to the McCleary house where she waited for the bus. At the city terminal, she bought a ticket for the only bus ready to leave. She would never lock her bedroom door again.

A few days later, she called her mother from Iowa City. She told her what had happened. Her mom started crying. "Oh, my god," she'd said. "What am I supposed to do now? You don't expect me to leave him, do you?"

"I don't expect anything, Mom. I just wanted you to know I'm alive."

"You should come home, Donna. Your father is going to be furious. What are we supposed to tell people? Everyone's going to think something bad happened."

Donna let her mother's words sink in. She could find herself nowhere in her mom's concerns. "Bye, Mom." And that was it; the last time she spoke to her mother.

After reliving the buried memory, Donna allowed herself to cry as long as the tears would come. *I don't like dogs.* She stayed home from work that day and the next one. And she stayed inside all weekend, too. She took long baths, drank tea and slept. She made herself toast with cinnamon and sugar. Sometimes she would cry as the memories sought footing, but gradually she would witness them and live them from a distance. They didn't scare her. Backwards from the day she'd left home, Donna paused before each horror and acknowledged it. She arrived at a time before the knocks came on her door and watched Jack go through the picture window at the front of their ranch style house. He'd gone to the hospital, and her dad had lied about an indoor wrestling match. And Jack had said, "Yeah, that's how it happened." And she continued back and observed her dad, drunk and mad with rage, crazed and inhuman, chase them both down; hitting her brother over and over.

On that Sunday night, Donna realized she'd gone four days without a drink. She poured out all the alcohol in every bottle. She ripped apart her last pack of cigarettes. And that was two years ago. She still, however, did not have a dog.

Donna returned from her reverie to look out the window again, this time focusing on the budding pear tree. She hated being alone; it wasn't her style; it wasn't what she had imagined. In a couple years she'd be 30. Who would want her? Surely the fact that she was alone proved she was undesirable.

Yet, she did have Bethanne. Of course, they wouldn't have been friends if David hadn't died in that fire. Donna gasped, choking back her shame when she realized how glad she was that Bethanne's husband had died. *What's wrong with me?* Immediately she began rationalizing. Bethanne never talked about him; maybe things hadn't been as perfect as they looked in the pictures on the tabletops and walls of Bethanne's house. She wondered what he'd been like. *I mean, who would be good enough for Bethanne?* Maybe Bethanne was secretly glad he'd died, too. Hadn't she moved directly to Iowa after his death? No one moves from New York to Iowa City. No one. It's the other way around; people move out, just as her brother had. *Maybe Bethanne had hated New York and had lived there only because David wanted to.* Slowly, Donna brought her runaway mind back into her control. *Right. I'm pathetic. It couldn't be because New York reminded Bethanne of David.*

Lady jumped to the windowsill compressing Donna's stomach and forcing her back into the present. Donna pulled her pillow to her side and lay flat on the mattress. She began examining the devious path down which her thinking had led her. She didn't turn away; she just observed what had happened. She looked at her feelings that had prompted the dark shadows. She was lonely. She was still a victim. She remembered. She was sober. She was all this. She needed to acknowledge every part of herself because until she did, she wouldn't be able to live without Bethanne's approval.

12

FIELD GENERATION

PART ONE: GENESIS

Thursday, 7:00 a.m. CDT

Bethanne woke Claire and Scott for their last full day of school. Tomorrow would be a half day. Bethanne had gone to sleep no longer seeking for the question to ask a professor, but seeking for the strength to go into battle. That night, she had received it, and the effect on her was powerful. Claire followed her mother into Scott's room so that she could see her wake Scott up. Scott woke to his mom's voice. Immediately held in the grasp of Bethanne's eyes, he felt like he was floating in space. Bethanne shifted her gaze to Claire, who was looking at Scott and smiling. Released from Bethanne's focus, Scott returned Clair's smile before fluffing his pillow up to get a better view. *This is big.* Scott was young, but he was observant. He saw the effect his mother had on his friends, on everyone. He knew she was special. But now he saw that he hadn't come close to understanding who she was.

Claire saw it with more depth. It was as if her mother had

always been this beautiful bird, her gifts dropped like feathers people would pick up and keep. But her mother wasn't a bird; she was the power of flight. Claire broke the silence. "Mom?"

Bethanne nodded. "I have to start experimenting." She looked at Scott. "Things—I don't know what for sure—but bad things have been set into motion." She turned to include Claire. "Last night, I had a nightmare, a premonition I'm afraid, of good people being hurt. I don't know much yet, but what I do know is that whatever is happening has been in the making for a long, long time. I can't explain it better right now; I'm just on the edge of understanding it. But what's clear to me is that I have to begin preparing for something big—something I'll be called on to do soon. I have to start practicing with my, um, I guess I'd call them energies."

"So, how are you going to do that?" Claire asked.

"What are you guys talking about?" Scott demanded. "I mean, are you a witch or something? Are we a wizarding family? I want to do magic."

Bethanne laughed out loud. "Wow, Harry Potter again."

"Well, are we wizards?" Scott asked.

Bethanne's smile faded. She grew serious. Taking up their hands in hers, she struggled to find the words. "I'm not sure what to call it, Scott," she began. "I have a connection to beings who don't live in bodies on earth. They are just as real as the people we know, but they don't live in physical bodies. I guess that's the best way to put it."

"Like Dad?"

Bethanne started, involuntarily squeezing their hands. She took a deep breath and looked at Scott. "Yes, honey, some of them are like Dad."

"Sometimes Dad comes to talk to me," Scott said. "I didn't want to tell you because I thought you'd feel sad."

Bethanne's eyes filled with tears. How could she have missed this? Gees, he was already 14 year old; he had kept this secret well for a long time. "Oh, Scott. I'm so sorry you felt you couldn't tell me that. But I'm glad that you see your dad. He talks to me sometimes, too."

"Me, too," said Claire.

Bethanne sighed. "Okay, from now on, no more secrets about this kind of thing. It's important; got it?"

The two of them nodded and waited for her to go on.

"So, here's my plan. I'm going to send my forces out there. A controlled burst. I've never tried it, but it's time. I don't know how far I can go, but I'm going to start by going up the Cedar River and see what happens—and I'll only keep it out there for say fifteen minutes or so. I don't know if I can even last that long. I already know I can focus it—that's what I did when I came into your rooms this morning. I've been working on that for a long time with my professors at school."

"So some people already know you can do this, Mom?" Claire looked frightened.

Bethanne squeezed Claire's hand, reassuring her. "Don't worry, sweetheart. I've been so careful; no one knows. I've been hiding in plain sight for years."

Claire looked at her mother. She saw that Bethanne was beautiful. She didn't wear make-up or style her hair or dress in clothes that would show off her perfect figure, so she didn't seem remarkable at all. *Mom must have rocked New York City.* She'd seen pictures, of course, of her mom and dad when they were young— both of them so beautiful they must have stopped traffic. It made the fact that her mother strove for plainness, for invisibility, more poignant. "Even Donna doesn't know?" Claire asked.

"No, not even Donna," her mother confirmed. She let go of her children's hands and got up from the bed. "Okay, you two get ready for school while I get breakfast going. The experiment will begin as soon as you leave."

PART TWO: OSMOSIS

Waterloo, Iowa, about 70 miles northwest of Iowa City, had been a thriving town on the Cedar River during the babyboom era of the mid-twentieth century. A job at the John Deere Tractor Company or Rath's Packing Company meant economic security. Suburbs were expanding and with them the shopping malls and new schools to accommodate the demands of the growing population. No more. In fact, those residents who had had the means were long gone. But at 7:30 a.m. that day, the people in these old neighborhoods from Cedar Falls, just north of Waterloo and the towns to the south—Vinton, Cedar Rapids, Coralville—were different. The sky, a robin's egg blue dotted with puffs of white cloud, hung its pastel tapestry above the trees and gardens in the backyards. The fragrance of fresh rain invaded the houses through their open windows. Parents took the time to eat breakfast with their children. Screens didn't get turned on; the singing birds took over the job of informing the residents about the day ahead. People spoke to each other kindly, made each other matter. No one, not one person, escaped Bethanne's influence.

Misery begins within us. The prescient citizens along the Cedar River began to sense their own responsibility for the quality of their lives. They remembered their dreams.

Sylvia Jackson looked at her three children around the table. They were all dressed and ready for school. She remembered how happy she'd been when she found out she'd be having Tyler's baby. *But he left, didn't he?* She was a fool—a stereotype. She'd been depressed for years, except for the brief romances that preceded the next two pregnancies. Today, this beautiful day, she loved her children guiltlessly. She asked the older two questions about school, grateful that they were still so young; she could start over, fresh, while it mattered. The children didn't seem surprised. They could see their mother's love straight through her eyes as they answered her questions. After they left for school, Sylvia picked up the breakfast dishes and began cleaning the entire mess that had accumulated in the kitchen. This apartment was going to shine; she could do that today.

People up and down the river regained the will to act on hopes they'd long ago buried. How this sense of possibility arose they didn't know, but as they went out into the world that day, they met other people who felt the same way. The thoughtful ones, well, they recognized their own part in the hopelessness of their lives; how the role they played was mirrored in the despair written on the faces of the people they were closest to. For these people, the stimulus from Bethanne would be a catalyst for some time to come. For others less aware, the effect would become a vague memory once they went to sleep that night.

For Bill Anderson, it was a change that would last. Professor Anderson surveyed the classroom from his podium. He'd already been awake for two hours. He went to bed early and rose early, a habit he'd begun as a boy on his father's farm near Fayetteville. His visual survey ended when he saw a bright yellow spiral notebook on a desk at the back of the lecture hall. *Idiot. Why take notes if you can't keep track of them?* He strode up the tiers toward the offending book.

Anderson was always in his office at 7:30, the time printed on the small cardboard sign outside the door and listed next to the syllabus of each of his classes. Now he was going to be late. *How ironic.* Right before finals he could actually count on a few students showing up. Not that they were interested in his class; they would come only to elicit advice about the final. Where had the desire to learn for its own sake gone?

When Anderson reached the notebook, he stopped, peering at it as if it were a foreign object. He slowly folded himself into the chair attached to the desk and opened it. Adam Margolis had taken down the course lectures almost word for word. The lectures were dated, with starting and ending times: starting promptly at 9:00 and ending at 9:50. Three days a week for an entire semester. Anderson skimmed through the first lecture's notes; a lecture he'd written several years ago. At the end of the notes, Margolis had posed four penetrating questions—questions piercing through the hard lamina of the lecture to the molten core of the subject itself. *Who is this kid?* Anderson continued leafing through the rest of the notebook; each set of lecture notes was followed by seminal observations or provocative questions. *Why was this kid sitting at the back of the class? Why didn't he ever ask the questions he'd written?* By 7:45, Anderson realized he had no idea who any of his students were. It had been a long time since he'd even thought about his students. He read Margolis' last question. "Why is this guy still teaching if he hates it so much?" *Why, indeed?* Except that Anderson didn't hate teaching; it's just that he'd been doing it by rote for the last few years. Three years, to be exact. The year his wife Sandy died, he'd simply recycled the lectures he'd given the year before. Depressed, he was without enthusiasm for life, let alone a fire for teaching anthropology to distracted teenagers. Sandy had been a professor, too, and they'd never run out of things to say to each other—about their subjects, their students, or the world they lived in. They traveled during their summer breaks to see the parts of the world that had been in the newspapers that year. Anderson hadn't packed a suitcase since her death. And he realized, with chagrin, that he hadn't taught a class since then either, even though he never missed a day of school.

He refocused on the notebook and realized with surprise that he wasn't crying; he was strangely elated, as he used to get when he'd tracked down a possible cause for a behavioral characteristic in a population. *Know thyself. The pronaos at the Temple of Apollo at Delphi. Know thyself—the I Am. My next project.*

He glanced at his watch. 8:00. *My office hours!* He picked up the yellow notebook and hurried down the tiers back to his podium where he placed it on top of the guidelines for the final he'd be giving at 9:00. Gathering the podium's contents into his briefcase, he strode from the room toward his office. A student was standing confused before the card listing his hours.

"Good morning," he sang.

Startled, the girl looked up. "Good morning."

"Sorry I'm late. Come on in," he added, unlocking his door. "Would you like some tea?"

"Um, no, actually I'm not one of your students. I'm waiting for my boyfriend. He thinks he may have left his notebook in the lecture hall yesterday, and what with the test, well, he wants it back. Anyway, I agreed to meet him here because he didn't want to miss you. Oh, he has a few questions, too."

"I've got it," Anderson smiled. "The notebook, I mean. I'll just leave the door open, shall I, and when Mr. Margolis arrives, you can join him, though you're more than welcome to wait for him inside." He walked into his office and turned on the tea kettle. He reached up for a book on the shelf behind his desk. *People of the Blue Water*; the Havasupai tribe still lived down inside the Grand Canyon. He'd have to go somewhere close by this year.

INTERLUDE

Bethanne pulled herself back in and sat still in front of her altar. She was not tired; she was exhilarated. *I can't believe it. I can't believe I can do that.* Her eyes filled; gratitude swept through her. She was immediately humbled by the gift she had been given. *Why me?* But she knew the answer to that question now, too. She'd come back for this; it was her destiny, and she had accepted it willingly many lifetimes ago.

PART THREE: SYNTHESIS

Scott noticed a change as soon as he got on the school bus. He and his friends were usually pretty crude, so when his best friend, Steve, greeted him with, "Hey, man. Did you notice how nice it is outside?" Scott was dumbfounded. He looked closely at Steve for clues and found an unguarded joy he recognized from their games together when they were little kids. Lately, Steve had become proficient at looking bored and apathetic. He made sure no one knew what he was thinking by keeping his observations monosyllabic whenever possible. When he did venture into complete sentences, Steve was sarcastic, witty and quick. Scott wasn't anything like his friend, but they'd been best friends since kindergarten. Scott struggled to redirect his usual response of, "Your mom's face," with a quick, "Yeah, it really is nice out."

As the boys approached the school building, Scott noticed that the kids were talking to each other, not into their tech. Their hands were free, gesturing to each other instead of attached to one form of tech or another. The sound of voices filled the air; a beautiful sound; an unfamiliar sound. And no one, not even Steve, looked bored.

The real shock came when he saw Bachman open the door to let Joey in. Joey was one of Neil Bachman's victims, which basically described everybody but his henchmen. Joey, however, didn't always remember how cruel Bachman could be because Joey was slow—really slow—mentally and physically. Mostly Bachman and his friends mimicked Joey and laughed; sometimes Joey laughed with them. Scott watched Bachman hold the door patiently while Joey, using his walker, struggled through.

Claire, too, immediately noticed a change at her school. Sitting in her first period math class, she watched her classmates settle down and take their seats when the teacher entered the room. *Are you kidding me?* Like the reformed kids from some movie like

Freedom Writers, which she'd found on vid a few months ago, the kids were acting respectfully toward a teacher that hadn't held their attention all year. Claire found Rick, the kid her class could always count on for disruptions. Rick caught her eye and grinned. She saw, instantly, that Rick had been trying all along to rouse his classmates out of their stupor and his teachers out of their complacency. He'd been trying to provoke a natural reaction, any natural reaction. But today he didn't have to and he knew it. He winked at Claire, and she felt herself blushing. *Is this why girls always go for the bad boys? Am I going to go for this bad boy?* Suddenly, Claire was grateful to her mother for an entirely different reason.

Bethanne walked into the library joyful from her walk to the campus. Like a powerful prism, she had taken the light streaming always toward the world and refined its beam, shooting it through the dense atmosphere of autonomous routine for a few minutes. Everyone in its rays had had an epiphany. She noticed students quietly studying individually at the tables. Nothing different there. Donna had just finished helping the star heavyweight from the school's wrestling team at the information desk; he was walking back to a small group of students sitting close by talking to each other with great intensity. The composition of the group gradually dawned on her, causing a short laugh to escape.

Donna looked up. "Oh, hi, Bethanne. How are you this fine morning?"

"Great."

"Yeah, me, too."

"So, what's going on?" Bethanne asked, nodding toward the group of boys.

"I know, right? I thought I was seeing things. The only people I've ever seen the wrestlers with besides each other are girls. Anyway, Tanner just came over and shed some light on this confab."

Donna paused, her face growing serious. She looked straight

into Bethanne's eyes. "I've got to tell you something, though. I don't know why I have to tell you, but I do, and I won't be able to relax until I get it over with."

"Okay, what is it?"

Donna lowered her voice and turned her back to the students. "When I first heard about your husband being dead, I—well a part of me, I guess, well, I was pleased. I was glad you were single so that you'd want to be my friend. I mean, I was horrified this morning when I realized I still felt that way. You know, like I was glad that you didn't have everything that the pictures on your walls said you had—the perfect life. I hadn't been able to admit it before; it was so awful, so evil. I just let myself think it without thinking *about* it, you know? But, for some reason, this morning I was thinking about how grateful I am that we're friends, and I realized this horrible thing, and I had to tell you. I'll understand if you don't want to be my friend anymore. That's the whole point; you should know who you're really dealing with." Donna stopped talking. Her eyes were dry, her face grim.

Bethanne looked at her. "You must have been scared to see that about yourself."

Donna broke their gaze and looked down at her hands clasped together. "Yes. I was scared at first. I tried to squirm out of it—like the other times—but I couldn't. And then I just looked at it, calmly, you know? And the longer I looked at it, the more I understood it. And the more I understood it, the less terrible it was. It's like I fixed it; like I accepted myself, my real self. It makes me wonder about other thoughts I just shove away because, basically, I've hated myself forever. Anyway, now you know. I'm so sorry, Bethanne."

Bethanne nodded. "Thank you for telling me, Donna. And you know I forgive you. Let me tell you something else: forgiving other people is way, way easier than forgiving ourselves. So, you're doing the hard work now, not me."

The two women were interrupted by Tanner Doyle, the

197-pounder from the team. "Sorry to bother you again," he said, looming over the desk. A person always felt small and fragile next to Tanner; his habitual demeanor did nothing to assuage one's sense of vulnerability whenever he was near, but today was different. "Mark and Randy from the chess club and the guys," he said indicating the boys behind him, "have been talking. We've been comparing chess moves with wrestling moves—you know, figuring out what the other guy's going to do and then what he'll do after you do what you do, you know. Anyway, it's pretty cool. We got any books on it?"

Bethanne and Donna flashed each other a look. "Comparing wrestling and chess, right?" Bethanne asked.

"Right."

"Let me see." She found a book currently in the library called *Beginning Wrestling*. Thomas Ryan, once the head coach at Hofstra, the author of the book, had said, "It's like playing chess with your body—moves and countermoves that outwit and overpower your opponent." She showed Tanner the quote onscreen, then wrote down 796.8124. "Here's the Dewy. I don't know how much is in there, but it's a start."

"Hey, thanks," Tanner said, turning and giving a thumbs up to the other boys.

"Will wonders never cease?" Donna murmured, shaking her head. "It's been like this all morning. Everyone's being nice to everyone. Weird."

Bethanne smiled and began sorting the books on the counter.

13

SECOND ROAD TRIP

Still Thursday, 8:00 a.m. PDT

"So," Morgan began, "I know something big happened back in LA, and if this guy's torus or star or whatever is even bigger than the last guy's, you could get even more messed up. Why can't you just do this on vid? I don't get the whole personal interview deal. Not that I'm complaining—I love the road... I love my car," he added, grinning wickedly as he gunned the r8.

After taking a circuitous route in and around San Francisco—just to be on the safe side—they stopped outside Sacramento for a fastfood breakfast. The car had been mostly silent, Morgan staring ahead at the freeway and Jeff staring out the passenger window lost in thought. When Morgan asked his question, Jeff shook his head, smiling. "My instincts are always right," he answered.

"Oh, really. Nothing like a little self-confidence... like you've never gone wrong following a gut feeling?" Morgan joked.

"No; this is different. I don't know why, but I'm always right about this kind of stuff," Jeff countered seriously.

"About what kind of stuff?"

"About how to get the job done right—you know, how to make

it all happen the way I want it to happen."

"Yeah. How about your instinct for knowing if it's *supposed* to happen?"

"Whatever. Anyway, my interview with the old man proved one thing. People with higher electromagnetic fields produce altered EMFs in the people who know them, and the effects seem to last even if those people move away. The anomaly of the first forever affects the field of the others."

"Jeff, I hate to tell you, man, but that's pretty elementary shit. I mean, a person who is influential in your life affects you for the rest of your life? Have you ever read a biography?"

"Ha, ha. I'm talking about the science of it, not the psychology of it."

"What do you mean?"

"I'm talking EMF transferences. That maybe EMFs get boosted by direct interference, I mean influence. And if it's measurable, observable, then it's probably controllable."

Morgan was quiet. *Shit. This is worse than I thought.* He loved Jeff, but this did not sound good at all. *What the hell is he up to now?* "Jeff, if it's controllable—if you figure out how to control it, *who* controls it, Jeff?"

"Hey, relax. That's not what I'm doing, man. No one's going to control it. It's just that most people operate within a certain frequency and that's fine. The differences are usually subtle, but identifiable, like fingerprints. So, I'm basically mapping and identifying people's electromagnetic profiles. I mean, that's what I'm doing for Delamater. This side thing is just for me."

Morgan was not reassured. "Why do you need to id everyone's EMF?"

"Look, the implant program was a success for the most part, but it's limited. The implants are cumbersome because they require a medical procedure to install them and a law to enforce their use. We still have groups of people protesting them—having babies at home and trying to keep them out of school. And every-thing between the coasts has sketchy participation. With an EMF registry, we don't need laws or regulations or doctors because we each have unique EMFs from the moment we're born. The electro-magnetic grid will recognize any field generated in any vicinity. It's perfect."

Morgan shook his head. "You know, you still haven't answered my question, little buddy. What for?"

"What for? So we know. Because we can. We should never *ever* set limits to knowledge."

"So the question *why* never enters into the equation," Morgan said flatly.

"I don't know what you're talking about. Look, this is cool shit, and I'm all over it; so, if you can't get it, stay out of it. Anyway, that's why we're going to Denver, well actually, Boulder. This guy's the first significant anomaly outside California that I can find—the program crossed the Rockies just before I packed up—so that's where we're going." Jeff paused a moment; Morgan said nothing. "Fine; you're an asshole. I have to take a piss, then we get back on the road."

Morgan set his jaw and turned his head away from the closing passenger door. *This is* so *not good.* He was beginning to see why he was along, though. He was going to have to convince Jeff to stop. And if he couldn't convince him, he was going to have to stop him another way. It didn't seem likely that Jeff would change his mind; he was nothing if not sure of himself. In fact, Morgan was pretty clear that the only time he'd been successful in changing Jeff's mind was on the first day of their friendship.

14

ANOTHER QUESTION

Thursday, 10:00 a.m. MDT

Reverend John Simms had acquired a congregation of over 4000 people. His ebullient manner and boyish good looks—dark tousled hair beginning to gray at the temples, blue eyes, ready smile—were currently projected onto a large screen behind him while he addressed his faithful flock. He presided over a congregation that was moderately wealthy, liberal, and spirit-minded. He had built the community with his sincerity, enthusiasm, and tirelessness. John was a good man. He was, however, embroiled in an internal battle. His congregation paid him well—too well. He lived in a large, fashionable, brick home on Highland Avenue. His beautiful wife, Michelle, was his assistant. He confided in her completely; she was the only one who knew the turmoil of his current state of mind. She was also twelve weeks pregnant with their first child, which somehow complicated his inner war.

"I could reach so many more people," John said that evening as they cleaned the dinner dishes.

"Yes," Michelle replied, inflecting a hint of a question.

"What, you don't think I could? Do you think I'd fail?"

"John, if you set your mind to something, you'll succeed at it. Of this, I have no doubt."

"Then what? Why am I agonizing over this? It's a tremendous opportunity. Why do I always suspect new possibilities are the devil's own temptations?"

Michelle looked over at her husband as she handed him a plate to rinse. She said nothing because the question wasn't hers to answer. She did know, however, that John was considering this new offer with the required depth.

She dried her hands as the teapot whistled and poured the boiling water onto the chamomile teabags lying at the bottom of their cups. John had fought demons the whole way, struggling for humility as his reputation and congregation grew. John had always had to make choices like this one. She carried the cups to the table and sat down across from him.

John often spoke at the university, but he'd declined a lucrative vid show that would broadcast his sermons weekly throughout Colorado. This new thing was big, though: a national show. *National! Coast to coast. Wait. No one on either coast would watch a church service except to make fun of it.* He quieted his thoughts allowing a question to form. *Is that what I'm really afraid of? Ridicule? Mockery? No, that would be a challenge.* "I don't know, honey," he said at last. "Maybe this would be an opportunity to show the materialists something they haven't considered for a long time. I'd get a chance to air my arguments, kind of sling them out there. You know, today's blind devotion to reason, as if that's all the brain is capable of, as if reason isn't just one of many possibilities... maybe not even the best one... certainly not the only one. Really, they're all so damned arrogant. A person has to make at least as many presumptions to disregard a spiritual world as a blind believer has to make to disregard so-called reason."

Michelle lifted her cup of tea. She met his eyes and raised an eyebrow, waiting for him to calm down.

He did and smiled sheepishly at her. "Ok, that was fun. If that's my motive, I have the answer already. Motive is everything. If that's clean, it's a good start."

Michelle reached out her hand. He took it like a precious gift, holding it with his full attention. Taking a deep breath, he let his rational mind take a break. *What would I do without her?*

He gave himself to the first level of relaxation. Immediately it became clear that powerful forces in the world were coalescing, gaining momentum and focus. The shadows were forever preying on people's weaknesses—their tendencies to be self-serving, their willingness to focus on the short-term without understanding or even considering the long-term, their fascination, even absorption, in decadence. The shadows had been gaining power rapidly ever since the first atom was forced to split. Most people didn't even recognize how bad things had become. He struggled with the realization that all his assessments about the state of humankind were right. His indignation was valid. He watched it survive his scrutiny. *Okay. I need to get my compassion on, here. This will take me nowhere.*

John needed more preparation. He relaxed his body, beginning with his toes and moving up to the crown of his head, all the while taking deep and rhythmical breaths. He allowed his thoughts to be quiet. *I have a destiny—show me.* He already knew he needed to wake people up to what they were losing, what they had already lost. If he couldn't gain a foothold on the coasts, eventually the tech would be impossible to penetrate. *Maybe a national show is the answer.* John let the question live as he descended deeper into himself. He saw himself on the screen, then preparing for air-time: the make-up, the advertising, the appeals for money, the directors, the producers, the shows on before and after his show, the entire 24-hour line-up. He shifted his internal gaze to the audience sitting in their homes using all the myriad tech that would bring his show to them. He saw them reacting to what he said then losing the thread as soon as the commercial came on, or as soon as the show was over, or as soon as any of a thousand interruptions occurred. *We're already too far gone.* He was amazed. Still inside himself, he heard the witty and clever, intelligent and reasonable people deriding his message, already too deep into their service to themselves to hear the truth of what he said. He heard their laughter. *No, a show is not the answer. Whew, no show.*

John smiled and opened his eyes. He started laughing, a joyful contradiction to the laughter he'd heard from his imaginary audience. He felt free.

15

EAGLE EYE

Thursday, 10:30 a.m. PDT

The security alarm sounded on his vid, its little bing invading the quiet car as it approached Reno. Jeff's quick investigation showed that Delamater, in his efforts to locate him, had passed his first level of defenses. Jeff wasn't worried; he had over 20, but he wasn't reassured that the first one had gone down less than 3 hours into his disappearance. "Asshole," he said under his breath.

"Eff you," Morgan answered, another code word from their first meeting.

"Not you, you moron. I'm talking about Delamater," Jeff replied.

"What's up with Delamater? I thought you weren't go to tell him where you're going," Morgan said.

"I'm not; he has no idea where I am. But that doesn't mean he isn't looking."

Morgan glanced over at Jeff. "Come on, dude. I know that you know that I don't trust Delamater, but you just keep working for him—you've never worked for anyone else. Why?"

"You're kidding, right? I get to play with my toys and live the way I want to and save the world all at the same time. It's perfect."

Jeff replied, edgy with annoyance.

"If it's so perfect, why are you so damned defensive whenever I bring it up?"

"Maybe because it's none of your *effing* business."

Morgan smiled. Jeff saw it and smiled, too, but he continued to look at his friend. He trusted Morgan on every other issue without exception. Hell, he trusted Morgan with his life. Yet this one thing, perhaps the biggest factor in his life, he couldn't peacefully discuss with his best friend. "Look," Jeff began, struggling to explain himself. "Like I said before, Delamater's an asshole, but sometimes being an asshole is what it takes to move things along."

"Really? So, the way it works is that assholes make things happen? Do you think maybe that's why the world happens to suck right now?"

"How does it suck? I'm happy; you're happy. I'll bet plenty of other people are happy too. And safe."

"And Delamater did all that with your cameras and implants?"

"Yes."

"So if you map everyone's EMF then the world will finally be completely, totally safe." Morgan allowed the sarcastic tone to fill every word.

"What is your problem? It's not like it's going to hurt anyone. It'll be a vast improvement over what we have now."

"Yeah, I'm sure you think so. I'm just wondering what the final goal is."

"The final goal is to get everyone's EMF. Are you retarded?" Jeff was starting to lose it.

"No, Jeff. That's not the final goal. Someone has to do something with all those EMFs, right? Think about some of the other stuff we've got going on. What's to prevent someone like Delamater from projecting whatever he wants into the electromagnetic field? If people with stronger EMFs affect other people, couldn't Delamater do some pretty significant damage if he had access to everyone's EMF?"

Jeff clamped his teeth and looked down at his computer. "Morgan. I'm telling you, Delamater is trying to make the world a safer place. That's all."

"Right. We're all one step away from becoming his own personal computer, Jeff. And you're going to give him the means. You'll never be able to take it back. I know you've always looked at this shit like a giant game. You've always wanted to be the best player; you *are* the best player. But, dude, you're getting played; big-time. And when you finally win this ultimate game, the whole world will be thoroughly, irreversibly screwed."

A cold sweat broke out all over Jeff's body. *Holy shit. Am I getting played?*

"The amazing thing right now is," Morgan continued, "you are invisible… Delamater can't find you. Something's working to get you on the right track, little buddy. So, let's go with that. This could turn out a bit differently than Delamater expects it to."

Jeff sat dumb and still. He closed his eyes; he was exhausted even though it was still morning. Morgan touched a few buttons, and Jeff's seat adjusted itself to a more relaxing position. They didn't speak again for a long time. Morgan noticed a golden eagle circling above the shimmering surface of the desert floor. Golden eagles lived everywhere in the northern hemisphere, from Alaska to Maine. Still. Collectively, they saw the entire continent; it was a beautiful thing.

16

EXPECTATIONS

PART ONE: PAUL AND MALLORIE

Thursday, 12:00 noon EDT

Delamater was having another bad day. He'd lost Jeff. Completely. The little shit was immune to his influence and the fact was, he needed Jeff. He was desperate to know what new tech he'd come up with. He knew it couldn't be a coincidence that Jeff had visited that teacher the morning before the old man's house exploded, but Jeff was a complete pacifist; he'd had nothing to do with the explosion, of that Delamater was certain. In fact, that's what had kept Jeff on his side all this time: the promise of an end to violence. Delamater needed to keep Jeff on his side.

On top of all this other bullshit, his wife wanted to meet him for lunch after some doctor's appointment. He'd been irritable, to say the least, when she called, and he'd tried to get out of going to lunch with her. Now she was pissed off; and Mallorie pissed off was not good. The problem was that she didn't yell; she just acted hurt in a dignified way that actually worked on him. He touched the screen to replay their conversation. "I'm sorry I bothered you at work, honey. I just thought it would be so nice to see each other during the day for a change." He'd answered, "Look, baby, you never bother me. It's just that sometimes I'm so busy. I can't always get away, you know?" And then she'd said, "Too busy for me? It's okay. I understand. But I remember a time when you would order me to come in for lunch just to be with me." And so on. *Shit. Of course I wanted you to come into town. I could count on getting some at least. What do I have to look forward to now—conversation? Screw conversation. I have conversation up the ass all day every day.*

Delamater's phone rang; she was calling him back. *Great.* "Hi, Mallorie. Did you forget something?"

"No, Paul, I didn't forget anything. But I'm afraid I have to insist that we meet for lunch. We have something important to discuss. It won't wait." She paused. "I won't wait. See you at Risotteria in half an hour." She hung up.

Oh, it just doesn't get any better. He hated Risotteria. One of the reasons he didn't like going out with Mallorie was her wheat allergy. He loved pasta, garlic bread, all things Italian, which is why he preferred Babbo—where he had his own table. Better food, better service, better ambience. High class; more his style. *And where does she get off ordering me around?* Paul was considering a no show when he realized that Mallorie never, ever asserted herself like this. He had to admit she'd gotten his attention. He pushed himself away from his desk and stalked out into the squad room.

He got into the back seat of his waiting car and began imagining what Mallorie had gotten herself into. An affair? She was, after all, one of the most beautiful women he'd ever seen. She was smart, too. Too smart to put her own life in danger by straying. She was too smart to tempt all the tech trained on her 24-7. *So, no affair.* Suddenly, Paul was stricken. Hadn't she just come from the doctor? Was she sick? *Oh bloody hell.* What if something was wrong with her? That would be bad for publicity. People don't like sick people.

It would mean he couldn't keep his own wife healthy. He needed to keep his image of perfection stainless. His car aimed for the Village, which was only a few minutes away because the only cars allowed on the streets of Manhattan were limos and official vehicles. Everywhere that mattered was just a few minutes away.

Mallorie sat alone at the table waiting for Paul to appear. She closed her eyes. *Oh, god.* She didn't know if she wanted to tell Paul; she'd already been keeping it a secret for so long. But she had to. *What's he going to do?*

"May I get you something to drink, Ma'am?" the young waiter asked.

Mallorie absentmindedly replied. "Yes. Sparkling water, please. Lime. Agava."

"Yes, ma'am."

Mallorie loved this restaurant. Its location on Bleeker. Its casual atmosphere. Its incredible breads, especially the breadsticks and pizzas—all gluten-free. She took a panini home for the following day's lunch every time she came here. She also appreciated the human staff. Many of the restaurants in town had converted to onscreen menus and robot service—cheap robots that didn't even approximate a human look. *Yuck.* The human staff was probably the only reason Paul tolerated the restaurant at all. He loved ordering, showing off his refined tastes. Mostly, he just loved telling other people what to do, something he never seemed to tire of.

Mallorie straightened the napkin on her lap and kept her focus there. *Oh, god.* She looked again at her phone: 11:58. The waiter returned with her water. "Would the lady like to order?"

"No," Mallorie replied. "I'll just eat the breadsticks until my husband comes."

The waiter stiffened. He knew who she was—everyone did; Paul Delamater was coming. The door to the street opened and Paul entered. His eyes adjusted until he could see Mallorie and the waiter. He put on his public, good-natured, man-of-the-people smile and walked to the table. Everyone looked up from their tables and smiled as he met their eyes and nodded to each one. The waiter, Joseph, held out the chair and, with an air of formality, laid Paul's napkin across his lap. "Wine, sir?" he asked.

"Yes. The same thing I had last time," Paul demanded.

"Right away, sir." Joseph hurried off.

Delamater finally looked at his wife. She was stunning; no doubt about it. Suddenly he was glad to be sitting across from her in broad daylight. She added to his virility index, put another attribute into his asset column. Of course, they were always featured in the society news, on webmag covers, in lifestyle media. They were probably the best looking, most famous couple in America—maybe the world—but it didn't hurt to flaunt it in real life once in awhile.

Mallorie stared back, unblinking, until Paul refocused. She had never been afraid of him, but she wasn't always sure that was a good thing. Lately, Paul had seemed dangerous in a new way, less in control of himself than he'd ever been. He was only five years older than she was, but at 34, Paul was already a master of the universe. As her twenty-ninth birthday approached, Mallorie was no longer able to underestimate Paul's hunger for more and more power. She was also feeling strangely vulnerable, as if a protection she had long enjoyed was retreating. Maybe it was just her condition. She smiled.

Joseph took that moment to set their drinks in front of them. "Would you like to hear the specials?" he asked.

"No, I would not like to hear the specials. I would not like to see you near this table again until I need you," Paul replied with a quick fake-smile. Joseph disappeared.

"Okay," Paul said, once again facing Mallorie. "What's going on?"

"I'm pregnant," she stated simply.

Paul froze, shocked by the unlikely words issuing from his wife's mouth. His eyes fell to her stomach registering a significant bump he hadn't noticed before. He briefly closed his eyes then opened them, fixing her with a fierce glare, disbelieving and furious. "That's impossible. We had an agreement. You'll have to get rid of it."

"No, Paul. It's too late for that. I'm at six months today."

"How can you be six months pregnant? I haven't noticed anything."

"You've been distracted the last month or so. Before that, I simply wasn't showing."

"And now you can't hide it anymore, so you tell me? Are you kidding me? If you could have made it through the entire thing without telling me, you would have?" Paul seethed.

"Paul, I couldn't take a chance that you'd demand an abortion. I am having this baby—"

She didn't need to go on. Paul knew that she would try to leave him or make his life miserable if he forced her to abort, but he wasn't used to losing—at anything. Suddenly a noxious force, like bile, rose up in him. "I could still insist on the abortion. If I decided to, there'd be nothing you could do about it. Nothing."

Mallorie sucked in her breath; her eyes widened. Her hands dropped reflexively to her pregnant belly as if to ward off danger.

Paul's eyes widened, too. *What the hell?* "I'm sorry. I'm so sorry. That sounded terrible; I don't know where that came from." He shook his head and took a deep breath and let it out slowly. He came back to himself. "Look, I just don't like that you kept it a secret for so long—that you didn't trust me."

Mallorie searched Paul's eyes looking for the truth. She saw that he was being honest—and he had a point. "I know. I know. I'm so sorry. I've been agonizing over it ever since I found out. I don't know why I kept it from you, Paul. I love you. I guess I felt I had to be in an unassailable position when I told you about it. Anyway, it's not like you've been around—even when you are around—lately. Are you okay?"

Paul let himself smile. "Let's not start talking about me yet, okay? I need to digest this awhile. Speaking of digesting, where the hell is that waiter?"

Joseph had been standing back transfixed by the strong emotions coming from the powerful couple. The second Paul's eyes sought him out, Joseph rushed to the table. "Can I take your order, sir?"

"Yes. We'll both take the risotto of the day. That will be all."

"Thank you, sir. Coming right up."

Paul began tallying the likely benefits of his new position. *Talk about virility!* Most women had trouble getting pregnant these days. If their eggs were okay, the guy's sperm wasn't or vice versa. Almost everyone used in vitro, which still didn't promise the desired for results. When someone did get pregnant naturally, it was almost newsworthy. Mallorie's pregnancy was definitely news-worthy. No, this would be fantastic. "Mallorie," Paul reached across the table and took his wife's hands in his, "I couldn't be happier about this. You'll be a wonderful mother."

"Oh, god, Paul." She burst into tears. "I'm so relieved. You have no idea."

"Have you told anyone besides me?"

"No."

"Not even your sister?"

"No, not even Bethanne; I wanted you to be the first. But I can't wait to tell her. She's going to be blown away. And Claire and Scott are going to have their first cousin."

"Hey," Paul said, "You should have Claire come out here. Didn't you say something about her dying to come to the big city?" Once again, Paul was confused. Words were coming out of him that he hadn't formed in his own mind. *What is happening to me?*

Paul wasn't the only one confused. Mallorie was uneasy with his quick transformation. Yet, he looked sincere. She shook her head and smiled. "She is desperate, poor thing. I still can't believe Bethanne moved back to Iowa. Yuck. Anyway, that's a great idea.

I'll see if she can come right away—school should be out for the summer soon if not already. Claire can help me get ready for the baby. I've been thinking about how I'd decorate the nursery..." Mallorie was excited, and didn't need much prompting to accept Paul's complete conversion. She realized that his acceptance made her happier than she had been in a long time.

Paul was happy, too. And not just about the pregnancy. He was also happy about Claire coming to visit. He didn't know why.

PART TWO: JACK AND TESS

Still Thursday, noon EDT

Jack was not happy. He'd been dead for less than two days, but he was already restless. He was making no progress in contacting Tess and the boys. Ironic, to say the least, since he'd spent almost no effort trying to contact them while he was alive. He was determined, though. He had to get them off their machines. How had things gotten so bad? How could everyone—not just his wife and kids—be so completely ignorant of the danger? The Rival had many assets in the so-called material world; in fact, one of the strongest was right here in New York City. He and his minions were active in many ways, clearing the way for his imminent incarnation. The most powerful resource he had, though, was the electromagnetic field. Look how subtly, how cleverly, the electronic media had conquered the human being. Why, they had even named the Internet's most valuable feature the World Wide Web. Web, indeed. Like a giant, venomous spider, the Rival sought to catch every soul in his beautiful and arresting web. Once there, his bite numbed his victim into oblivion, into a world existing only onscreen. Some people saw it for what it was—they saw its potential for entrapment—and used tech carefully, purposefully; most did not. Though very few escaped once trapped, it was still possible. But not for long. Jack saw it all in horror.

During his life, Jack had been as ignorant to the danger as everyone else, but now he could see it. He'd been surprised to find himself conscious after death. Maybe it was because his death was so sudden, so unlikely. He watched Lance walk away, leaving his body on the sidewalk. He watched Tess wake up cursing him. He watched Alek register his absence for his birthday breakfast. He saw Matt's anger. He couldn't blame them. Then he saw how little Tess cared when she heard the news of his murder. He fled the scene and rested in the presence of some kind of angel or something that was trying to ease his pain; showing him how to accept it. He longed to go back to his life, his former life. He wanted to do a better job. *Too late. Too late.*

He went to see his sister while she was thinking of him after she'd received the family vidcard of Alek's birthday breakfast. Donna looked great. She'd been a mess for so long that he'd given up on her. As he watched her now, her love for him obvious as she looked at the vidcard, their whole tragic childhood together flashed before him in minute detail all at once. She'd come to stay with him in the city for a few months after he and Tess had first moved there. She'd been such a basket case, though. One night he told her she had to leave; he couldn't take care of her. She left the next morning, and that was the last time he'd seen her. Oh, she'd call every once in a while, drunk on her ass, trying to sound sober, sophisticated, so that he'd stay onscreen with her. He always got off as soon as he could. Why hadn't he just refused to pick up? Some bizarre sense of responsibility toward her. He'd been disgusted by her, not just for her drunkenness, but for all their dad had done to her. He felt the scorn on his own face whenever he saw her. He'd blamed her and she knew it. When he finally told her that she was a whore, had always been a whore, and that he never wanted to hear from her again, she'd stopped calling. He recalled feeling the same relief as he had when she'd left home suddenly all those years ago. *Oh, my God. This was me?* Another failed relationship. And even when Tess had gone with the boys to visit Donna once, he had refused to be a part of it. Now look at her. Donna was better than healthy. He could see that she had righted herself. *How did she do that? Does Dad know?*

Jack immediately found himself in his father's living room. He wasn't surprised by what he saw there. Bitter, angry, and unrepentant, his father was plugged in 24-7 to the worst of the angry talk shows and to sports—both venues meaningless, violent engagements. His father was completely cut off from the rest of the world. Jack felt revulsion first, as usual. Then he felt pity as he watched from his new perspective. Soon he felt a broad and blameless compassion for this human being who had been his dad. This was a surprise. Jack allowed himself to explore the origin of the unfamiliar emotion. He saw before him his dad as a child, an unwanted child, come late into a family already formed. Already two boys and a girl; the least he could have done was even the score. When his mother found out he was not the girl she was hoping for, she pushed him away. His brothers were popular, his sister the delight of his mother. He was small for his age. He started drinking early and never stopped. Jack could see now why his dad had plugged in. Who wouldn't? The mistakes his dad had made with his sister and him, mistakes his dad had been horrified by when he'd realized he'd made them, haunted the few sober moments he had. *Oh.* Jack left the room and returned to his own family.

He took a closer look at the origins of this group. *Why Tess?* He saw her Facebook page; the first time he'd ever heard of her. He was at Penn; she was, too. When Jack was written up in *Knowledge @ Wharton* for his ideas on reaching untapped markets in Africa, Tess had looked long at his picture before reading the article. She was a cheerleader: small, blonde, gorgeous. Tess asked to be his friend on Facebook the very same day. Jack, serious and academic, was feeling influential and destined for success; he acquiesced. Tess quickly realized by reading his page that Jack's pursuit of wealth was all that mattered to him. He'd had little exposure to the fun things in life. She decided that she would be that exposure.

They arranged to meet Friday night for dinner. Tess invited him back to her place, which she had carefully prepared: sound system playing old Billie Holliday, scented candles musky and aglow. Jack's head was on fire. Then Tess did things to him that he had never even imagined, and he was hers. He'd always been attracted to a slightly slutty look, but he wanted to marry a good girl. Tess was his dream. The contrast between her classy upbringing—discernable in her accent, in the words she chose—and her appetite for sexual adventure fulfilled every need he had from a woman. They were engaged before they graduated and married shortly after Jack got his first job in New York City.

Their marriage was perfect in the beginning. Neither of them wanted intimacy; both of them wanted wealth. They were beautiful to look at; Tess enjoyed making vidnotes and sending them to everyone she knew. She peppered their online ids with pictures of their intimate moments. And when she became pregnant, the first child, Matthew, and the second, Alek, became part of her onscreen dedication to her life. No moment too precious or too trivial for a vid.

So, Jack looked at Tess's life. Why had wealth been so important? Why was she content to live onscreen? And he saw that Tess's family, comfortable, bourgeois, had only one standard for success: money. Tess didn't know what she wanted for herself, but she knew what her parents wanted for her, so that became her goal. But she'd never discovered her own dream. Over the years, she grew indifferent to everything in their lives, even the wealth, but she knew that on the surface she looked successful and happy. So she lived to support that surface. Of course, it wasn't enough, so she started medicating herself. Never too much to obstruct her care of the boys, but then, they didn't need much of her. She'd plugged them into all the tech early.

Jack saw how perfectly he and Tess had worked together. He disengaged from the family; she disengaged from herself. He'd never even looked at it. Or her. The stasis they'd achieved was interrupted only on special occasions, like Alek's birthday. He'd never wanted to disturb the waters during his life, but now he was compelled to plummet into them. He had to find a way through. *Maybe tonight when they fall asleep.*

ALAINA'S NOTE TO READER:

I want to bring your attention to the fact that, as you can see, the Record shows none of these people meant any harm. Yes, ultimately bad things happened around them, but it's clear to me, and should be to you, that in trying to reconstruct cause from consequence, these people simply did not have the deplorable motives that have been submitted by the state through the media. This distortion of context is a common tactic of leaders throughout history—I see it all the time in the Record—and thus their lies become the story everyone believes.

ALAINA AMUNDSON

17

THE RIVAL

The darkness emanating from the third floor archives had always been uncomfortable to Bethanne. Today it was positively evil. No one else felt it through the haze of pleasantness Bethanne had produced, but Bethanne felt it and knew it was stronger because she'd tempted the Rival—a moniker for the adversary that she had no idea how she'd acquired—with her little experiment that morning. On the other hand, she knew that the powerful joy reverberating throughout the campus would support her if she decided to confront the malevolent force directly. She nudged Donna. "I'm going up to the third floor archives."

"You're kidding; today? That place sucks."

"I know, but I have to do a little research. I'll be back down in less than an hour. Can you cover the desk?"

"Of course. See you," Donna said, turning to the student standing in front of her. "Did you find everything?" she asked, taking the small stack of books.

Bethanne climbed the last of the stairs—she purposely avoided the elevators—and unlocked the doors to the stacks holding all the works of the professors and grad students that had been written since the college opened in 1947. Well, not exactly everything because from 2005 on, everything was written and stored digitally. No one really explored this old accumulated knowledge; it wasn't important enough to be preserved online or republished in any form, so it sat here collecting dust. Besides, most of what had been written in these pages had been disputed or disproved by now. In fact, the exact opposite theory might have been embraced within a few decades or less. The physical world is a phenomenon—its so-called laws and evidence no more "real" than a rainbow. And everything our senses tell us is just one side of the truth—one facet—and never the whole truth. No one questioned the evidence of their senses, even though, ironically, scientists and psychologists had learned that senses could be fooled and people could be manipulated by leading their senses astray. Standing in a room like this made that particular fact indisputable, though. All this stacked knowledge was useless, which made it a favored haunt of the Rival and his shadowy minions. *Too bad all this hadn't been in the basement; the flood in '08 would have destroyed it.*

Within seconds of her arrival, her hair was standing on end. The Rival, aware and ready, spoke. "I can teach you more than anything contained in this room. I can teach you more than all that exists in the known world. You can know everything. Your knowledge would spread across the world, powerfully, instead of the pathetic little happiness bubble you floated out today. Knowledge would make a *real* difference; knowledge would be worth your effort."

Bethanne listened. His promises soaked into her being spreading hope for the world, for the future of the world.

"Imagine," he encouraged.

Bethanne imagined. She knew the Rival could do this, could make it possible for her to spread herself out and permeate the energies of the world's people. What a gift. What a powerful gift.

She sat seduced, imagining the world as a more perfect place.

"You would become the most powerful person in the world."

And that, of course, was the Rival's error. As much as he could see, he couldn't see that a person might not want this goal. He'd made the mistake before.

"No thanks," Bethanne replied, sincerely, quietly. "Not my cup of tea."

The voice returned, reasonable. "But *you* came to *me*. You knew I would be here. Come, now. What can I do for you?"

"Join me. It's not too late for you."

"Hah! I've said no since the beginning. The people are mine now. No one with reason would follow you anywhere. Far more advanced are the educated than the faithful. Faith is not just ridiculous, it is dangerous. The evidence is everywhere. Reason alone must rule the world, and I am the master of reason. People who believe in god are considered fools. Atheism is no longer perceived as a threat; it is rightfully considered to be the antidote to stupidity. Granted, I still have work to do, but, as you can see for yourself, far less to do than has already been done. We're all wired together now. So few left to join me, you see. Why would I join you? It would stop the whole show. No thanks. Not my cup of tea."

"If your work is almost done, why bother with me? Why deign to meet me here?"

"I like to condescend almost as much as I like to conquer. They go together so naturally, I've found.

"Do you still condescend if you cannot conquer?"

The silence stretched out, the malice coagulated, pulling Bethanne's hair off her neck. *I knew I should have had my hair cut.* She laughed.

A blast shook her to the floor. "Laugh at me! I'm winning, you fool."

But he wasn't winning here. Not this time. Bethanne lay on the floor, rolling in the dust, laughing until tears squeezed out of her eyes. A clap of air announced the Rival's departure. Bethanne lay still on the tiles in the silent room. She closed her eyes. "You know that if I win, I'll take you with me," she whispered. Getting to her feet, she dusted herself off and walked to the door. *Well, not bad for a first encounter.*

18

CONNECTIONS

Thursday, 6:00 p.m. CDT

When Bethanne got home from work, Claire rushed to the door to greet her. *Uh oh.*

"Hey, Mom. How was work?" Claire was trying to act normal but was not succeeding. Besides the fact that her mother could read even her subtle emotions, Claire was never good at hiding what she was feeling when it was big.

Bethanne laughed. "Work was fine. So, what's up?"

"Aunt Mallorie called. She wants me to come to the city to help decorate the baby's room. Oh, yeah, she's pregnant."

Bethanne's smile disintegrated. She set her bag down on the kitchen table and pulled out a chair for herself. *I don't believe it.* This had been in her dreams for the past year. It had seemed so unlikely, yet here it was. Mallorie and Paul were going to have a baby.

"Mom? What's the matter?" Claire's voice betrayed her self-interest. "Mom, you're going to let me go, aren't you?"

"I don't know, Claire. Let me absorb this a minute. When did she call?"

"Just a couple hours ago; as soon as I got home from school."

"What exactly did she say?"

"Mom, is something wrong?"

"No, honey, just indulge me. How did she tell you?"

"Well, I answered the phone, and she said hi and then she said that she was lucky that I answered the phone because she wanted to talk to me. And I was all surprised and then she asked me if I wanted to come out to stay with her this summer, and I started, you know, losing it and then she said that she guessed I wanted to come and that was good because she needed help decorating the baby's room. And that's how it went."

"Did she ask to talk to me?"

"Of course. She doesn't know your hours or anything, so I told her you'd be back after 6:00, so she said she'd call back sometime after that." Claire paused weighing her mother's mood against her desire for an answer. "Mom, you'll let me go, right?"

Bethanne looked up into her daughter's eyes. The mixture of emotions—desire, fear, excitement, hope—clutched at her, begging her to acquiesce. Claire had always romanticized Mallorie's life. Mallorie, New York City, classy, glamorous, sexy, rich, beautiful; the city and the woman, the same. And here she was, with a fantastic aunt like that, stuck in Iowa City. The modest celebrity of the Iowa Writer's Workshop barely put her town on the map.

"Claire, I know how badly you want to go, but I'll need to talk to Mallorie first, and I'll have to think about it in light of everything else that's going on right now."

Claire knew that anything she said at this point would work against her. Her eyes registered the decision to let it be; her mom's registered her approval, acknowledging Claire's fledgling ability to control her will. They parted friends as Claire went up to her room to study for her final test of the year.

Scott got home from skateboarding a few minutes later. Bethanne was still at the table. "Hi, Mom. Are we going to go somewhere for supper?" he asked glancing at the inoperative kitchen.

Bethanne was forced from her reverie. "I guess we'll order a pizza tonight. How was skateboarding?"

"Okay. I met this guy. He's good. Guess we'll hang out."

"Hm." Bethanne was already far away again. Scott didn't take it personally, though. His mom was distracted a lot lately. He went upstairs.

A minute later Bethanne heard voices raised and then Scott pounded down the stairs to confront her. "Is it true? Does Claire get to go to Aunt Mallorie's?"

"Scott, I don't know yet. I haven't talked to Mallorie. We'll see."

Claire raced down the stairs to join them in the kitchen. "Scott, I told you I don't know for sure." She looked at her mom to make sure Bethanne heard what she was saying. Her attention returned to Scott. "You're such a jerk," she continued, hitting him on the shoulder.

"Claire! That's enough. Both of you go do your homework; we'll discuss this tomorrow. I don't want to hear another word about it. I'll call you when the pizza's here."

Claire and Scott shot dirty looks at each other and left the room. Bethanne shook her head and smiled grimly to herself. *Oh, boy; here we go.* This was not what she needed now. Slowly, the tone of her smile changed—when was anything what anyone needed now? That's life. She picked up the phone and ordered a pizza and salad then went upstairs to get into her sweats. *Might as well be comfortable.*

The family was still eating when the phone rang, halting everyone's movements. Bethanne got up and answered. Iowa was one of the twelve mid-western states that still had landlines. Though compatible with the tech on the coasts, they operated much as they always had.

"Bethanne?"

"Hi, Mallorie. I can't believe it's true. Claire told me you're pregnant."

"I know, right? I'm pregnant. Actually, I'm really pregnant; six months."

"Six months?" Bethanne went silent. How could she be six months pregnant? How could she have kept that a secret from her? Surely they'd spoken in the last six months.

"Bethanne, are you still there?"

"Of course. I'm just… surprised." The hurt tone finally registered on Mallorie.

"Hey, oh no, please don't be mad. I didn't tell anyone before I told Paul. Only my doctor knew. I told Paul today."

"You told Paul today? He didn't know you were six months pregnant? How is that possible?"

"Well, you know, I'm pretty tall and, well, thin, so I didn't show until about five months and then I just wore clothes that hid it." Mallorie sounded proud of her accomplishment.

"Mallorie, what was the point? Why did you keep it a secret from Paul?"

"Um. Well, see, I never told you this, but when we got married, I had to agree not to have children. Paul just didn't want kids, you know? But after awhile, I realized that I wanted a baby more than anything—especially watching Claire… and Scott too, of course. I just wanted to have a baby so bad. And so I decided to try, and it worked out. I didn't even need help. I think Paul's really proud of that. Most couples need help, but we didn't. He's feeling very manly now."

"Right." Bethanne was careful to keep the disapproval from her voice. She had almost lost Mallorie when she was too forceful in her warnings against Paul in the beginning. Mallorie had given her an ultimatum: accept Paul or lose her. Bethanne's opinion of Paul, however, had never changed; she just didn't trust him. At all. "So he's okay with it now?"

"Absolutely! I haven't seen him this happy in months. In fact, it was his idea that Claire come out to help. I mean, he wants all of you to come eventually—it's just that you'd need to take off work and get a housesitter and stuff, right? But Claire could come right away, couldn't she? And she wants to so bad."

"So this was Paul's idea? Wow. That's unexpected."

"I know. I could hardly believe it myself. He's just really pumped about this. And I just really, really want Claire to come. We would have so much fun together. And, you know, I've seen her artwork and everything. She'd probably have great ideas about decorating the baby's room. Oh, please, Bethanne. Please let her come out here."

Bethanne, who had been pacing between the living room and kitchen while she talked, sat down on the edge of the couch. What would she gain by saying no? Well, she'd have Claire close by. That was worth something. But it wasn't worth the disappointment both Claire and Mallorie would feel. She sighed and answered, "Ok, Mallorie. Ok. Claire can come out." She heard a whoop from the kitchen. "When do you want her?"

"Well, that's the thing. I want her to come right away. See, Paul's going to have this big assembly for teenagers and he thought Claire would like to be part of it."

"That sounds interesting; what's it about?"

"Top secret, Bethanne. But it's going to be great—that's all I can tell you. Honestly, the whole idea to get Claire here came up over lunch today. And it just so happens that Paul's jet is taking someone to Chicago Friday morning, so it would be nice if it could come back with a passenger instead of empty."

"Wait. Mallorie, are we talking about this Friday, tomorrow Friday? You've got to be kidding."

"I'm not kidding, Bethanne. Paul's assembly is the day after—on Saturday morning. Come on, you know doing something spur of the moment makes it more exciting. You used to do it all the time.

Remember that time you came into my room yelling *Road Trip* and we went camping overnight at Lake Macbride. Remember? Besides, Claire won't be able to stand waiting for no reason and she should really be at this assembly—it's such a great opportunity."

Bethanne decided to relent; what difference did it make really? Claire was going regardless. "All right, Mallorie. It sounds like you've thought of everything. Fine. Tomorrow's the last day of school anyway. Claire's final's at 9:00 and then I can get Claire on the bullet train to Chicago. Will someone be there to meet her?"

"Oh, Bethanne! Thank you, thank you, thank you! This is going to be great. Um, yes, one of Paul's people will pick her up at the station and get her to O'Hare. Paul's crew will take care of her until she gets to our house."

Bethanne sighed. "Ok. That's settled. Now, tell me how you feel, Mama." Bethanne heard Claire pounding up the stairs with Scott right behind her. Dinner was officially over.

"I feel great, Bethy. I've never been so happy in my life. I think it'll make us closer, too, because I'll need all this advice from you, you know?"

Bethanne smiled and softened. Even though Mallorie was sophisticated and successful, whenever they talked, Mallorie's voice reflected the family's humble roots that had supported them both before they'd escaped to the big city. Bethanne's smile widened as she thought of how completely Paul had underestimated a beautiful girl with that kind of upbringing. Paul lived only in the rarified atmosphere he'd been in his entire life. Mallorie, however, could go anywhere, which ended up being an asset to Paul in his ambitious quest for higher and higher office. Now, in the 21st century, the police commissioner of the east coast was one of the most prestigious offices in the world, and Mallorie's grace and affability had helped him achieve it at an early age. Who knew where he'd end up? Bethanne regained the present moment. "Yes, we *will* be closer, honey. I love you. I'm so happy for you."

"Thanks, Bethanne. Thank you, too, for Claire. By the way, she doesn't need to bring much because we are going to do some serious shopping when she gets here."

"I'm sure you will. Don't forget to make the arrangements in Chicago, Mallorie. I don't want Claire to be stranded at the train station."

"I won't forget, Bethy. Don't worry. I'll call you as soon as she's safely in the air. I love you. Bye."

"Bye," Bethanne said and lowered the phone into its cradle. She relaxed into the darkened room and cleared her mind. She perceived the release and spin of a tumbler; heard it click into place. Whatever she was unlocking, Claire's visit to New York City was one piece of the alignment. *Oh, God, please let Claire be all right.* She dabbed a tear forming in the corner of her eye; no time for that. She would need to get Claire ready now... in more ways than one.

19

LOVE

Still Thursday, 4:30 p.m. MDT

Jeff finally spoke when Morgan reached Salt Lake City six hours later. He had been drifting in and out of sleep, disorientated by the drive and his dreams. "So, let's grab some dinner and get you a few hours of shut-eye. I need to sleep without moving down a highway, and I'm starving."

"You're sure we won't show up on Delamater's radar if we stop someplace for more than a few minutes?" Morgan asked.

"I've got it covered. Seriously, man, we are completely invisible. Undetectable. We are free to roam, remain, whatever."

"I believe you, but why not just stay in the car? We can grab some fastfood, sleep a few hours, and get back on the road. I don't mind," Morgan answered.

"Ok, have it your way. No reason to use up safety at this point. Probably the less we test the system, the less progress Delamater will make on his search. We'll be way more visible once we get into Denver—I'm sure it'll still hold, but we'll have more time if we wait till we get there to be in public."

"Roger that," Morgan said. He kept to the northern route until they reached the junction of the 15 and 80 and they stopped at a Taco Bell for a bag full of tacos and a couple cokes. "I want to eat real food in Denver," Morgan said. "You can tell this stuff has never been touched by human hands."

"You miss your mama's cookin'?" Jeff laughed.

"Damn right," Morgan answered. "Now, how do you want to do this? 15 south to the 70 or 80 to Cheyenne?"

"Something tells me we need to go south. I guess I just don't want to stay straight on anything for too long. This'll mix things up a bit."

"Okay." Morgan turned onto the 15 and headed south. They got off the freeway on West Center Drive and headed for Utah Lake. They parked in the campground, and Morgan pressed an icon on the dash to turn his seat into a bed. "You ready for some sleep?" he asked holding his finger in place over the icon for the passenger seat.

"Not really; I've been napping off and on the whole way. I'll make my bed later."

Morgan fell immediately to sleep, but Jeff opened his computer. *John Simms, a minister. Who still goes to church?* Jeff shook his head. Mass delusion. Poor slobs. Yet this guy did have an enormous EMF; his star at nighttime was gigantic. All evidence to the contrary, some people still believed in God. It was pathetic, really. So what was this Simms telling his congregation? Jeff sifted through the data on Simms and saw that, as in Thompson's case, the people close to him—lots of people—had elevated EMFs. *Damn.* Jeff's program had continued to teach itself so that he could now look wider into the present and deeper into the past. Every person who had spent any significant time with Simms had a higher EMF than the so-called normal population. He wondered just how long the exposure had to be for affected results. He set the question into his program and closed it up.

He pressed the icon on the dash and lay back into his seat

feeling the contours shift as it morphed into a bed. The roof of the car was opaque from the outside, but he could see the stars through it. *Stars.* Why had he chosen the star icon? It didn't seem as random anymore, but he didn't know why. *The brighter stars in the heavens are closer, closer to us here on earth. What are the brighter stars on earth closer to?*

* * *

Friday, May 25, 2008 2:00 a.m.

When Jeff and Morgan arrived in Denver, they drove straight to Tremont Street and the Brown Palace Hotel. Morgan had been to Denver several times for ski trips; he always spent a few days in the city before going up to Breckenridge, usually at the Four Seasons on 14th. They would remember him well, so no Four Seasons. The valet took the car, and the two men entered the famous lobby with its soaring atrium. Fifty years ago, this would have been the most conspicuous place in the state, but nothing deep between the coasts was conspicuous now, and Jeff's device took care of the rest.

In front of them at the counter, an almost unbelievably beautiful woman turned around and smiled at them briefly, resting her eyes for a moment on Morgan before she strode with a bellhop to the elevators. The two men just stood there watching her walk away until the reservationist cleared his throat the second time. Morgan looked at Jeff and grinned conspiratorially; Jeff answered with a firm headshake. *Not this time, buddy.*

Jeff had reserved two staterooms on the ninth floor. Once the clerk saw Jeff's decoy account, the bell captain, with alacrity, got two young men—not the idle robots lined behind his desk—to take their luggage to their rooms. They rode up the elevator, exhausted and silent. When they got out on 9, Jeff turned to Morgan. "Six hours; pick me up." Morgan walked on to his room. Luxurious and well-appointed, his room, in hues of peach and gold, coerced him into relaxing. He took a quick shower and pulled down the gold-striped cover of the large bed. He set the alarm for 7:45 and slipped naked between the sheets. *Ellyngton's for breakfast; perfect.* He fell asleep.

* * *

"Don't look now," Morgan whispered, gesturing with his eyes. The six hours of sleep had done wonders, and both men were eager for the breakfast buffet awaiting them.

Jeff looked. Two women were sitting at a table near the windows. Both of them, young and gorgeous, were checking them out; one of them was the woman who'd been in front of them when they'd checked in. "Oh, man. I sure could use some of that," Jeff sighed.

"I know. Me, too. Let's do it."

"Right. Come on, man; we're on a mission. I have to meet this Rev. Simms guy this afternoon. I don't have time to mess around." Jeff's voice indicated a lack of conviction.

"That's what I thought," Morgan answered. "Let's get some buffet."

After filling their plates with poached eggs, bacon, sausage, miniature quiche, crabmeat, pancetta-wrapped figs, and strawberry and banana filled crepes, Morgan led Jeff on a detour toward the girls' table. He stopped in front of them and locked eyes with the one he'd chosen. "Can I get you anything from the buffet? Or perhaps there's something else you'd like."

Jeff groaned. Only Morgan could say something that ridiculous and get away with it. Once Morgan smiled, women's brains froze.

"Mm. It all looks good to me," answered Morgan's choice.

Jeff looked her over. She was Ethiopian; she matched Morgan's skin tone almost exactly. Jeff had long held the belief that Ethiopian women were the most beautiful of all human beings; this girl affirmed his conviction.

"I'm Morgan." Morgan's attention didn't waiver. "And you are?"

"Lakia," she said breaking into a dazzling smile.

Jeff realized he wasn't really breathing. They were almost too beautiful together. With effort, he tore his eyes away from them and looked at the other girl.

"Hi," she said, obviously used to the effect her friend had on men and ready to accept the guy Lakia hadn't chosen.

"Hi. I'm Jeff."

"Hi, Jeff. I'm Brandi."

Jeff swallowed, then smiled ineptly. *Brandi. Perfect.*

Morgan broke in. "We almost met last night at the front desk. If it hadn't been so late already, I would have asked you to join me for a drink in the lounge. Perhaps you would you allow us to join you now?"

Lakia smiled and turned to Brandi with a raised eyebrow. Brandi grinned back and nodded. Lakia turned back to Morgan and Jeff, "I think you'd better; those plates must be fairly heavy by now."

The two men sat down; Morgan erased some of the distance between his place and Lakia's when he pulled in his chair. "Well, bon appétit," he said, his accent perfect.

Lakia smiled again. *This one could be good.*

"Are you here for long?" Brandi asked Jeff after allowing him to get in a few bites.

"Probably just today, maybe tomorrow."

"So, you busy later?"

"Yeah, I'm pretty busy—" Jeff looked over at her and then back down at his plate. He glanced at Morgan who was steadily clearing his plate without really taking his eyes off Lakia. Clearly, Morgan was not going to rescue him. "Um, how about you?" He wasn't really listening to her reply as he tried to formulate what he would say next when he heard Lakia place her knife and fork across her plate; she was done with her meal and so was Morgan. *Well, that's it then.*

"So, we're going to take a walk," Morgan said as he offered Lakia his hand. He reluctantly shifted his attention to Jeff. "I guess I'll be seeing you later on; when?"

"I'll meet you at noon in the lobby."

"You got it. Excuse me," Morgan said nodding to Brandi and then to Jeff. He pulled Lakia to her feet and pressed his face into her neck. "You *are* a found treasure," he whispered into her ear.

"You speak Amharic?" Lakia asked, surprised.

"A bit."

Lakia's looked into Morgan's eyes and made a decision that Morgan read. They left the restaurant hand in hand.

It wasn't the first time Jeff had found himself in an awkward position signaled by Morgan walking away with some girl. Still— hard to get used to. He looked at Brandi. "I could use another cup of coffee. You?"

"Absolutely," she said.

Jeff signaled for coffee. He couldn't remember the last time he had even talked to a woman. Though he had never been much good at it, some women found this deficiency charming. Others thought he was too handsome to be bad at this, and after a stilted conversation went nowhere, the interested party would assume he was either uninterested or gay and they'd move on. Jeff was not gay.

"So, where you from?" Brandi asked responding to Jeff's apparent inability to advance the conversation.

"I'm from… the west coast."

"Well, aren't we mysterious? Are you hiding from someone?" She grinned.

Jeff looked up, alarmed. "What do you mean?"

"Nothing. Oh, shit. You are hiding. This is not a good place to be." She glanced up at the ubiquitous cameras.

Jeff followed her glance and shook his head. *Perfect.* "Ok. I'm not hiding; that would be ridiculous. I'm just kind of in-between places. I just moved out. I haven't figured out where I'm going to live yet."

"Denver's nice." Brandi smiled again, indicating that she would not pursue the subject.

Jeff blushed. He needed to get out of here.

Brandi sensed he was ready to bolt. "Hey… Jeff… relax. This can be easy. Let's go to your room." She leaned toward him, her breast touching his arm on the table. Jeff felt his cotton shorts get tight and knew that he needed her now.

* * *

Morgan unlocked the door to his room and gestured Lakia inside. She readied herself for the theatrics that all couples had adopted for the cameras. She faced Morgan and stopped short.

Morgan was looking at her with a focused intensity oblivious to the cameras. Suddenly, Lakia was unsure of herself. He put his hands on her shoulders and pulled her into his chest as he bent his face toward hers and kissed her. His eyes were closed. *What the hell?* She closed her own eyes and felt the kiss. She felt herself expand and fall—that always weird stomach drop like when a swing reaches its zenith and begins its backward descent. Without tools, without visuals, without warning, Morgan had penetrated the outer barricade of her fortress.

Morgan disengaged, pressing her away with his hands still on her shoulders. She opened her eyes and fell into his. They'd always been together though they hadn't met before today. The flame of recognition danced between them until Lakia realized she was crying. She had never wanted anyone more. The heaviness of her desire was mirrored in Morgan's eyes. He slowly unbuttoned the tiny buttons that ran the length of her short dress. When he got to her waist, he dropped to his knees in front of her. She put her hands on his head, her whole body quaking with awakened passion. Every button was an agony of anticipation. When he finished, he leaned back on his heels and looked up at her, waiting, admiring. Lakia slipped the dress off her shoulders and stood naked in front of him. She had distained lingerie her entire life; Morgan approved. She knelt down next to him and reached for his shirt, but they'd both had enough of waiting. They surged toward each other, wild and hot and without inhibition. They both understood that their lives were going to be different now; they had crossed a threshold they'd never before approached.

Meanwhile, Jeff and Brandi quickly fulfilled their sexual contract. Brandi spent the time preening in front of the camera, pinching, licking, smiling her way through an emotionless fornication. Jeff didn't have the heart to tell her the cameras weren't recording. He did, however, manage a powerful release that tore through his system and left him gasping lungfuls of the oxygenated air of his penthouse suite.

Brandi got up and walked naked to the kitchen area and opened the small refrigerator. "Do you want something to drink?"

"No thanks. Actually, I've got an appointment soon. You're going to have to leave now."

"Oh, ok. Hey, this was fun. If you want, I can come back up here later on."

"No. Thanks, anyway…" He paused and reconsidered. She was good to look at and seemed harmless enough. Besides, Morgan was probably going to be otherwise occupied tonight. "Well, I'll call you. Swipe your number on the screen."

Brandi did and then got dressed. "I'll see you later then." She stood by the bed looking down at Jeff.

"Sure, maybe," he said, once again awkward.

Brandi left. The lock clicked and Jeff closed his eyes. *God I needed that.* He fell asleep until his alarm woke him at 11:30.

Morgan looked at the screen. Time to go. He cupped Lakia's face in his hand. "I don't know how long I'll be."

"It doesn't matter. I'm not going anywhere."

"Good."

He got up and went into the shower. Lakia decided not to join him; she'd lose his smell and, besides, she didn't want anything to start that they couldn't finish. She lay under the light layer of the thin sheet outlining her perfect body, the cameras blind the one time something worth seeing was in front of them.

20

LESSON PLAN

Still Friday, 12:00 noon MDT

In the lobby, Jeff called Simms and spoke to his secretary. "Yes, Mr. Clark, Rev. Simms is expecting you at 1:00. Do you know how to get here?"

This was, of course, a mere courtesy. Everyone knew how to get everywhere now. "Yes, ma'am. I'll see you at 1:00. Thank you."

Morgan walked up as Jeff disconnected. "So?" Jeff asked, eyebrow raised.

Morgan wasn't playing. "Leave it alone, Jeff."

Jeff had already framed his retort, but he could see that Morgan was as serious as he ever got. "Hey, no problem. Let's just go then."

By the time they walked out of the lobby doors, the car was out front. The alternate ids Jeff had set-up on the way to Denver meshed perfectly with the tech inside the small local system of the hotel. To the larger world, they simply had ceased to exist. Morgan was constantly amazed by how little value was placed on evidence provided by the senses. Tech told you who was who.

* * *

"What do you think Delamater's doing without you?" Morgan asked as they merged onto the 36 from the 25.

"I have no idea. He can't be too happy. I imagine he's got his best minds on the problem. I haven't detected a breach though."

"Doesn't that seem odd? Delamater is not the type to give up, Jeff. How sure are you of your system?"

"I'm sure." But doubt had now crept in under the curtain of Jeff's certainty. He reached down to his laptop and opened it. He ran it though the checks and alarms that would indicate attempts to penetrate, but everything looked in order. In fact, it looked like it hadn't been tampered with at all. It looked unchallenged. *Shit. This can't be right.* Jeff glanced over at Morgan who was purposefully staring ahead—his method of allowing Jeff room to acknowledge he could be wrong about something. It worked every time. "Ok. I think there must be a problem. I need to figure out what Delamater is up to."

"I agree. Why don't you give him a call?"

"What if he doesn't know where I am?"

"What if he does?"

"Shit. This sucks. If I call him now, I open every door that's closed."

"Yeah, unless you make the call from home."

"Of course. I'm at home. Duh. Besides, we'll be moving on right after the meeting with Simms."

"What do you mean?" Morgan didn't manage to keep the sharp edge out of his voice.

Jeff looked over at his friend more closely. "What do you mean, what do I mean? I mean we're packing up and leaving after I meet with Simms. I just checked on the progress of my little program, and I've found the next person we have to see. She's hard to track, though. Her field is volatile; I can't understand it. Sometimes it's huge; way more intense than any of the others. And sometimes it's not even there. Gone."

"Where is she?"

"Iowa City."

"And we have to leave today? How about tomorrow morning?"

"Oh, I get it," Jeff laughed. "You have some unfinished business to take care of?"

Morgan chose to ignore the lewd gesture Jeff was making. He consciously decided not to get angry; it wasn't as if Jeff could understand. "Hey, it's not like that, so don't. I'm not leaving town until tomorrow; you can give me that."

"Sure, no problem." He paused, "Where was I? Oh, yeah. So let's pull off so I link back to my house from somewhere besides the car.

They pulled off in Superior, a small support town for Boulder. Morgan stopped at a roboshop for gas while Jeff went around the corner of the building where he could log onto a phantom base.

Delamater picked up on the first ring. "Hey, Jeff. Nice of you to call." He paused for a second. "Back home?" Delamater's voice was friendly. He was smiling, looking relaxed and self-assured.

"Yup," Jeff answered. "So, I'm guessing you've been trying to reach me."

"I was. What are you up to, Jeff?"

"Still researching. Still a little freaked by the old man's house blowing up, you know?" Jeff stopped talking and waited.

"Listen, you've got to let that go. Accidents happen—accidentally. So do coincidences. We both know you had nothing to do with it—wrong place at the wrong time kind of thing. So, you getting close to supplying me with the new tech?"

"Not really. Just thought I'd call to see how things were going. And, I'm not quite ready to just let the LA thing go. Have you heard anything new?"

"Look, the police found no evidence of wrongdoing. The

house's electrical system just went crazy. They're checking other houses on the same grid to make sure they're okay. Anyway, we're off the hook. Coincidence—that's all."

"Right. Well, I need to go now."

"Jeff. One moment. I know I was a little short with you the other day. I'm a bit out of it. My wife is pregnant in the middle of all this, and..."

Delamater's wife was pregnant? "Wow, man. Congratulations. That's amazing."

"Yeah. I'm sure you can imagine my state of mind. Anyway, I'd like to move forward as soon as possible. Now that I've got a kid coming, I want the new system in place more than ever."

"I can imagine." Jeff could *not* imagine. "Well, I'll call you later then." He tapped off. He stared at his blank screen awhile, trying to fit this new piece into the mosaic he'd made of Delamater. He returned to the car and relayed his conversation to Morgan. "Morgan, do you think we could be wrong about Delamater?"

Morgan, however, was more suspicious than ever. Something was up. He looked over at Jeff. "I'm not ready to change my assessment yet. Let's see what happens after you meet with Simms today."

"Sounds good to me," Jeff answered. Morgan pulled out of the station and continued on 36. He got off at Broadway and turned left onto Spruce. Boulder was still one of the prettiest towns in the country. Settled against the red angles of the Flatirons and the hulking wildness of the Rockies, the population still regarded itself as spiritually in tune and had kept itself apart from the insatiable metro urges of other cities. It had had its low-life problems like anyplace else toward the latter half of the 20th Century, but those days were past now as the troubled youth moved away from the now quaint atmosphere of anti-tech sentiment pervading its confines. People still spent free time out in the mountains and parks, hiking, biking, skiing. Over 900 miles from San Francisco and 1600 miles from New York City, Boulder was left alone as a relic inhabited by technophobes. The streets were more beautiful than they'd been at the end of the century. No power lines obstructed the view. The city, unlike most, had had them removed once wifi made them obsolete. They'd even re-used the poles after shaving off the chemical-laden exterior to create the wood paths that now ran through the town's parks.

Jeff dug through his pocket as they turned onto Pine and spotted the house. He pointed a metal pen into the air and the cameras stalled in position. The arrival of the two men would not be recorded. Nothing in the 600 block of Highland would be recorded. "Extra precaution," he said grimly. He didn't want another explosion.

Morgan stopped beneath a shade tree. The house was a large, two-story red brick with white pillars holding up the balcony stretching over the front porch the width of the house. The lawn was terraced above the street level, which augmented its impression of calm, secure dignity. Morgan turned off the car and looked over at Jeff who was making no move toward leaving. "So, you going to take a nap or what?"

"Or what, I guess. What are you going to do?"

"I think I might take a walk around the neighborhood; it's really nice here."

"Uh, how about coming in with me?"

Morgan examined Jeff's face. *What's going on?* Jeff looked rattled. The old teacher must have really spooked him; maybe he was afraid of what would happen with this guy. "Fine," he said making an effort to appear nonchalant.

They exited the car and walked up the steps to the front door. Jeff rang the doorbell, amused by his own pleasure at the novelty. A doorbell. It had been years since he'd seen one. It chimed two pleasant tones in a descending third. Jeff heard footsteps on a wood floor approach before the door opened wide. A petite, blond woman, her blue eyes sparkling, greeted him. "Hello. You must be

Mr. Clark."

"Yes, I am. I'm pleased to meet you." He shook her outstretched hand and stepped back a bit to indicate his friend. "And this is my colleague, Morgan Davis."

Michelle felt suddenly awkward. Though her husband was a handsome man, Morgan Davis was the most beautiful man she had ever seen in person. He was almost hard to look at. His face just stopped a person. Perfectly proportioned, his cheekbones and jaw the easel on which his large hazel eyes conveyed his intelligence and integrity. Michelle realized she was holding her breath. Embarrassed, she slowly let it out and opened the door wide. "How do you do," she said offering Morgan her hand. "Please come in." She returned her attention to Jeff. "My husband has been looking forward to your visit."

Jeff, who had become used to Morgan's affect on every, single goddammed woman they encountered, smiled a friendly smile and entered the foyer. He glanced around the front room. It was furnished tastefully with an overstuffed carnelian couch strewn with abundant pillows and two large chairs, a massive teak coffee table sitting on a patterned wool rug, and a tall floor lamp between the baby grand piano and one of the chairs. The quiet elegance was presided over by an antique chandelier with varying sizes of crystals. The walls had original art by artists Jeff didn't recognize. *Beautiful.*

Michelle noticed his gaze. "These are paintings done by some of the young people in our congregation. Many of them want to be artists; I think they already are."

"I agree," Jeff replied.

"Well, why don't you follow me to Rev. Simms' study. He probably didn't hear the doorbell; he never does." Michelle's tone indicated that this was not a dig but a simple fact. She led them down a wide hall lined with more paintings to a closed set of double doors at the end. She knocked lightly and turned the knob. "Rev. Simms, your guests are here. This is Mr. Clark and Mr. Davis."

Simms, who was talking to his screen, quickly said goodbye and stood up to greet the men. "John Simms. It's a pleasure to meet you," he said shaking hands with Jeff. He turned to Morgan. When their eyes met, they realized they were of the same cut; they spoke a language silently, composed not of words but of meanings. Simms read Morgan's concern about Jeff's intentions as soon as they shook hands.

Jeff watched the exchange, slightly annoyed by the obvious warmth passing between the two men. *Why the hell did I bring Morgan?* By the time he could feel surprised by his own thought, the two men were facing him.

"I have been looking forward to your visit, Mr. Clark. My wife said you were interested in my work. She also said that you are conducting interviews of people who influence others. Is this some kind of sociological study?"

Jeff realized that Michelle, the secretary, was Rev. Simms' wife. *Where was this guy's entourage?* The quiet privacy of the couple's lives didn't mesh with the onscreen images of little, budding stars emanating out from this man's sun.

Simms looked at Jeff. "It's my day off. I have two days off every week. One of them I spend in the mountains, the other I spend reading or puttering around the house. This is one of the latter. I don't look upon our interview as work, though. It isn't, is it?" He smiled.

Jeff, startled at the answer to his unasked question, stuttered a moment before clearing his throat to speak. "Uh, no. At least, I don't think so." He tried to smile but managed to look only more uncomfortable. He felt his forehead getting damp. *Shit. I'm beginning to hate these star people.*

"So, why don't we sit over here away from the desk and screens." Simms indicated a comfortable sitting area to the right of the doorway that Jeff hadn't noticed before. The wall facing the desk was dominated by a large brick fireplace and hearth. The mantle held framed photos of Simms' family and friends. His attention focused on a photograph of a sculpture. It was a man with his left arm pointing down to one corner of the sculpture and his right had slanting away from him and lifted toward the right corner of the sculpture. Disturbing figures appeared at the corners to which the figure seemed to point. The central figure's expression was tragic. Jeff did not like the picture. The figure's eyes seemed to look right through him. *Way too intense. Why would anyone put a picture like this in his house?*

Morgan was already sitting in one of the comfortable leather chairs facing the loveseat on the other side of the coffee table. Simms stood in front of the loveseat until Jeff tore his gaze away from the haunting picture. Jeff took the vacant chair next to Morgan and then Simms sat down, too.

"So, what can I do for you, Mr. Clark?"

Jeff, struggling to get comfortable, snapped into focus. The last time he'd heard these words was when Stuart Thompson had asked them. And now Stuart Thompson was dead.

Morgan glanced over at Jeff, sensing how off-balance he was. He checked out Simms' perception; Simms looked calm and patient, inscrutable, as if he were oblivious to Jeff's confusion. But he wasn't.

"You can call me Jeff." Jeff began to gain his equilibrium again as he had that day with Thompson.

"Jeff." Simms spoke his name and paused. "Fine, Jeff it is." He waited.

"I'm investigating the effects pastors have on their congregations. Not just on Sunday, of course, but every day. You know, do the effects last? That kind of thing."

"So, how did you hear about me? My wife says you're from California; did you read one of my books?"

Jeff stopped short. *Right. Shit.* "No, I didn't read a book." *Yeah, how the hell did I hear about him.* He looked out the sliding glass door onto the wood deck in Simms' back yard while composing a plausible answer. He looked at Morgan who imperceptibly shook his head before looking away. Jeff sighed, smiling, amused. *Ok. I'm incompetent.* "So, that's probably a question I should have prepared for." Now, the look that passed between he and Simms was honest.

"Let's do this right," Simms suggested.

"Yeah, I guess we could do that." He looked over at Morgan and was surprised by the approval he saw in his friend's eyes. He realized he didn't really know Morgan—he'd just assumed he was the same kid he'd grown up with. The consequences of his oblivion were beginning to dawn on him. *Ok. I'm incompetent and self-absorbed.*

"Ok," Jeff began. "This is what's going on. I know a thing or two about computers… Actually, I know probably as much as anyone in the world. Anyway, the thing is, I've created a program that allows me to find people who influence other people. Big time. This wasn't my original purpose, but it's become the program's most interesting feature. See, originally I needed a baseline for personal electromagnetic field so that I could map the country so that, well, so that everyone would be identified by their EMF. It'd be so simple; we wouldn't need to attach or implant any tech because we're all born with our own unique EMF. But, as I began mapping, I found a guy whose EMF peaked way higher than anyone else's. Like this quantum leap—this huge spike leaving everyone else's EMF in the dust."

"Are you using localized EMF, say from the heart torus, or are you using the entire field?"

Jeff swallowed. "What do you know about this?"

"Jeff, the knowledge of auras is centuries old. You know that. You can call it EMF if you like. Not that the aura is the EMF just like man is not his physical body. But the electromagnetic field is evidence, let's say. I was just wondering, since we know that the EMF from the heart is significantly stronger than that of the brain, if you're using the heart or the entire thing. It would make a difference you know."

"I'm using the heart's torus."

"Fine. Please go on."

Morgan was grinning broadly. Nothing pleased him more than seeing someone matching wits with his friend. He was so glad Jeff had brought him along. This was going to be fun.

"So, anyway, I decided I would go meet this guy who had the strongest EMF on my map, which still isn't completely done. Now I have everything west of the Mississippi, but the day I met this guy, I had only the west coast. Anyway, Morgan and I drove down to LA and I met the guy and then we went back home and then, when I looked at the map again, I saw your EMF and decided to come here. Yours is even bigger than the one in California."

Simms closed his eyes. Of course, he'd known he was different. It was one of the reasons he'd chosen this profession. When he was little, he'd been told he was going to be a leader and that he needed to decide what kind of leader he was going to be. Usually, this point was used as either a punishment or an enticement to create a desired behavior. It wasn't always effective. In the end, though, he had realized that he wanted to do good work; he wanted to change the world for the better if he could change it at all. Now, here was scientific proof of his difference, which brought him no comfort—no increased understanding—only recognition. Here was the tech that he'd known would come—that he'd dreaded for years. What he could not have anticipated is that its creator would show up at his door.

"That's quite some tech you've got. And why, exactly, did you create this program?"

"I wanted to see what people with high EMFs are like. I wanted to meet them to see if I could tell they were different just by being with them."

"No, I mean, why did you create the program to identify people through their EMFs in the first place?"

"Well, the world needs to be safe, right? I mean, that seems clear to me. And, after this guy was murdered in New York City the other day, the guy who murdered him evaded the police for awhile because he'd tampered with his tech, wore a disguise, you know, got around the system. So Delamater..." *Shit!* Jeff slumped back in his chair. He felt sick. In all the years he'd worked for him, all the millions of dollars he'd earned from him, the only rule that was ironclad was confidentiality.

Morgan sat on the edge of his seat. He had no idea what Jeff was going to do now. He'd never imagined Jeff would slip up like this. This was not good. Just hearing Delamater's name out loud was alarming.

"Jeff." Simms' calm voice broke into the panicked atmosphere. "Jeff. It's okay. It's better that I know. Remember, we can do this right."

Jeff took a deep breath as he held Simms' gaze. *Right.* He made the decision to continue. Besides, the damage had already been done; it wasn't like Simms was going to forget Delamater's name. He went on, "Ok, so Delamater asked me to fix the problem. I just started working and came up with this EMF tracking idea and realized how perfect it is because it doesn't need tech."

"What does Mr. Delamater think?"

"I haven't told him yet." Jeff stopped talking once again. *I haven't told him yet.* This fact was important. Jeff had never considered the human element in any of his work. He'd never wondered about the effect his creations had on people. He'd never even thought about the underlying purpose of anything he'd done. He'd simply tackled a problem and solved it. That had been a mistake.

"Jeff, I'm going to go get us something to drink from the kitchen." Simms rose from his chair and left the room.

Jeff closed his eyes. *What an idiot I've been; what a pawn.* He looked with new eyes at the world he was living in—the world he had helped to create. The big cities crowding the coasts seemed already lost. Every person's every move watched, retrievable in the clouds of invisible tech encircling the globe making the past and present strangely intertwined. Yet, the more tech there was to record everything, the more confusion there was. People altered their own memories, creating better ones with tech. Reality was less real than it had ever been before. Every sense could be confused, every memory could be altered. There was no reality anymore; it was all up for grabs.

The coasts were the worst. By the last decades of the 20th century, nothing in between the coasts mattered much—at least in the minds of the people on the coasts. The middle of the continent still had some peace; had somehow evaded the most intrusive tech, though, of course, they were supposed to obey the implantation laws. The people who'd resisted, who'd refused to comply with implantation laws, wouldn't be able to escape Jeff's new program. The real id was someone's heart and mind, and the last of the free people were going to belong to Delamater when Jeff followed through with his contract.

21

THIRD FIRE

Still Friday, 2:30 p.m. MDT

Simms returned with a tray holding three cups of tea and a plate of pecan cookies. He placed them on the coffee table. Jeff hardly dared to look up as the heavy grains of thought filtered down through his layers of guilt. He had been a fool. An ancient tableau opened before his mind's eye. The tree of knowledge. Temptation. Ignorance. Sin. Knowledge. Jeff returned gradually to the present. Simms was waiting.

"Something happened," Jeff began. "I don't know exactly what, but the guy in California is dead. He and his wife. Some electrical accident at his house. The house just exploded. At first I thought Delamater did it, but he was pissed as hell—he knew I'd been there and called me with the news. Anyway, I got off the grid as soon as I found out, and Morgan and I came here."

Jeff looked down at his hands. The whole thing was so unbelievable.

"So, how are you doing?" Simms asked.

"Not so good."

"That's a matter of perspective, Jeff. I would say you're doing much better."

"Yeah, sure. Well, it's hard to do worse than curse the entire world."

Simms threw back his head and his laugh, resonant and genuine, filled the room. "Ah, Jeff. How nice of you to take the blame for all the ills of the world. I'm afraid, however, that blame cannot rest on your shoulders alone. The current state of affairs has been a long time coming. A long time. Almost from the beginning. But we humans have always been given the tools to fight." He pressed his hands in a gesture of prayer.

"If you're talking about religion, I'm not interested. I think it's all bullshit." Jeff's defiance flushed his face. He was suddenly no longer interested. *Figures.* Simms was a preacher, after all, what did he expect? *What a waste of time.*

"We don't need to talk about religion, Jeff, we can talk about history. But before we embark on that journey, why don't you tell me about your interview with the person you met before me." Simms fixed him with a steady and potent gaze.

Jeff struggled for stability. *I must be losing my mind.* He remembered feeling the same imbalance when he'd talked to Stuart Thompson. He made a mental note to investigate this feeling—was it a response to the elevated EMF? Nevertheless, he launched into his story of meeting the old man. Since he was unwilling to reveal the content of his reveries during his time with Thompson, there wasn't much to tell; his whole story took less than a minute. Simms and Morgan exchanged a glance that acknowledged Jeff's resistance to his own feelings. Jeff, who may have been naïve in the heart realm, was quicker than most in every other. He did not fail to register their exchange.

"Screw you guys. Sorry, Reverend. But, what the hell? Did I miss my own joke?"

"Yo, Jeff. I know you're a sensitive guy and all..." Morgan's complicit look with Simms was gone, replaced by one of levity.

Jeff turned to face Morgan, saw the look, and grinned. "I have no idea what happens to me, man. I was just like this the last time."

"Cognitive dissonance. Both the teacher and Simms make you feel things you'd discounted long ago. You're being forced to look in a mirror and you don't recognize your own image—you aren't who you thought you were. It sucks for you. But, I think you should just get on with it; you'll have plenty of time to explore all of this later. Tell the reverend here what actually happened in L.A."

Jeff nodded and began. "His name was Stuart Thompson—"

Simms' gasp stopped Jeff short. "History teacher? Married to Patrice?" Simms asked.

Jeff's mouth fell open. He looked from Simms to Morgan and back again. "Are you kidding me? You knew him?"

"Just briefly. He taught a class at NYU once; I have no idea how he happened to be there, but I remember feeling so lucky to have him. He really took me under his wing; he mentored me for awhile even after he left the school and moved back to California. He was a real inspiration for me." Simms looked down into the cup he held in his hands. "I can't believe he's dead. And Patrice, too." He involuntarily looked toward the door through which his own wife could be heard working in the kitchen. He got up and closed the door. "I am so sad to hear this news, Mr. Clark. Please, tell me everything that happened while you were there."

When Jeff was done, he refocused on Simms who had listened with his eyes closed and his hands folded on his lap. Simms opened his eyes and looked into Jeff's. "So, what did Mr. Delamater do when you reported to him after that?"

"Well, I didn't report back right away. I woke up at 5:00 and called him and he told me that Thompson and his wife had been killed in some freak electrical explosion and that Derek Burns knew I'd been there that morning. Well, not me, specifically, but someone who had major tech working for him. He figured something was up and wanted to know who'd been there. Burns assumed Delamater had something to do with it. I've told you the rest."

Simms stood up and walked toward the fireplace deep in thought. Morgan and Jeff exchanged looks and waited in silence for him to speak. Finally he said, "It's begun. I thought so."

"What?"

"It's a long story. Lots of myth, superstition, rumor. Lots of truth, too, if you can see it. I can see it. I don't think what happened to Stuart and Patrice was an accident. It was a direct attack to destroy Stuart's influence."

"But that doesn't make sense," Jeff retorted. "What influence? With an EMF that powerful, Thompson lived in almost total obscurity—barely anyone even knew he existed."

"Sometimes that's the point, Jeff. How did Thompson make you feel when you were with him, besides uncomfortable?"

Jeff blushed again. He looked at his hands noticing the round and perfect cut of his fingernails. He had no idea what to say.

Morgan reached over and nudged his arm. "Hey, are you okay?"

Jeff looked up and saw Morgan's look of concern. *Damn it all.* He turned to Simms. "Thompson brought up these old memories I'd forgotten about. At least I think it was him. He didn't say anything, but somehow he made me remember how Morgan and I met." He kept his eyes locked on Simms. "I guess I realized how my life would be different without him." *There. I said it.*

Morgan laughed. "True that. Your life would suck without me."

Jeff's breath burst out as if he'd reached the surface of a deep lake. Suddenly, things were fine. He hadn't drowned in warm emotion after all; he'd survived. He looked at Morgan, his eyes filled with gratitude.

"I love you, too, man." Morgan smiled. And it was so clean, so true, that they both laughed.

Simms smiled too, but quickly got serious. "Love is important. It is usually predicated on interest—interest in someone other than ourselves. If people lose interest in each other, we will become more and more like the robots we've created—form and function with no being. We will lose our capacity to carry our individualities within our earthly lives. We will be homunculus not human. Stuart Thompson was interested in people; he genuinely loved people, and as a result, people loved him back. Each person he knew felt special, cared for, seen—that always proliferates."

Jeff was trying to follow. Some of it made sense and some of it was foreign. He recognized the words, but had never heard them put together that way. "What do you mean 'lose our capacity to carry our individualities'?"

"It's a long story. It starts with creation. It starts with God."

"Oh, come on. You can't be serious. Evolution disproved God long ago—long ago. No one believes that creation bullshit now. I thought you said this wouldn't be about religion."

"Intolerance of ideas doesn't suit any of us, least of all people who have as much influence in the world as you do, Jeff. However, I'm not talking about religion, and I'm not discounting evolution. That would be ridiculous, of course. However, what existed before the earth? Would you be surprised to know that human beings did?"

"So we are the progeny of space aliens. Good. This is getting better all the time."

"Jeff. Give the man a chance," Morgan interrupted. "You don't have to buy any of this, but presuming you know what he's going to say is just plain rude. What's your problem?"

Jeff didn't know what his problem was, but he recognized his disrespect and apologized.

Simms began again. "It's not space aliens we share the world with, Jeff. We are spiritual beings, we humans, but we are not the only ones. In fact, we are to be the tenth hierarchy when we survive the earthly incarnations. We don't really have time to go into this. Have you ever heard of the Akashic Record? No? It's like a library, a spiritual library, written in energy. If you can read it, if you've prepared yourself inwardly to read it, then you can observe all events from all of time. The story is too big to go into now, but the upshot is that we have to thwart the powers that wish to bind us to the earth. These beings have made extraordinary progress in the last hundred years or so. They've prepared for the incarnation of a being who will lead us astray, away from our destiny as mankind. Many will follow him. Many have already sworn allegiance to him without even knowing it. Something ties these two deaths together—the one in New York City and the one in Los Angeles. You may be the key."

Jeff sat still trying to find one solid thought to hang on to. It was all too fantastic—too ridiculous; he turned his back on it. "Well," he said, moving forward in his chair, "this has certainly been interesting, Rev. Simms. I used to love science fiction. I liked the stories about Odysseus, too, and the Cyclops and the Sirens. Lots of dangers in those places, you know? But, I know none of that shit is real, so this is where we part company. I get that you believe you're trying to help, but I can't go where you're leading. I don't know about Delamater; maybe he's nuts, a megalomaniac, but this stuff is pure insanity."

Simms sat back in his chair and allowed a gentle smile to play on his lips. "Delamater's far more dangerous than you think, Jeff. And, if I'm just a misguided fool, then how do you explain the EMF?"

Jeff looked to Morgan, whose one raised eyebrow told Jeff way more than he wanted to know. *Okay. Just a few more minutes. Might as well finish it up.* "Fine. Tell me how Delamater is so dangerous?"

"Well, for one thing, he isn't working alone. He's got some immoral, self-aggrandizing traits, to be sure. He's also the dangerous type who abuses his power. But even his substantial power proved insufficient for his ego. Now he doesn't just want power, he wants absolute power. And, in a real life catch-22, he's become vulnerable. He has come under the power of the influences I was referring to before and, due to those influences, his quest for power is insatiable."

"How do you know all this shit?"

"I've already told you."

"So what makes Delamater so powerful? The media?"

"Well, the media certainly helps. It has been creating a magnificent image of this man. Most people are believers. He is, as far as the media is concerned, courageous, virtuous, selfless, not to mention charming and good-looking. Right? He would be hard to miss. Commissioner of New York, actually the entire east coast, is one of the most powerful jobs on the planet, wouldn't you say? He has all the tech at his disposal. If he wants it to, the media can convince the rest of us that we need complete surveillance. It's not like he's trying to keep secret the fact that he is responsible for making the world a safer place with each new tech innovation. Go back a few decades. You'll find he studied and analyzed MySpace, Facebook, YouTube, Twitter—all the wonderful sites that allowed us to share ourselves with millions of others. A while back, an odd artist, Andy Warhol, promised people they would all get their 15 minutes of fame. Warhol was prescient. People wanted it. If other people weren't watching you, you didn't exist. If it wasn't recorded, it didn't happen. By the time we had no choice but to be recorded, most of us couldn't have cared less that we had lost all our privacy. And that's the world we live in today. If your EMF tech gets out there, the struggle will be over. Total control. I've been following Paul Delamater for a long time. I still don't know if I'll ever meet him face to face, but actually, this is even better. I'm talking with the person who creates the tech. Did you know that every single technical creation poses a moral question we no longer think to ask?"

Jeff heard every word. And the discordance between what he told himself about what he was doing for Delamater and the reality of what was happening, manifested before him, shattering his complacency. Stunned by the clarity of its awful truth, Jeff sat immobilized until her heard Morgan clear his throat. He hadn't expected that a moment of such transcendence would come with the sense of trumpets blaring. So that's what people were talking about: a sudden burst of insight that was total. He swallowed hard and opened his eyes. "Ok, now what?" he asked.

Simms had observed Jeff's transformation. He leaned forward. "I don't have time to explain any more of this. We will have time later, though. I do need you to understand the cosmic challenges we are facing. The more you understand what you're up against, the more powerful your assault will be."

"What assault?"

"That's what I've been alluding to. I can see that you aren't interested in pursuing your tech advances for Delamater anymore. This is good."

Jeff looked over at Morgan. Morgan's look of triumph was softened by the gratitude he felt for Jeff's conversion.

"You had lost touch with the simple truth that every single decision has an ethical consequence," Simms continued. "Each new creation has a counterpart in the moral realm. Prosperity and success are not the same thing. We've all gotten confused over the years about what constitutes truth, and there's a price to pay for that."

"So what's the truth, Rev. Simms?"

"As I said, we'll have to get to that later. We've just begun. Meanwhile, keep away from Delamater. He'll be able to tell he's lost his acolyte the second he sees you."

"I'm not sure I can keep hiding from him. He might find me even though my cloaking tech is practically flawless. Unfortunately, Delamater has a lot of tech too."

"Well, do the best you can. We'll try to tie this up tomorrow." He paused and smiled. "I know this will sound terribly mundane

under the circumstances, but Michelle and I have company coming for dinner this evening, and I promised I'd help make the
dinner. Life goes on."

The three men rose at the same time and Simms led them
to the door. Suddenly the lamp on his desk exploded, firing glass
missiles into the room. The ceiling lights shattered deadly hail on
their heads. Simms yanked open the door to find the hallway lights
detonating like a string of fireworks.

Morgan and Jeff ran down the hall following Simms who
was yelling his wife's name. The kitchen noise was unbearable,
dishes, glass-faced cupboard doors, light fixtures all bursting at
once spewing glass everywhere into the room. The gas stove was
obscured by the solid wall of flame exuding from it. The toaster,
blender, microwave, oven, stove, refrigerator, all of it—every appli-
ance—a ball of flame igniting the cupboards, pealing the wallpaper.
The heat, intense and inescapable, held the men back. The room
was already full of smoke. Simms dropped to the floor. "Michelle!
Michelle! Where are you?" His voice grew frantic. Suddenly, the
roar changed tones. Nothing was left to explode—now the flames
took over.

Michelle lay in the middle of the floor. She was a mélange of
cuts, bleeding from uncountable punctures the length of her body.
Glass quills protruded from her skin. Her hands were black; she'd
been at the sink. Before the explosions, she'd been electrocuted. As
Simms bent over her, the smoke descended to the floor.

"Simms; we've got to get out of here. Now. This place is going
up." Morgan grabbed Michelle's shoulders. Simms responded by
grabbing her feet. They fought their way through the smoke to the
front door and got out. "Keep going! Keep going! Get out of here!"

Jeff was behind them. As soon as they cleared the door, he
helped get Michelle over Morgan's shoulder as the three men ran
out into the street. They crossed the road and leaped down the
slope on the opposite side of Highland.

Simms pulled Michelle from Morgan's side and sheltered her as the house across the street shrieked like a captured animal before igniting. A dark cloud punched the air as flames crackled high above its roof. Seconds later they could hear the sirens.

Morgan picked up Michelle and they all sprinted toward the car. Simms lunged into the backseat, and Morgan thrust Michelle into his arms before throwing himself into the driver's seat. Jeff's head snapped back and forth between windows and mirrors; no one was in view; the neighbors apparently gone in the middle of a work day. The car sped away before the fire trucks turned into the street.

Morgan drove without haste once he turned off Pine; they couldn't afford to draw attention to themselves. He looked over at Jeff who was calculating the fastest route to the hospital on the car's console. "Go south on 9th then..."

"Find a place to pull over." Simms voice, grave, interrupted them. "She's gone."

Jeff whipped around to meet Simms' stricken eyes. Then he looked down at Michelle, lying across the backseat with her head cradled in Simms' arms. "Oh, man. You've got to be kidding me. I can't believe this. Oh god." He turned back and looked at Morgan, hoping for some kind of guidance.

Morgan gripped the steering wheel, eyes straight ahead. He found a place to park on Walnut. For a moment he kept staring ahead then looked in the rearview mirror. He found Simms returning his gaze. Neither knew what to say. Finally, when Simms returned his attention to Michelle, Morgan said, "It's our fault. I don't know what else to say. This can't be real."

Jeff turned around again. "Rev. Simms, I never would have approached your house if I'd thought there was even a chance of danger. I don't get it. I disengaged every piece of tech. No one—not even Delamater—knows where we are. I can't believe this. I just can't believe this. What is happening?"

Silence descended as they listened to the pinging of the car settling itself; no one moved. Then Simms' began whispering prayers over his wife, punctuated by low, cello moans as he stroked her hair.

Morgan finally turned around in his seat. "Rev. Simms— John—I'm sorry." Morgan paused hoping for insight, but he knew he was on his own. "I hate to say it, but we've got to figure out what we want to do now." Simms looked up. "We've got to get out of here; we've got to get to safety. What just happened, well, I'm guessing it's only going to get worse."

Simms was watching Morgan's lips as if he were deaf. When Morgan finished, Simms said nothing for a moment then took a deep breath, held it, and let it slowly out. "I've got to take care of Michelle. We can take her over to Golden; there's a mortuary just off the 93."

Jeff began to key in a guidance request, but stopped. Shouldn't trust tech until he could figure out what happened. "You'll have to give me directions"

"Yes, of course... A friend of mine—a good man—runs the place. I met him years ago when I was just starting out. He helped me get through my first funeral." Simms paused, caught in his thoughts. "Strange, I have always empathized with their suffering, you know, the survivors, the ones left behind. But, I felt strongly in the purpose of life, in the promise of the spiritual life to come. How arrogant I've been. I can see that now. Even knowing all that I know..." He trailed off, leaving his unfinished sentence suspended in the thick stew of guilt and remorse and grief.

Morgan pulled away from the curb and looked again into the rearview mirror, his eyebrows raised in question.

Simms looked up and returned to himself. "It's easy to get there. Just stay on Walnut and take a right on Broadway. Broadway turns into 93."

Morgan nodded. He glanced over at Jeff to find him staring

unfocused out the side window. He could only imagine what was going on in Jeff's mind. He turned back to the view in front of him and applied more pressure to the gas pedal.

"Simms, can I bother you for a minute?" Morgan looked at him in the mirror.

"Sure. Michelle's fine now."

Morgan's eyes widened. "What do you mean?"

His tone brought Jeff out of his own exile. Jeff looked at Morgan then back at Simms. "What's wrong? What just happened?"

Simms' grim smile flashed and disappeared. He looked at Jeff. "I just told Morgan that Michelle is fine. I think he misunderstood. I mean that she's made the first transition; she's fine. She knows I'm here and that I love her and that we will always be together."

"Right." Jeff was embarrassed for him—people can make themselves believe anything.

"I want to rent a car and do this myself. I think we'll attract too much attention if we all show up at the mortuary. Jimmy wouldn't care, but he does have people working for him who would ask questions."

Morgan and Jeff thought about it; they had to agree. "I can get you a car. Do you know of a place nearby? I've been sitting here thinking of different ways for us to get around the system; obviously we've been found out. Anyway, I think I can just lock onto someone's implant and access his account. It would take a while for anyone to figure out what was going on."

"Sounds good. There's an Enterprise on Colfax right before 6th. The cemetery is right there. You just drop me off and go down 6th to the 25 and get back into Denver. Where are you staying?"

"The Brown Palace." Jeff's thoughts raced ahead of the conversation. "You can meet us for dinner. Let's say Panzano's; it has booths. When do you think you can be there?"

"Well, Jimmy won't keep me long. What time is it now?"

"It's 4:00." Jeff's pronouncement stunned them all. They had met just three hours ago.

Simms eventually replied. "Let's say 7:00 at Panzano's. What do you want me to do with the car when I'm done with it?"

Morgan and Jeff exchanged glances. *What indeed?* After thinking a moment, Jeff said, "We'll have to leave Denver tonight." Morgan closed his eyes, his jaw clenched, as Jeff continued looking at the map. "Why don't you leave it at the Performing Arts Center and walk over to Panzano; it's just a few blocks down Champa."

"Fine.

"Great." Jeff returned to his blistering reverie. *What the hell is going on?*

Morgan glanced once again into the rearview mirror. Simms looked up at his reflection and answered Morgan's unspoken question. "I'm good, Morgan. I'm probably in some kind of shock, but I'll be all right. I don't have a lot of choices here."

They passed the 470 interchange and drove past the southern edge of the cemetery on their left; and then, just a half-mile down the road, they saw the Enterprise. Morgan pulled into the lot, and Jeff got out and went inside. He returned just five minutes later and got into a white Altima.

Jeff, with the cemetery's green lawns haunting him from the left, stayed close behind Morgan. Morgan turned right into an empty school lot; Jeff pulled up next to him. The three of them transferred Michelle's body into the rental's back seat, and Jeff handed Simms the keys. Looking each man in the eye, Simms nodded and got in the car. He pulled away leaving Jeff and Morgan standing mute next to their car. Finally, Morgan broke the oppressive silence. "We have to get back to Denver. If we're leaving tonight, I have a lot to do."

"Me, too," Jeff added grimly.

* * *

Thursday, 5:00 p.m. MDT

They didn't speak again until they were at the hotel. As they reached Jeff's room and Morgan prepared to walk on, Jeff grabbed his arm. In a maniacal whisper, he raged. "This is unbelievable. Somehow I've killed three people. It can't be a coincidence. It's got to have something to do with the program, but no one else knows about it but you, me and now Simms. We could have all died in there. What the hell?" His fists clenched, his veins protruding from his neck, Jeff himself looked ready to explode. He main desire was now to do some serious damage to whoever was responsible.

Morgan faced Jeff and waited for his friend to take a breath. "Jeff, listen carefully. Whatever is going on, we're going to have to play it out. You're the tech wizard of this outfit; you've got to figure it out. I'll take you wherever we need to go, but here's what I won't do. I won't go one more step with Delamater. If you change your mind again, if you let him in, I'm out. It's not an ultimatum, Jeff, it's a fact. Somehow he's behind this; I know it and so do you. So, what's it going to be?"

Jeff looked at Morgan. Morgan never lied. He also never gave an empty threat. Ever. It just wasn't in him. He meant this. Jeff nodded his understanding, turned, and swept his wrist in front of the door's lock. Morgan continued to walk down the hall thinking only of Lakia. His eyes grazed the room. There she was. She sat on the peach colored divan, one of the hotel spa's white robes loosely draped around her. She was reading a book. A book. Morgan was impressed. No one read books anymore; everything was onscreen. She looked up and held his gaze. Her smile faded as she grasped Morgan's state of mind. "What happened?"

Morgan's eyes filled. Lakia lay her book down and walked toward him. Morgan hadn't moved. "What is it? What happened to you?"

Morgan didn't say anything; he just opened his arms and Lakia walked into them. His hands reached under her robe and he felt desire flood through him overpowering the horror and guilt he'd been holding at bay since he'd looked in the mirror at Simms' eyes.

Lakia felt him rise and knew that no conversation was possible until he had release. Locked in his embrace, she let him walk her backwards. When they reached the bed, she let the force of Morgan's body press her down onto its surface. His lips found hers and pressed them apart, his tongue animate and hungry. His need became a desperate prayer to a benevolent deity. She answered his prayer.

Afterwards, skin glistening in the late afternoon light, Morgan and Lakia finally spoke. Morgan told her everything; Lakia listened without interruption, without judgment. She knew he was a good man; she also knew he was in danger. And now she was, too, though that didn't matter. She, who had never belonged to anyone but herself, now belonged to Morgan.

When he arrived at the present moment, Morgan stopped. He'd been reciting to the ceiling, replaying the visual stream in his mind. Now he looked at Lakia and saw her betrothal. He arranged his pillows so he could lean against the headboard with Lakia snuggled against his shoulder, but Lakia removed herself from his arms and sat between his knees facing him so she could look into his eyes. "So now what?" she asked.

"I have to leave," he said. "I'm meeting Jeff and Rev. Simms at 7:00. We'll eat and go. We're driving to Iowa next, from there, I don't know. What about you?"

"I'm leaving for New York City tomorrow morning. I was here for a meeting."

"Oh. With that girl?"

"No," she laughed. "She's my old college roommate; we catch up with each other once a year. That dorm room is the only thing we'll probably ever have in common though."

"So, you were here for a meeting…"

"Yes. I'm a lawyer; civil rights. Right now my firm mostly

represents organizations that are challenging the surveillance tech. We have an office here in Denver—we're trying to keep the tech from expanding here and in the Midwest." She paused. "I've met Delamater. In fact, I'm a big pain in his ass."

Morgan couldn't contain his ironic laugh. "I can't believe it."

"I know. I can't believe it either."

"Destiny isn't being very subtle these days, is it?"

"No, it isn't." Lakia paused. "Thank God."

"Yeah," Morgan agreed. "Well, I imagine Jeff and I will be heading out toward New York before long. We're going to have to confront Delamater in person at some point."

"Sounds likely."

The room fell silent again. "Morgan," Lakia began, "You're in middle of something truly horrible, and I know that you feel responsible somehow. But I don't believe you could have prevented anything that has happened so far. I believe you're involved in all this because the world needs you to be right where you are. You're going to help this turn out right. I believe in you."

Locked in a timeless moment, they both saw that it was indeed possible to believe in each other, to trust each other, to love each other even though they were practically strangers. The powerful forces of evil had their counterpoint in love. Lakia moved back to Morgan's shoulder, and they lay content in each other's embrace. Morgan, though, had to be somewhere soon, and he was going to have to start moving. "Are you hungry? I can get some room service," Morgan asked.

"No thanks. I'll get something after you leave."

"What do you want to do until then?" Morgan asked, smiling.

Lakia smiled back.

22

ANOTHER

Friday, 5:00 p.m. EDT

Claire laughed when her mom picked up the phone interrupting its first ring. "Claire! How was your trip?"

"It was great, Mom. I'm in the back of a limo; it's awesome. And you should have seen the jet. It was like this amazing living room. And the food was amazing, too. Everyone has been so nice. The chauffeur told me it's only about a half hour to Aunt Mallorie's. I can't believe I'm here. I can't believe how tall the buildings are." Claire hadn't been to the city since she was a young child still living in Brooklyn; she had no memory of her visit except the ice-skating at Rockefeller Center with Santa Claus ringing a bell on the corner. She'd been too afraid to tell Santa Claus her wish. "How could you ever leave this place?"

Bethanne, despite her misgivings, found herself smiling. *Does a teenage girl exist who doesn't love New York City?* "I'm glad you had such a good trip, honey. You must be so excited."

"Yeah, I can hardly wait to see Aunt Mallorie again; it's been forever." Paul and Mallorie had visited Iowa just once after they got married; the families had since kept in touch with vid. Now

Claire's aunt and uncle lived in a huge mansion on West 76th Street. Of course, Mallorie had sent a 3-D vid to the family, beguiling Claire beyond reason, but now she was about to see the real thing. "Anyway," Claire continued, "I have to go, Mom. I just wanted you to know I got here safely."

"Okay, baby. Thanks for letting me know. I love you honey. I'll talk to you later." Bethanne did her best to hide her apprehension. Something terrible had just happened—this time in Colorado—and more than anything, Bethanne wanted her family close by.

"Yeah, ok, Mom—talk to you later. Love you. Bye." Claire clicked off and leaned back in the plush, leather. This was going to be the best summer of her entire life. *Maybe I can stay even longer.* Surely her aunt would need help with the baby. *I could go to high school here.*

Delamater, sitting at his desk, watched his screen with great intensity. He smiled as he observed his niece lean back. He was so happy Claire had been able to come.

The car pulled up in front of a wide, limestone mansion five stories high. A doorbot saluted the chauffeur as he got out of the drivers' seat and walked around to open Claire's door. As the doorbot approached the car, the front door opened and Mallorie stepped out onto the staircase leading down to the street. Claire leaped from the car and ran past the bot and up into Mallorie's waiting arms.

Mallorie embraced her a long minute before she pulled away and held Claire at arms' length. "Oh, my god! Look at you. You've grown up so much. I can't believe it."

Claire's laughter joined with Mallorie's. "I can't believe I'm here, Aunt Mallorie. I'm so excited."

"I know what you mean. Me, too. How was your trip, sweetheart?"

"It was perfect. It was incredible. I can't believe you have your own jet. I can't believe you live here. You're so lucky."

"Yes, I am. Only one thing was missing, and now I'll have that, too." Mallorie patted her protruding belly.

Claire looked down and stared.

"I know; it's enormous, isn't it?" Mallorie spoke with pride because, of course, it was hardly enormous—barely noticeable, especially since she had retained her perfect figure everywhere else. "Well, let's squeeze through the door and get you settled in. I'll show you to your room first and then I'll show you the rest of the place."

Claire walked arm in arm with her aunt into the house. The polished wood of the entryway floor was laid out in long v's that continued down the broad hallway and up to the edge of the gracefully curving staircase. Claire stood in the entryway unmoving, transfixed by the opulence of her aunt's home.

Mallorie was aware of the effect. Even people used to luxury found themselves envious. "Claire, this is going to sound weird, but here goes: you're just going to have to get used to this place—and you will."

Claire tore her gaze away from the staircase and looked once again at her beautiful aunt. "No way. I could never get used to this."

Mallorie smiled. "People can get used to just about anything. Anyway, I'm putting you into one of the suites on the fourth floor. Your luggage is being taken there."

Fourth floor? Claire looked back at the sweeping staircase, then up at the enormous chandelier.

Sensing that Claire needed some comforting, Mallorie led her to a little divan in an alcove off the entryway. "Let's sit for a second. So, did you call your mom yet? Does she know that you've arrived safely?"

"Oh. Yes, yes I called her. She answered before the first ring was over."

Mallorie laughed. "That's great. Sounds about right. It's pretty amazing that she let you come—and on such short notice."

"I know. I was afraid to even talk to her once she said yes; I thought maybe she'd find a reason to change her mind."

"But she didn't," Mallorie affirmed.

"Nope. Unbelievable. And now I'm here for the whole summer. Maybe you should pinch me."

Mallorie laughed again, the sound of which returned Claire to her early childhood. Mallorie had moved to New York after Clair had moved back to Iowa, so she'd only seen her aunt a few times on short visits. Nevertheless, she had fallen in love with Mallorie immediately. Warm, friendly, and gorgeous, Mallorie was perfect; and her laugh invited the world to join in.

"I don't think pinching you on your first day would be very nice. Let's get you settled, okay?"

Mallorie pulled Claire up and walked past the staircase; she pressed a button on the same wall. An elevator opened and Mallorie walked in. She turned around and giggled upon seeing Claire's shocked face. "Ok, come on; it's safe."

Claire became aware of her mouth hanging open and snapped it shut. *You have got to be kidding me. No one will believe this.* The elevator opened on the fourth floor into a laundry room area, which they walked through before turning left down the hallway. "This is the bigger bedroom on this floor, plus it overlooks the back garden. The baby's room will be on this floor facing the street. There's a playroom, too—"

But Claire wasn't listening. Her room was enormous, with floor to ceiling windows. She had a queen-size bed with canopy in turquoise and royal blue, two colors she loved. The bed was sitting on a huge wool rug with a geometric design incorporating the two colors and adding an emerald green; Claire noticed the same color on the edge of the many bolsters and pillows against the headboard.

"I took the liberty of asking our chambermaid—she's a bot—to unpack your bags and arrange your toiletries. She's pretty logical—duh—so I'm sure you'll be able to find everything."

Claire knew about bots, of course. Everyone did. But she'd never actually seen one before today when she saw the doorbot. Mallorie led her into the bathroom, a large, luxurious room of marble in a peach palette. Facing the mirror was a robot that looked a lot like her friend Alison Blake's mom. Mrs. Blake had always fascinated Claire because she'd been born in France and had retained her exotic European elegance in spite of living in mundane Iowa. The bot was just over five feet tall with perfect, lightly tanned skin and dark hair pulled into a bun at the nape of her neck.

Mallorie addressed it. "Gabrielle, this is Claire."

The bot held out her hand and Claire took it. "I'm pleased to meet you, Claire. You must be sure to let me know if you need anything," she said with an alluring French accent.

Claire's instincts warred with her reason. The bot's touch was unnatural and its eyes, though expressive, lacked something Claire couldn't define. Yet, here it was addressing her. She had to respond. "It's nice to meet you, too," Claire said before quickly withdrawing her hand.

Mallorie, watching their encounter, thanked Gabrielle and dismissed her. "Claire, you don't need to use Gabrielle at all if she makes you uncomfortable; I can have her stay out of your room when you're in it.

Claire didn't want Mallorie to know how freaked out she was, so she pulled open the drawer in front of her. She found her comb, brush, and hair ties arranged neatly inside. She took out her brush and locked eyes with her reflection while Mallorie walked to the closet opposite the bathroom doorway. Claire brushed her hair until she could feel her heartbeat slow to normal. *Okay. I can deal with this.*

Malorie continued, "But, you know, it took me awhile to adjust to the bots, too. Now I'm totally comfortable around them. In fact, bots are way better for this than people. I always felt a bit guilty having people wait on me hand and foot. Bots aren't real people, so I don't mind having them do everything for me—that's what they're built for."

Claire nodded, unconvinced. *Why not just do things for yourself?* But, then, why not take it easy if you have the money to do it? Claire had done a report on AI in tenth grade; no one thing was more expensive than a lifelike robot with AI, and Mallorie had at least two.

Claire finished brushing her hair and turned to Mallorie who was examining an enormous walk-in closet filled with clothes— lots of clothes; lots more than Claire had brought. She joined Mallorie as she walked inside and realized that all these clothes were for her.

"I hope you don't mind," Mallorie said. "I couldn't help myself; I had them delivered this morning. We can return anything you don't like, but I was just so excited, and I remember only too well the pathetic options you have in Iowa City."

Claire ran her hands through along the row of designer clothes. Several pairs of Affliction and Apricot jeans; Prada shoes and Fendi bags; Mela, AX Paris, Misumi, even Kira Plastinia dresses. These labels did not appear in the malls Claire had been to; in fact, she was completely ignorant of their existence. "Um, wow. I don't know what to say. This is crazy."

"I know," agreed Mallorie. "Anyway, let's get out of here so Gabrielle can finish up. Come on; I'll show you around." Mallorie put her arm around Claire's shoulder and led her from the room. "Let's use the stairs now; I need the exercise."

"We'll go upstairs first, since you might want to come up here a lot—especially this time of year." On the fifth floor, they turned right and walked down a hallway lined with Lautrec prints. The bedroom they entered was dominated by a wall of French doors leading out onto a terrace that ran the width of the house. Flowerbeds filled with blooming tulips, lilies, daffodils, and irises crowded the stone walkways. A little table and four chairs sat off to one side near the vine-covered outer wall. The water cascading over the alabaster bowls of a three-tiered fountain sparkled in the afternoon sunlight.

Claire became aware that her face was feeling the strain of smiling for so long. "I can't believe it. I've never seen anything so beautiful in my life. I love these flowers; there're the same ones my mom has."

"I know. I love them, too. This is my perennial garden; almost everything you see here is either a bulb or corm. Your mom and I learned all about them from your grandma."

"If I were you, I'd spend all my time out here," Claire said.

"Well, it's pretty dismal in the winter time. Then, we keep the drapes closed most days because just looking out here makes you feel cold. But this time of year, nothing beats it. Well, nothing but the rooftop. We have a solarium up there; come on, I'll show you."

After exploring the glorious rooftop and the third floor, which consisted of a huge master bedroom, an office, and the biggest bathroom Claire had ever seen, they glanced quickly into the enormous living room and dining room that occupied the second floor. "We don't spend much time on this floor at all unless we have company. I'll show you the basement," Mallorie said. She led Claire down past the first floor to the lower level. To the right of the stairs was a wine cellar filled with racks of bottles. Mallorie smiled. "This is locked," she said, winking at Claire. "And Paul knows every bottle in here—it's one of his passions. He's got over 1900 bottles, some of them worth thousands of dollars."

Claire was fascinated by the racks of bottles, but her attention was immediately grabbed by the room across from it, a home theater with cushioned leather chairs set on tiered levels and a curtain drawn across the a stage with a massive screen behind it. "Oh, my god! Are you kidding me?"

"I know; it's a bit much, but since Paul and I attract so much attention when we're in public, we wanted to preserve the feeling we used to get going to movies, you know, in style, like the good old days."

"I love it," Claire enthused running her hand over the old-style popcorn machine just inside the door.

"Me, too. Hey, I want to show you one more thing." Mallorie led Claire through a much bigger laundry than the one upstairs and into an enormous gym as big as the living room. All the latest equipment, a dance floor with mirrors and a ballet bar, filled the space. "Both of us are pretty psycho about being fit. It's vain as can be, I know, but there it is."

Claire was overwhelmed. All of it was so over-the-top that she had run out of nice things to say.

Mallorie sensed her mood. "Hey, I bet you're exhausted. Why don't we take the elevator back up to your room? Gabrielle is probably done unpacking now, so I'll have her run you a bath and then you can take a little nap before dinner. It's a little before 6:00; Paul will be home around 7:00 or so and we'll eat around 8:00. That gives you plenty of time." She led the way into the elevator and pressed the 4. She kissed Claire on the cheek and briefly took her hand. "I'm so glad you're here, honey. Honestly. This is going to be so great. If you need anything, just press for Gabrielle or me on one of the room screens. If I don't hear from you, I'll know you're fine. Gabrielle will check on you at 7:00 so you can get ready for dinner. I love you." Mallorie waited for Claire's eyes to meet hers.

"I love you, too." Claire said as the doors opened. She stepped out of the elevator and stood still for a moment in the quiet of the small laundry room. She was uncomfortable. Something was wrong here, but she didn't know what. She began to feel a bit of panic as the sense of being pursued rose to the surface of her mind. She closed her eyes and sent her thoughts to her mom so far away. Immediately she felt her mom's reassurance and love. Tears sprang to her eyes. *What am I doing here?* Claire took a few deep breaths as Bethanne had taught her to do whenever she felt overwhelmed. She began to reason with herself; after all, her mom had told her she could come out. If her mom said it was okay, it was okay. She regained herself and opened her eyes. Taking another deep breath, she walked toward her room.

Gabrielle was just leaving the steamy bathroom in which a tub full of warm water and bubbles beckoned. Gabrielle saw Claire and nodded a greeting. "I've taken the liberty of drawing you a bath. I will leave now. If you need anything, just ring." Gabrielle smiled, her eyes twinkling with good-natured warmth. Claire felt her stomach turn. She looked away, trying to dodge the conflict that the person/bot caused her. As Gabrielle shut the bathroom door behind her, Claire looked at the tub of water waiting for her. *Might as well.*

23

THE CHASE

Still Friday, 7:30 p.m. MDT

Simms put down his glass and turned his intense gaze on Morgan and then Jeff. "I'll go back a ways. Around 1915, a little book called *War and Christianity* by Vladimir Soloviev, the greatest Russian philosopher of that time, was published. The text contains three dialogues, each one about a different social problem. In the third conversation, Soloviev describes in great detail how our world will prepare to welcome the coming of the Antichrist. I think you'd find it interesting, but the upshot is that Soloviev describes a guy not unlike our Delamater as, let's say, a very adversarial force in mankind's evolution."

Morgan had nothing to say. He was familiar with the Russian thinker who'd died at the turn of the previous century and, when confronted with the clear lines that Simms had drawn, realized that his suspicions of Delamater had been well placed all along.

Jeff, however, was beyond astonished; he was indignant. "Let me get this straight; are you implying that Delamater is the Antichrist?" He snatched the napkin off his lap and threw it across his plate. "You've got to be kidding me. This is the 21st goddamn century. This religious crap is for backwater Neanderthals and every intelligent person in the world knows it. Please tell me you are *not* serious."

Simms' eyes rose to meet Jeff's. Jeff was suddenly helpless, held by a powerful and irresistible force. As he sat, caged by the reverend's sheer will, the room abruptly disappeared and Jeff was thrust into a golden light, bright and warm, that enveloped him completely. Suffused in its glow, he became aware that he was buoyant, almost weightless, and that nothing existed but where he was right now. He was learning things; being instructed without words. He was okay. He'd always been okay. He experienced truth as if it were tangible. He was complete. He was blameless. He was on a journey. Everyone was on a journey. He was loved. He was planned for. Jeff accepted it all without question. And then, slowly, he became aware once again of the room around him. He looked at Morgan, who raised one eyebrow in response. Jeff looked back to Simms' gentle smile.

"Okay, what was that?"

"A little welcoming party. Now that you've got through the door, you may decide to return once in awhile. Most people do. I decided to take you there because it's important for you to see that just because you think you know everything about the world, you don't. You have built certain limitations for yourself, but you don't need to keep them. Meanwhile, I would like to suggest that what I've been telling you isn't religious crap. Religions have nothing to do with this; they've long ago lost connection with the truth of things; in fact, most religions are more materialistic than atheism. What I'm telling you must figure into the decisions you make from now on."

Morgan spoke into the silence that was stretching uncomfortably between Simms and Jeff. "Rev. Simms. We have to go. We've got to get to Iowa City. If we leave soon, we'll get there before dawn. What are you going to do?"

"I want to go back to Boulder because I'd like see Michelle before Jimmy cremates her, but I know I can't; it's not safe there. So I've decided to go to this place I know—quiet, remote, no tech—in the mountains. I work there sometimes; no one but Michelle knows—knew—about the place. I would like to get off the grid, though. Any chance of that, Jeff?

Jeff had been silent, listening to the two men talk as if he weren't there. Hearing his name called him back. "Yeah, sure... of course. No problem. You need to be invisible, too. I've got a little something," he said pulling out a small packet. "Hold out your arm."

Less than an hour later, Morgan and Jeff were heading northeast toward Interstate 80 that would take them all the way to Iowa City. It would be a long drive speeding across the flat plains of eastern Colorado and Nebraska, but Morgan was energized on a cellular level. He couldn't sleep if he wanted to. Finally, a mission had been given him that required all that he had, all that he was. He looked back in gratitude at everything he had done to prepare himself for this without ever knowing the reason why. Always he was attracted to the edges of things, the occult understanding of even the most mundane or practical ideas. He'd learned to meditate in college and had kept it up ever since. His body, which had been the means to his higher education, was as important to him now as it had been then. He was in perfect condition. And at this moment, miraculously, he was in love. He was the whole deal. He would need it all because he was going into a heart of darkness that made Conrad's story look like a sandbox catastrophe engineered by a child. The evil he meant to confront could alter the course of human evolution forever.

Morgan glanced over at Jeff to see how he was doing. Jeff had opened his vid, wincing as a bright light filled the screen. He began manipulating the data to try to get the star emitting the light reduced to a size small enough to pinpoint exactly. Jeff sensed

Morgan's attention and looked up from his work. "This is weird, man. This star doesn't make sense, but I've checked the program and everything is working like it's supposed to."

"So what does that mean?"

"Well, it looks like it means that this star is bigger than all of the others—massively bigger than all of the others. Which means that this Iowa lady is off the charts."

"Good thing we're going there then, right?"

"Hell, I don't know what's good anymore. I just wonder how she's managed to stay alive this long because if whoever's exploding anomalies thought it was worth killing off Thompson and Simms, this one's got to be driving him crazy."

"Maybe he can't see these people until we get there. I mean, we must be the worst kind of omen."

Jeff sat motionless, contemplating. *I'd be the instrument of another death.* But if they didn't continue on, Delamater would get her anyway; of that Jeff was certain. *Delamater?* "We have to take that chance," he said. "Maybe she already knows, like Simms seemed to know, that bad things are in the air. Maybe she'll just run if we tell her to. Maybe we can meet her outside somewhere—away from her house."

"Maybe."

Jeff went back to his work as Morgan drove off into the night. Their course was set.

* * *

Still Friday, 10:00 p.m. CDT

Bethanne sat on the edge of Scott's bed listening to his steady breathing. *I love you.* She was being pursued; she'd felt the focus pressing against her, disturbing the field surrounding her. She couldn't get a clear read, though, so she didn't know whether to wait or flee. She got up and walked to the door, glancing back before silently moving toward her own room. She knelt beside her bed, childlike, with her hands folded. Sufficiently humbled, she asked for guidance. *Open yourself... NOW!*

Bethanne rocked back, gasping. She crawled to her rug and focused on her breathing. Her attention slowed its pace and calmed her terror. Never had she been directed so strongly or with such urgency. Her slowing breath calmed her mind, and she began to clear herself of all thoughts, all emotions, all awareness of the external world. She saw Claire and Mallorie. Claire, her nascent power exposed, faced Paul Delamater. Paul was instructing Claire, his impatience barely contained. He would make her strong; together they would rule the world making it a safe and beautiful haven for all life. A heaven on earth.

Bethanne felt a sudden rush of malevolence as a shadowy face rose out from Paul's head and looked toward her, locking her eyes with its own, traveling through the open channel toward her. Bethanne, stunned, contracted herself, panting in fear. But then she was lifted from the floor by strong hands on either side. She found the courage to defy the fear pulsing through her; she illuminated the darkened channel with love. She fortified the walls with luminous warmth overwhelming the flow of darkness as she directed its current toward Paul. The light overcame the darkness effortlessly as it surged toward its goal. Bethanne watched Paul collapse on the floor. The shadow stayed outside of Paul, though, and glowered at her as their eyes connected once again. Then it smiled. The trap was set.

Bethanne returned to herself, amazed that she was still sitting, still facing her altar. She closed her eyes, issuing thanks to those who had assisted her before returning to the question that had brought her to her room. Wait or flee? The answer was neither. She didn't know who was stronger, she or Paul, but she knew it was her battle—maybe her final one—to fight him. She had been preparing, without knowing it, her whole life. She stood up. Taking a deep breath, she reached for the telephone and dialed Donna's number. They'd have to leave immediately.

* * *

Friday, 9:15 p.m. MDT

Jeff dimmed the screen for a full second before he could make the star visible without killing his eyes. The star he was observing exceeded the power of Simm's exponentially. He watched as the star shot out an arm of light eastward. He backed up until he could see its destination. New York City. As he watched, he noticed a ripple flowing back against the current through the Star's arm. It was swirling like a tornado through the arm's center. The light dimmed as it advanced, a black hole swallowing the light. *What the hell?* Mesmerized, Jeff watched the celestial slaughter, awaiting an outcome that seemed inevitable as the light was devoured instantly, the black menace pulling it into its gaping and ravenous mouth. Suddenly, a burst of power reversed the current again and dazzling light filled the arm throwing off sparks that ignited the dark shadows. The darkness fled back to its source and disappeared. So did the star.

"Holy shit!" Jeff attacked his keyboard, demanding answers that were coming too slowly.

"What's wrong?" Morgan, lost in his own thoughts, had missed the mounting agitation glinting off his partner.

"I think something really big just happened. Shit. Bethanne's star is gone. I don't know what's going on. Some weird kind of battle, but it looked galactic on the screen. Star Wars.

"Between who?"

"Between Bethanne and someone in New York City."

"Delamater?"

"Wait a second; I should be able to figure that out." Jeff replayed the event and focused this time on the source of darkness. All the same numbers, but negative. He fast-forwarded to the end of the battle and confirmed, "Yeah. Wow. It *is* Delamater."

"So what do you want to do?"

"Well, he obviously knows about Bethanne, but it looks like she beat him back. Except now I can't see her star."

"So, what does that mean?"

"Hell if I know."

"Do we to go to Iowa City or do we go straight to New York?"

Jeff thought about it. Iowa City was on the way. It couldn't hurt—it's not like he'd be leading Delamater to her. "Iowa City. No stops."

"You got it." Morgan steadily pressed the gas pedal. At 120 miles an hour, they'd be in Iowa City in less than five hours.

* * *

Friday, 11:00 p.m. CDT

Bethanne had gathered all her energy in, holding it close, before she'd picked up the phone. Donna would be here any minute. Claire was safe for the moment. David—*Oh, David, how I love you*—had teamed up with Donna's brother, Jack, to protect her. Poor Jack; he had died a horrible death, but he was eager to help out. She wondered whether or not to tell Donna, but decided it was too dangerous now.

Small world; really small world. But most people could not imagine the intertwining lives they had with the people they knew—and how they were connected to those they loved who had already passed through the gates of death. David had become a skillful communicator since he'd died, and even though Bethanne had left him free to go, he stayed near. Jack, however, whose life had been extinguished abruptly just a few days ago, had been working relentlessly to find a way to alert his family. Once Jack had recognized Donna's connection to Bethanne and Bethanne's connection to David, he too, had been staying close. When the Rival threatened Bethanne, both he and David had been there, savagely fighting by her side.

Bethanne grabbed a small duffle bag from the closet and threw an extra set of clothes into it. She left her room and re-entered Scott's. "Wake up, honey."

"Mom, school's over; let me sleep." He opened his eyes into the darkness of the night. "What are you doing? What time is it?"

"Road trip." For years, those words had conjured two-lane highways through fields of growing corn. She'd traveled over them to get to the highways that would lead to Chicago, Minneapolis, and finally, New York City. As children, her father had taken the family all over the country. It had been her job to distract Mallorie, strapped into her car seat, bored and restless as they traveled mile after mile. All that had been a long time ago, and the words she always loved to hear had never before carried the dire import they did now.

Scott's body responded to the tension in his mother's voice. He kicked the covers off and jumped out of bed, wide awake, alarmed. "What happened, Mom?"

"Claire's in danger. We have to get to her right away."

"Did she call?"

"No, Scott. I don't think she even knows. But I do."

"Can't we just call her?"

"I'm thinking that she will be less vulnerable if we don't alert her. Now, grab an extra shirt and underwear—basics; we've got to go. Donna's on her way."

"Why's Donna coming?"

"It's a long story; don't worry about it now. Besides, we need her car." Bethanne smiled briefly as she recalled the many times she'd kidded Donna for keeping her car. No one drove anymore; it was ridiculous to spend the time and money keeping a car in running condition. But Donna hadn't budged. This car was her first car; her first real possession. *Thank God she didn't listen to me.*

Scott threw underwear, socks and another tee shirt into Bethanne's open duffle. They hurried downstairs and into the kitchen. "Put some apples and protein bars in there while I fill the water bottles. Grab some cheese and that loaf of bread, too."

Donna knocked lightly before walking in the kitchen door. "I brought some food, too. We can get coffee while we fill the gas tank. Of my car." She raised one eyebrow at Bethanne, who managed a short laugh.

"Yeah, yeah. I've already thought of that. Get over yourself."

Donna smiled and took the duffle from the table. "Scott, run back upstairs and grab a couple pillows and the blanket from your bed. It'll be a long night; you're going to want to sleep for at least some of it."

Scott tossed the pillows and blanket into the back of the old Volvo 750 and climbed in after them. Donna settled into the driver's seat and started the car. Bethanne stood outside the passenger door and glanced back at the darkened house. *Will I ever see it again?* She slipped into the car and closed the door as Donna backed out of the driveway. Bethanne wouldn't be able to help with the driving because she needed to focus every bit of her energy inward; she had to remain invisible to the force working through Delamater and whoever seemed to be approaching from the west. Even if the Volvo managed to keep close to its top speed, it would take over 12 hours to get to the city; a long time to stay small enough to escape notice.

The road was a lonely place these days. Interstate 80 all the way. It was just 200 miles to Chicago and another 200 or so to Toledo; they'd be there in 5 hours and they could look for a place to stop and stretch and grab a bite to eat. After that, they were just

150 miles to Youngstown, the last city they'd have to go near on the interstate. Then, 5 hours later, they'd be in New York—around noon. How perfect; showdown at high noon.

Bethanne looked over her shoulder to check on Scott. His head was cradled deeply into his pillow; he was sound asleep. Donna caught her eye as she swiveled her head back around. "You ready to tell me what's going on?" she asked.

Bethanne grinned briefly then shook her head. "There's not much I can say. I do know that Claire's in trouble. Something is wrong with Mallorie's husband, Paul. I never really liked him, you know? I always thought he was, I don't know, kind of slick. And not in a con man way, more ruthless than that. Like world domination ruthless. But he was always so good to Mallorie, and she worshipped the ground he walked on, so I decided that I would never think anyone was good enough for her, right? I didn't want what I thought of Paul to be true, so I decided it wasn't true based on nothing. And, of course, my gut was right. Too right. He really does want world domination."

Donna felt her soft hair lift off the back of her neck as if a light, chilling breath had blown through it. A current of electricity escaped through her fingertips before she clenched the wheel in trepidation. Holy shit. Bethanne wasn't kidding. Donna took several even breaths before speaking. "Um, Bethanne, what the hell?"

"I know. It sounds pretty intense—it *is* pretty intense. Sorry. God, the word sorry doesn't even come close. This story is huge and ancient and dark, and I'm just starting to grasp it myself. And I hate that I need your help to do what I have to do. But I can't sugarcoat it for you, Donna. This is the real deal. I am the Real Deal. And I've got some serious responsibilities. I feel like even just talking about it is going to draw attention, though. So we're done. You've been warned. I'm sorry to bring you into this, but you're supposed to be here. That's already clear. You've been chosen, too… But I'm done talking for now. I've got to close things down here and disappear."

Donna, for some odd reason, understood what Bethanne was saying. She left her friend alone and turned up the tunes. It was, after all, a road trip, and she loved the oldies. *Crimson and clover, over and over.*

INTERLUDE II

Still Friday, 7:00 p.m. EDT

Something was definitely wrong with Paul. Mallorie had been alarmed as soon as he'd walked in the door for dinner that night. He was pale, and his eyes sparkled strangely. He held himself rigidly upright; his smile unnatural and forced. "What's wrong?" she had asked immediately.

"What do you mean? Am I late?" He looked at the clock—7:00—right on time.

"No, you're not late; you look terrible. Did something happen?"

"No; I'm fine. I mean, it was a long day. Plenty of bullshit coming my way, as usual. I guess I'm just a little tired. Where's Claire?"

"She should be down any second. She was exhausted from her trip, so I left her upstairs to take a hot bath and a nap."

"Did she let Gabrielle help her?"

"A little. She seemed pretty freaked out, though. It'll take some time."

"She'll get used to her. Before you know it, she won't want to live without her."

"Maybe." Mallorie wasn't so sure. Clair's mother had certainly never gotten used to it. She called it slavery—and she didn't mean the bots. *Geesh.*

"Well, get her down here," Paul insisted. "I can't wait to see her."

Mallorie went to the console and commed into Claire's room. Claire said she was on her way and Mallorie clicked off. She looked at the blank screen and saw the worry in her reflected eyes. Why was Paul so interested in Claire all of a sudden? *Is it her age? Is it because I'm pregnant? Is he a perv? Did I marry a pervert?* She shook her head to banish the evil thoughts. She'd known Paul a long time now; he didn't even like porn. No way was he a molester. She turned to face Paul again and caught a foreign glint of sardonic humor before he blinked and gazed innocently back at her.

The dinner, though, went well. Claire had less difficulty accepting the robot assistance at dinner and was delighted to receive Paul's unwavering attention. Soon he had her chattering away about school and how boring Iowa was. She asked countless questions about the city, and Paul answered every one by mixing historical facts with elaborate stories. Mallorie, however, could barely breathe. Something was very, very wrong.

Later, lying in bed, she looked again at the bedside clock. 11:15. This night was never going to end. Paul was breathing evenly beside her. They would be taking Claire around the city in style tomorrow after the big meeting Paul had scheduled. What would Claire think of all their fame? She was impressed by their riches, but Mallorie was sure Claire had no idea how important or powerful her uncle was. Or how loved. And that's when Mallorie's breath caught. If anyone else had seen the glint of malice, sly and treacherous, spring out of his eyes tonight, that love would turn to doubt. Anyone. Herself. She placed her open hands against each side of her pregnant belly. *What have I done?*

11:30. Mallorie couldn't take a sleeping pill—nothing while you're pregnant, the doctor had said. She finally got up and walked to the baby's room. She sat in the corner away from the windows and began to cry.

* * *

Field Anomaly

Saturday, May 26, 3:00 a.m. CDT

Morgan pulled in front of the small house on East Jefferson. The lights were off; it felt empty. Jeff turned away from the window and met Morgan's eyes. Yeah. She was gone. "How did we miss her? Can't you tell when she's moving? You just lost her entirely?"

"I know. I don't get it. Maybe she has some kind of cloaking device."

"Somehow this place doesn't seem like it's techno elite."

"Well, if it was, I'd know about it. Nothing in tech world gets past my little darlings. They'd be so jealous."

Morgan shook his head. He hated when Jeff personified his tech. "Do you want to go check it out at least? Maybe she left something behind."

Jeff glanced down at his screen. A brilliant flash erupted and vanished. If he had blinked, he would have missed it. He stared in disbelief for a second then his fingers rushed over the keyboard. "I found her," he said. "I can't believe it. She's got a few hours on us, but she just showed up east of Chicago. Let's get out of here."

Morgan put the car in gear and pulled a quick u-turn. "So if she's east of Chicago, that probably means she's going to New York, right?"

"Where else? It's all coming together."

24

CLOSER

Saturday, 8:00 a.m. EDT

Bethanne and Donna leaned their heads back on the headrests. They'd just crossed the Meander Creek Reservoir in northeastern Ohio and had pulled off at Salt Springs Road for gas and food. Donna held her eyes closed as the autopump filled the Volvo's tank. The pump finished its job and withdrew its arm. Donna started the car and pulled forward into the restaurant parking lot. She turned the car off and looked over at Bethanne. "Hey, are you awake?"

Bethanne smiled without opening her eyes. "Yes. I'm awake and hungry." She looked back at Scott. "How about you?"

Scott grinned back at her. "Nah, I'm not hungry, Mom. I could go a whole week without eating. Really." He reached for the door and then stopped midway to the handle. "Wait a minute; are we safe?"

Bethanne looked at him seriously for a moment before speaking. "I can't really explain it, but I know the attention is off me right now. It may not be good for everyone else, but it's great for us. So, let's take advantage of it and eat some real food. We're going to need it later."

Denny's. The smell greeted them like an old friend. Donna and Bethanne ordered coffee; Scott ordered juice. They each ordered eggs and toast and Donna got a waffle for the table. Bethanne sat quietly looking across at Scott. *How beautiful he is.* She was impressed with how well he seemed to be adjusting to all this—evidence of his trust in her.

Scott looked up and met her gaze. He smiled; his eyes reassured her—he was cool with everything. He knew two things about his mom: one, she was different than anyone else he knew, and two, he could trust her with his life. Actually, anyone could. He tried to picture what was waiting for them in New York, but he couldn't. Though he had no idea what kind of trouble his sister was in, he knew his mom would handle it, and she didn't seem particularly worried right now. He figured they'd go straight to his aunt's house; and he was stoked about being in the grand house he'd seen on the vids she sent. He knew, of course, that his uncle was an important man, famous, but Scott had never cashed in on that with his friends. Come to think of it, he'd never told anyone—even when friends had been at the house and Uncle Paul had appeared on the news. That's weird. "Mom, want to know something weird? I've never told anyone I'm related to—"

"Stop," she hissed, reaching as if to put her hand over his mouth. "We don't want to attract his attention."

Scott's eyes widened. *What the hell?* He looked over his shoulder. "Whose attention?"

Bethanne shook her head. "Scott, whatever you were going to say, we'll talk about later." She changed the subject. "So, are you excited about getting to see the big city?"

"Sure," he responded, confused but willing to play along. "I feel like I've already been there—every cool vid in the world is set there." By the time he was finished with his thought, he had completely forgotten about Paul. Completely.

Bethanne relaxed her mental grip. *Such an intrusion.* She

smiled. "I know. It seems like a million years since I've been there."

Donna laughed. "Yeah, it's always the other way around. My brother, Jack, did it that way. As soon as he could leave Iowa, he did. He's been in New York ever since he graduated from college."

At the mention of Jack's name, Bethanne reached out to divert Donna's mind, too.

Donna went on, "Have you thought about where you might want to go to school once you graduate, Scott?"

Bethanne quietly took a deep breath. Everything was connected to everything else. She wouldn't be able to hold on much longer. Just then, their food was delivered and mercifully all the talking stopped.

As they eased back onto 80 and the last leg of the trip, Bethanne immediately closed her eyes again. The only bump she had felt since they'd left Iowa was the psychic one she got at breakfast. Paul was about to make his first overt move—and Claire, somehow, had to be protected. How? Bethanne widened her scope enough to sense Jack and David. She pulled back. Good. They were there. They would be helping out.

25

HELPLESS

Saturday, 9:30 a.m. EDT

"Look, I don't have a choice," Matt answered, looking Alek square in the eyes. "Our whole class has to go. Anyway, every sophomore in the borough has to be there. I already told you, I don't know why we can't just watch Delamater onscreen. He's onscreen for everything else. I mean, do you think I actually want to go to police headquarters?"

The boys hadn't been apart once in the four days since Jack's murder. They had, in fact, been spending a lot of their time together offscreen for a change. It was weird.

"I hate that guy, Matt. He didn't really give a shit that Dad died." Alek had watched the conversation between Delamater and his mom a hundred times on the vid in his room.

"Well, you didn't seem to care that much either," Matt retorted.

"I did so."

"No you didn't. You barely looked up from your game when Mom told us."

Alek was sitting on the edge of his bed. He bowed his head and thought about what Matt was saying. When he finally looked up, his eyes were brimming with tears. "You're right. I didn't care right away, but I've started thinking about him so much lately. Especially at night. It's like every morning I wake up, I feel like I've been with him."

"Wait. No shit? Me, too," Matt exclaimed.

"No way. Why didn't you say anything?"

"I didn't want to freak you out."

"Well, I'm freaked out now," Alek said. "What do you think it means?"

"How the hell should I know? Look, don't think about it for now. We'll talk when I get home."

"Matt, are you sure you have to go? I really don't want to be alone." Alek looked down, embarrassed by his feelings."

Matt squinted at Alek. *What's got into him?* "I'll probably be gone for just an hour or so."

"Okay then; fine. See you," Alek mumbled.

Matt really didn't want to go that much. He had always hated going to school, even though it was only on rare occasions that he had to attend actual classes. But Paul Delamater sparked his interest. And Paul Delamater knew as much as anyone about his dad's death. Dear old dad. Matt tried to brush away the electric tingle that occurred every time he thought about his dad now. It was as if just the thought of him brought him close. Whatever. Besides, he was going to be in the same room as the man: Paul Delamater. Everyone's hero. Making the city and the entire nation safe and secure. He was in the news again, too, because his wife was pregnant. *Big deal. Like she's the only woman who's ever been pregnant.*

Matt shook himself out of his reverie and locked eyes with Alek. "Okay. I'm out of here. See you." He stood up and offered his hand to his brother.

Alek let himself be pulled from the bed, then wrapped his arms around Matt, who struggled to pull himself free.

"Look, I really have to go, Alek. Take it easy, will ya?" *Seriously, what is up with this kid?* He turned and walked out of their room, down the hall, and out the door. He didn't bother saying good-bye to his mother. She was keeping herself busy by re-watching every home movie she had, about 20 years worth. If she loved her life with his dad so much, why hadn't she shown it while he was still alive? *Whatever.* He went down the steps to the subway at Lexington and 59th, two long and three short blocks away. Matt had never lived anywhere but the Bristol on East 56th. His entire worldview began and ended there. He knew exactly how long it would take the 6 train to get to the Civic Center; a clump of intimidating buildings fronted by massive columns. All of them now belonged to the police—to Paul Delamater.

When he arrived, he immediately spotted the mass of teen-agers gathered in front of the Municipal Building. It was bizarre to see so many kids his own age in the day time. Most of the large gatherings that occurred now that schools were all online happened at night in locations announced just minutes before events occurred. Matt went once in awhile, but always felt out of place. He didn't use drugs or the muse or anything else for stimulation. He was no moralist; he had tried everything. It's just that everything made him sick—really sick. And puking his guts out wasn't his idea of fun. He had no best friend, no one he confided in. He didn't have a girlfriend. Not that girls didn't throw themselves at him; they did. He knew enough about the world to know he looked good. And it was a natural good, not a manufactured one. Girls had radar for that. Sure, he worked out, but his face was the one he was born with. So was everything else. The problem with the girls he'd bothered to date was that they were basically brainless and easy. He figured it was some fault of his own that he attracted that type, so a few months back, he'd just stopped dating. Screw it.

He joined the mass of students under Muni's arches right as the loudspeaker announced that the proceedings would occur at City Hall. *What the hell? Now they had to walk over to City Hall? Why not just meet there in the first place?* Matt surmised that this was all some kind of lesson in intimidation—control. *Ooh. Big, bad powerful Chief Delamater. Fine.* Matt was curious about City Hall anyway. No one had been allowed in there without a pass for decades, and even tours had been stopped long ago. He realized he was going to be one of the few people living in the city to see the rotunda. Supposedly this thing was for all the sophomores from Manhattan. The sophomores from the other four boroughs would get their chance over the next two weekends; Manhattan was first—of course. The students followed the robot guide's lead toward City Hall. Because he had been at the back of the line at Muni, Matt was at the front as the group turned to go to City Hall. *Nice.* He'd be in the first row to see Delamater in the rotunda—this was going to be awesome.

* * *

Saturday, 9:30 a.m. EDT

Paul was grinning broadly at Claire. "You're going to enjoy this morning, I think." He winked at Mallorie, who had spent an hour trying to look as if she'd slept.

"What are we going to do?" Claire asked, picking up her glass of fresh squeezed orange juice.

"We're going to City Hall. That's where I work. I'm going to give a speech to sophomores from all over Manhattan. You're a sophomore, too, right?"

"Well; I'll be a junior in the fall."

"Perfect. We don't really have many traditional schools here in the city anymore; most of the students go to school online."

"I don't think I'd like that at all."

"Oh, you'd get used to it. It has lots of advantages. No bullies, no early classes, no mean teachers."

"Yeah, but how do you make friends?"

"New York City gives kids lots of opportunities to meet each other if they really want to, but from what I've heard, most people your age meet on vid."

"What about lunches and—" Claire protested as a list of things she loved about school began forming in her head.

"You know, you should give it a chance before you judge it, Claire," Paul interrupted.

Well, everyone knew that New York City was a great city, so just because they had school online didn't mean she shouldn't give it a chance... just because she hadn't tried it didn't mean it wasn't cool. Still, no school, no daily contact with kids her age, didn't seem right at all.

After breakfast, Paul led the way to the elevator. Mallorie held Claire's hand. Paul seemed fine today; maybe she had imagined his scary look last night. After all, she couldn't be much more hormonal than she was right now. She was probably seeing things. She'd have to ask her OB about it when they got back. She squeezed Claire's hand, and they shared a glance as Paul pressed a panel under the elevator buttons. The panel swung open to reveal another button, which he pushed. The elevator descended below street level and kept going down for several seconds. It opened to reveal an opulent subway car sitting on a track in a tunnel tiled with beautiful mosaics depicting the city above.

"Oh, my god!" Claire exclaimed.

Paul smiled and winked at Mallorie, who winked back. They followed Claire off the elevator and walked straight toward the waiting car.

"Are you kidding me?" Claire stood at the car's entrance, looking in. "You have your own subway?"

Paul expelled a one-syllable laugh. "Not a whole subway, kiddo, just a car. It takes us to a stop beneath City Hall. It was closed for a long, long time, but since I wanted to be able to come and go as I pleased without interference from my adoring public—ha, ha—,

I had it fixed up and voila, here it is. Mallorie and I used to be the only people the car recognized. Now it will recognize you, too."

"What do you mean?"

"I mean that the tech that operates it will recognize you and take you to City Hall too."

"Wow. Even if I'm not with you guys?"

"Yes, even if you're alone. It will recognize you no matter what."

Paul's voice indicated a deeper meaning that sent a cold shiver up Mallorie's spine. What the hell was the matter with her? She looked at Paul, who was looking at Claire with an indulgent, favorite-uncle look. She closed her eyes as she sank into the plush yellow leather of the sofa facing forward. As soon as Paul and Claire took their seats, the car eased into motion and rapidly gained speed.

"How do you know when the other trains are on the track?" Claire asked.

"This is a private track, Claire. No other lines use it; this is the only car on it. In fact, no one really knows about it besides my staff, and they aren't allowed on it. It's just for us." Paul put his arm around the back of Claire's plush seat and expounded on the history of New York's subways and all the different lines as Claire sat silently drinking in every word he said. She loved New York City again. Every inch of it.

Soon, the car began to slow. It stopped before an ornately tiled entrance leading to a stairway. Paul reached for Mallorie's hand and pulled her up off the couch, smiling as he patted her stomach then looked up into her eyes.

"You poor, tired baby," he said.

"I know. I feel like I'll never get a good night's sleep again. Sometimes I think I'm losing my mind," she added.

Paul tilted his head and looked sideways at her. His hair had fallen in front of one eye; he looked particularly gorgeous this way. Mallorie wondered briefly if he knew it; if he'd done it on purpose. *Wow. I am definitely losing it.* She looked away and found

Claire waiting for them. She smiled as she held her hand out again. "Ready?"

"Ready," Claire chirped. *How cool was this?* They approached the elevator, which opened immediately.

"First we'll stop in my office and check the status of everything," Paul remarked hitting the button for the second floor. They walked by the uniformed bots and into the Governor's room. Magnificent portraits and marble busts embellished the borders of the room. George Washington's desktop had just one vidscreen on it; nothing else. Paul walked over to the screen while Mallorie, docent-like, led Claire around the room, pointing out the historical artifacts.

"Mallorie, what's going on today exactly? I mean, I'm starting to feel a little nervous," Clair whispered.

"Oh, don't be nervous," Mallorie said aloud. "Paul has been worried that the teenagers here are becoming too wrapped up in themselves. He wants them to care more about the city they live in. So, he decided to get all the sophomores together—one borough at a time—to talk to them."

"Why sophomores?"

"Well, apparently sophomores are mostly at a stage of, well, anger I guess you could say. They're mad at the adults for messing up the world so bad—especially their parents. Before they're 14 or so, they can't really see it—or if they see it, they don't know they can act on it. But at 15 or 16, kids do act. They stop playing along; you know? Sometimes they even leave home..."

Startled, Claire looked up sharply. *Is this true? Is this why I left home?*

"Ok; let's go," Paul interrupted. "All the kids are here and waiting."

They left the room and walked toward the grand staircase under the dome of the rotunda. Now they could hear the voices of hundreds of students.

Claire stopped short and whispered, "Wait a minute. You want me to stand in front of all those kids with you?"

"Of course," Paul answered.

Claire pulled back on Mallorie's hand. "No way, you guys. I can't. No."

Mallorie smiled and shook her head. "Come on, baby. Don't make me do this without you. Your uncle just wants to show the kids that he knows people your age; he gets kids, you know? They'll see he has his very own niece the same age they are. Besides, as soon as he introduces us, we'll step off to the side."

Paul gestured impatiently. Claire got the reassurance she was looking for in Mallorie's eyes, so she walked back up to Paul's side. The three of them descended the stairs together, Claire in the middle.

As soon as the students saw Paul and Mallorie, they erupted into cheers and applause. This couple was a big deal—and being here at the rotunda made the students feel like they were important, too.

Matt watched the three beautiful people walk down the stairs as he applauded with the rest of the kids. *Who's the girl?* The intercom loudly announced Paul, Mallorie, and their niece, Claire. *Oh.*

Claire couldn't believe how many kids were in the room. She was nervous, but Mallorie's hand clutching her own kept her heart from exploding. As she got closer, Claire began to see individual faces. So, these were New York kids. She scanned the front row and stopped dead as her eyes locked with those of a tall, good-looking boy. A blue line of electricity, or so it seemed, blazed a path through the air between them. It lasted an instant but was unmistakable, undeniable.

Matt wasn't breathing. *Holy shit! I know that girl.* He flashed back to his mom's weird ass trip to Iowa to see his dad's sister one summer a long time ago. He couldn't remember why his mom and taken them there, but he remembered his dad wasn't with them; he'd stayed in the city. His mom had posted tons of pictures showing the loving extended family. Come to think of it, that's probably why they went—to fill out her vidfile. Aunt Donna's best friend had a daughter his age, Claire. They had played a game of baseball together after church. She'd been dressed in a pink dress with white tights and white shoes. She hit a home run, and as she ran the bases, he fell in love with her. He left the next day and pined for her the rest of the summer. He had mostly forgotten about her, but sometimes he would remember her as he was falling asleep. She was like the perfect girl. And here she was on the steps of the rotunda. Paul Delamater's niece. *Holy shit!* His mom would trip if she knew she was just one degree of separation from Paul Delamater.

Claire recognized Matt, too. He was her dream—the one she imagined touching her when she in bed at night. She'd felt his hands on her, molding him into her dream. *Oh, my god! It's Matt.* She broke into a fast sweat and dropped Mallorie's hand. Paul was stepping down one more step, ready to engage the audience. What should she do? Should she go to Matt? She read deep into his eyes; all her longing was matched by his.

Paul introduced Claire. He didn't say she was from Iowa, a fact that, normally, would have earned him her eternal gratitude, but she wasn't even paying attention. Mallorie nudged her. *What? Oh.* She smiled at her uncle and gave a small wave to the audience. Paul spoke about his child on the way; Mallorie took that as her cue to smile lovingly at him before returning her smile to the audience. Paul dropped her hand indicating that she should leave the podium, so she took Claire's hand again and led her over to the side of the stairs where they took a place next to the students standing in the front row.

Claire didn't hear a word Paul said. Neither did Matt. Matt unobtrusively made his way to Claire. The students he brushed against as he moved did not react; they were held immobile by the power of Paul's speech. The room was silent except for Paul's voice; no shifting of feet, no coughing, no whispers in the back. Paul had them in his control, though he was no longer in control of himself. A voice of hypnotic authority emerged quietly and persuasively from Paul's mouth. Logic—pure, clean, clear, irrefutable—washed through the young audience. Here was The Way. No more doubt or fear. Laced with moments of cutting humor, the kind they liked, biting and satirical, the speech overpowered them; with each word Paul uttered, they pledged their allegiance to him in the silence of the hall. The only movement in the room was Matt's. Claire, who didn't take her eyes off him, watched his careful progress toward her.

Paul sensed the movement, knew his influence was incomplete, but couldn't find where it was coming from. Something was blocking its source; something powerful. He was briefly divided as he realized he couldn't keep the crowd entranced and find the disturbance in the field at the same time. He let the disturbance go. *Later... plenty of time. Tackle the big things first.*

Matt, meanwhile, had arrived next to Claire. Claire looked up at Mallorie, who was facing Paul, mesmerized. Snapping her attention back, she leaned cautiously away from Mallorie toward Matt. He reached out his hand. As their fingers touched, a spark like a memory forced their hands apart. Suddenly, both were self-conscious. Matt raised a finger to his lips and shook his head. He didn't know why. He didn't feel completely in control of his own actions. What the hell was going on?

Claire saw confusion enter his eyes and quickly grabbed his hand. She almost gasped aloud with the power of the connection. But, through that potent connection, she understood that she could not tell her aunt and uncle about Matt. *This is huge.* She was going to have to come up with some excuse to be with Matt; she had to figure out what was going on with him. It definitely had something to do with the danger she had discussed with her mom the other night. As soon as that realization hit, she knew what she would do. She nodded to Matt and held up one finger. *Hold on.*

She reluctantly let go of his hand and leaned back into Mallorie's side. She looked out at the mass of students and saw how completely they had given themselves to her uncle. She focused for the first time on what he was saying.

"There will come a time—soon— when I will call on you," he exclaimed, his eyes shining. "I will call on each one of you to enter the future with me. A future of peace and contentment. A future of answered questions. A future where you know who you are and why you are here. A future unimagined; a future heaven on earth. We shall overcome all obstacles in our way. We shall recognize the true leader of humanity. He is among us. Be ready to heed the call when it comes. It will come. I will call. Thank you." Paul closed his eyes and stepped back.

The crowd unleashed its wild approval. Applause and bravos, crying and whistling, high fives and back slapping all resounded under the dome of the rotunda. They would remember forever the sound of Paul Delamater's voice, and they would always be ready to heed his call. Claire looked again into Mallorie's face. Tears were streaming down her cheeks. Mallorie, in the months of her pregnancy, had forgotten her husband's power to dazzle and entice; she was under his spell once again.

Claire leaned back toward Matt and handed him her phone. He understood and punched in his number. She took the phone back and looked away from him. She slipped her hand, unnoticed, back into Mallorie's. She waved the fingers of her free hand, and Matt nodded and moved away.

Paul opened his eyes again, looked out at the crowd and blessed them with his broad, sincere smile. The kids cheered again. Paul waved and turned around, slowly mounting the stairs as the students continued to applaud and whistle.

Claire tugged a bit at Mallorie's arm. "Hmm, what is it,"

Mallorie asked.

"Are we supposed to follow him?"

Mallorie watched Paul round the curve of the massive staircase. "Yes. Yes, we should get upstairs," she said, clutching Claire's hand with excitement. "Wasn't he wonderful? Claire, wasn't he just wonderful?" Mallorie repeated, her eyes shining.

"Sure was," Claire responded. They mounted the stairs together while the crowd turned as one toward the doors and began filing outside.

When they re-entered the Governor's room, Claire saw that her uncle had gone to the vid to replay the event. He was utterly absorbed, searching for the disturbance he hadn't been able to find during the speech. Claire was weirded out by his intensity, and suddenly wanted to get as far away from this place as she could. Turning toward Mallorie, she asked, "What are we going to do now?"

Mallorie didn't answer. Slowly, she shook her head. "Wow, that was intense. What did you just say?"

"I was just wondering what we're going to do now," Claire replied.

"Oh, oh, right. Of course. Well, Paul thought you'd enjoy seeing some of the sights. Maybe we can have some lunch and do some shopping. Later tonight, we can go see a play if you'd like. But right now I have to pee; it's like I always have to pee. It's amazing what your body's like when you're pregnant."

While Mallorie went to the bathroom, Paul stepped aside from his vid to accept accolades from his staff. Claire took the opportunity to look at her phone. There was a message attached to the number. *Don't say a word.* So Matt knew they needed to keep their friendship a secret, too. *Why?*

* * *

Saturday, 10:00 a.m. EDT

Morgan pulled up in the Denny's parking lot. They were just an hour behind Bethanne now. He might have caught up with her, but Jeff was worried. Morgan could tell that he didn't want to screw things up again. He didn't want her to get hurt, either, but he knew that Bethanne was key. He had no idea what would happen if he and Jeff got between her and whatever it was she was supposed to do in New York. Something, though, was telling him that it would be very, very bad.

The two men had breakfast taking lots of refills on their coffee, hoping the way would become clear. When they finally got on the road again, Jeff cleared his throat. "Look, Morgan, I know you know we're headed toward some kind of danger. And, well, I just want to tell you that I wouldn't blame you if you decided to wait this one out. You can go to the Ritz or whatever and hang out while I go talk to Delamater."

"Right. Yes, that's what I'll do. Because I'm never interested in seeing things through. So, isn't there some computing you have to do—the talking thing isn't working so well." Morgan stared at him.

Jeff grinned sheepishly at his screen. *Well, I tried.*

26

COME TOGETHER

Matt shambled outside after the others. Mixed with his elation at having found Claire, he was surprised that his dad was on his mind again. *Why?* As he stood back outside City Hall, he wondered if Claire would call soon; he had no idea where to go in the meantime. His phone rang; it was Claire. "Hello?"

"Hello." Her voice was muffled. "Is this you… Matt?"

"Yeah. What the hell? I can't believe you're here."

"Me either. I mean, I can't believe you're here either. I can't talk long. I'm in the bathroom in my uncle's office."

"Your uncle is Paul Delamater. That's so nuts."

"I know. It's weird, though. I never really thought about how famous he is and everything. Until today. Watching all the kids react—"

"Yeah, that *was* weird. Something about that whole thing feels wrong. Wait, is that what you meant? I mean, do you think the meeting was okay? Do you think your uncle's okay?"

"No. I don't think my uncle's okay, but I don't know why. He's being so nice to me. And he loves my aunt. They're even going to have a baby, right? So, the question is, why am I talking on the phone in the bathroom trying to keep you and our whole thing a secret from him? I don't get it."

"Me either. Here's the thing, though. I really need to see you. I know this'll sound insane, but I still think about you. I can't tell you how mad I was that I never got to see you again after that baseball game. My parents didn't talk about Aunt Donna once we got back—I think my dad was even pissed off we went to visit her. I don't know what happened."

Claire only half-heard the words after 'still think about you.' *Oh my god! He thinks about me too.* She slowly became aware of the silence on the other end of the phone. "Sorry; I spaced out. Listen, I want to see you, too. I don't know how to do it though. Let me call you later when I know more about my day."

"Okay. I'll wait to hear from you."

The moment stretched out a ways before they realized neither of them were talking. They both spoke at once, "Well, bye." They laughed "Okay, bye." Same thing. The silence returned; each waiting for the other to speak first. Finally, Matt said, "Okay. Call me back as soon as you know something."

"I will," she said. "Good-bye."

"Bye."

Claire put her phone away and looked at her reflection in the bathroom mirror. Her eyes were shining and she was flushed with excitement. She giggled. Her own eyes held her, though, and she felt her pleasure jolted by a mounting fear that was visible in the mirror. *Stop it!* She jumped when Mallorie knocked on the door calling her name.

"Claire, are you okay? Claire?"

Claire broke away from the mirror and shook her head to clear it. "Yeah, I'm okay; I'll be right out." She flushed the toilet and ran some water over her hands. She finished up and opened the door.

Mallorie was standing there with an apologetic smile on her

face. "Guess what? Surprise, surprise. Paul won't be able to join us today. This is something else you have to get used to. I can hardly count on him for anything."

Claire looked at Mallorie; her question unspoken but evident.

"No, don't get me wrong. He's wonderful. But he's also the busiest person on the planet." She looked down. "I wonder what kind of a father he's going to be."

"Oh, Mallorie. Don't even think about it. We're going to have the best summer; I'm fine with just you and me." Claire hoped she was hiding her relief successfully. "So where are we going?"

Mallorie looked exhausted. "I don't know, now. What would you like to see?"

"You know, I'm going to be here all summer. We don't have to fit everything into the first day, and you look exhausted. Why don't we just go home? I want to see the—um—the Empire State Building, but that's something I can do all by myself."

"No you can't." Mallorie glanced over at Paul whose back was turned to them as he continued to talk with his staff. "I mean, I don't think that's such a great idea."

"Why not? Hey, I know, why don't we go home now, have some lunch, and then you can rest while I'm gone? Besides, I won't feel like I belong here until I can get around by myself. Really. And you need the rest."

"Claire, Claire, Claire. You are so like your mother. Always taking care of everyone else." She stood still looking into Claire's eyes as if her answer was there. "Tell you what. If you let our driver take you there, I'll agree to your little plan. What do you say?"

"Sounds good to me."

Mallorie quietly approached Paul and waited for a break in his conversation so she could tell him they were leaving. She touched his arm, and he jerked it away and scowled down at her. "You still here?" he hissed.

Mallorie's mouth dropped open, her eyes filling automatically before Paul recovered himself and hurried to make amends. "Oh, sorry, honey. You startled me. You leaving now? Yes?"

Mallorie nodded, her eyes averted.

"Okay, then. I'll see you two later," he looked past her and smiled at Claire.

They took the subway car home. Mallorie felt better as soon as she walked into the house. The two of them hung out in the kitchen while Mallorie decided what to have for lunch. Claire left with the driver shortly before noon. Matt would be waiting for her on the observation deck at the top of the Empire State Building; no longer the most impressive building in New York City, more a relic of bygone days, a bit of nostalgia. Claire had no idea how cliché their meeting place was.

Matt took out his phone again. Claire would be here any minute. He paced nervously in front of the main doorway on the observation deck, oblivious to the impressive view below. He jumped when his phone rang in his hand. Alek. "Hey, little dude. What do you want?"

"I'm just wondering how things went. Can you talk or what?"

"Oh, no, it's cool. It's just that I'm getting ready to meet someone. Are you all right?"

"Yeah, I'm fine. Nothing's going on here. So, how was it?"

"We ended up listening to Delamater give a speech in City Hall. I was right in front; I got to see the cupola. It's awesome. Anyway, Delamater's pregnant wife was there and so was his niece—"

"What was he like? What did he say?"

"He was okay. I mean, he had all these kids in the palm of his hand. I don't know what he said, though. I wasn't actually listening—"

"What do you mean you weren't listening?"

"Well, that's what I'm was trying to tell you. Delamater's niece—I know her. We both do. Well, kind of. Remember when we went to Iowa with Mom to visit Dad's sister? Aunt Donna, remember?"

Alek thought back. He remembered his aunt's back yard mostly. It had lots of trees and green grass and flowerbeds. Petunias. He remembered the name because he loved them. The soft, velvet petals he had plucked and rubbed on his face; purple and pink and white. But he couldn't remember his aunt very well. He couldn't picture her face at all.

"Ok, I can tell you don't remember. You were probably too little. Anyway, while we were there, we were playing a game of baseball with some other kids in the neighborhood, and this girl—Claire's her name—showed up still wearing her dress from church or something. I can't remember if you were even there. Anyway, she hit a homerun—blew us all away. Well, like I told you, she's Delamater's niece and we saw each other and we decided to meet. So that's who I'm waiting for."

"Wow. Delamater's niece ... scary. Does she seem okay?"

"Alek! She's more than okay. She's beautiful. I—oh, here she is—gotta go. Later."

Claire had already seen him. She walked through the open doors and stopped a few feet away. Neither moved, but the energies passing between them were frantic and raw. The world vanished around them; they could see only each other's eyes.

* * *

Saturday, 12:30 p.m. EST

Donna pulled up outside the house. The doorbot immediately dislodged itself from the front entrance and began walking down the sidewalk toward them. Bethanne waited for Mallorie to answer her call.

"Bethanne? Hi! I was just getting ready to take a nap. I can't believe how tired I get now that—"

"Mallorie. I'm outside your front door. With Scott and Donna.

Come let me in."

"You're what? Oh my god! I'll be right there."

The doorbot stepped aside when Mallorie appeared. Bethanne rushed up the sidewalk to catch her little sister in her arms. Suddenly, Mallorie was sobbing into Bethanne's neck. She had no idea why.

"Oh god, oh god. I can't believe you're here."

"Yes, darling, I'm here," Bethanne cooed. "I'm here. It's okay. It's all okay. Oh, honey. Look how big you are."

Just as suddenly as the tears had come, Mallorie began to giggle towards the edge of hysteria as she pulled back from her sister's warm embrace. "Oh, god, Bethanne. I have no idea what's going on with me. It must be hormones." She saw Scott and Donna standing a bit down the sidewalk and let go of her sister. "Scott! Oh, my god, Scott!" She ran, arms open, to her nephew. "I'm so glad you came. This is amazing. Look how big you are. You're going to be taller than your dad." As she held onto Scott, she looked over his shoulder and smiled broadly at Donna. "Hey, Donna. It's good to see you, too." Then she noticed the car. She pulled back from Scott and looked from Donna back to Scott before turning around to confront Bethanne. "Tell me you didn't drive here all the way from Iowa."

"As a matter of fact, we did."

"Why on earth would you do that?"

"Well, that's part of what I need to talk to you about. Why don't we go inside."

"Of course. You must be famished. Come on." Mallorie led the way up the stairs into the commanding foyer. "Let's go sit in the kitchen. We can catch up in there. I just had lunch with Claire. This is so crazy. Oh, maybe I should call Claire; she just left. Did she know you were coming?" A suspicious spark lit Mallorie's narrowed eyes.

Bethanne caught it. "No, honey, I promise. Claire has no idea.

She definitely would not have welcomed it. I'm here for a different reason. Anyway, you don't need to call her just yet. She's fine… She's more than fine."

Mallorie's arms dropped to her side as her face sobered in defeat. "Oh, Bethanne, not this again. Are you telling me you *know* how Claire is?"

"Mallorie, that's not the half of it. We need to talk, and I'm sorry, but every single thing I have to say to you is going to upset you. I tell you what. I'll just tell you the stuff you need to know; how's that?"

"Oh, by all means. Edit away. You know how I can't take care of myself, right? Mallorie can't handle the big stuff, right? Shit. I'm 26 years old, Bethanne."

Bethanne stood quietly for a moment before answering. "Sorry. Reflex," she said.

Mallorie's eyes met hers and she relaxed. "Me, too."

"So, let's get to the most important thing. Let me greet that baby." Bethanne reached out and put her hand on her sister's stomach. She felt the baby, so near still to heaven, but here, too. She talked to the baby with her thoughts. The baby answered, agreed, and fell deeply asleep.

Scott, unsure of what to do with himself, stood behind his mother. He'd felt tense and ready to run out just moments before. Now he was relaxed and reassured. *Women.*

Mallorie was smiling blissfully with his mom's hand on her stomach. Donna had moved to the table to get out of their way. He decided to join her. He sat down across from her and noticed she was crying. *God, are you kidding me?* He seriously doubted things could get worse.

Donna wasn't sad, though. She was filled with joy as she listened to her brother, her dear Jack, share his feelings for her—the ones that resided beyond his capacities while he had been alive. So Jack was dead; she'd missed him by less than a week, yet instead of feeling remorse, she felt an enormous burden being lifted from her. He didn't hate her... he didn't blame her for anything. He loved her.

Bethanne lifted her hand off Mallorie's stomach and gave her sister another hug. She turned around, eyes glowing, and smiled at Donna and Scott. "Okay, then. Let's eat," she said as she joined them at the table.

Mallorie directed the kitchenbot to deliver food to the table before sitting down herself. "I just ate with Claire," she reminded them. "You guys go ahead. I'll watch."

Scott grinned. "You might not want to; I'm starving. It could get ugly."

They all laughed and, for a moment, the world looked safe and right as it often does around a kitchen table.

Before dessert was served, Bethanne set down her fork and put her plate aside. "We have to talk now," she said. "Mallorie, you need to hear this in the right way. It won't be easy, but I think you'll be able to attest to the truth of what I'm about to say. Paul isn't himself anymore."

Mallorie gasped. Tears welled in her eyes. She put her hands up to her face without removing her gaze from Bethanne. *It's true.* She didn't need any more proof than her sister's words. She'd been seeing it for a long time, but now it was terrible. She was losing Paul completely. She slowly calmed under Bethanne's influence—her loving gaze and steady, deep breathing. Mallorie became aware of Bethanne holding her hands across the table. "Do you know why he's changed?" Mallorie asked, the desperate tone in her voice contracting the distance between them.

Bethanne sighed. "It's his time, is all. Paul was designed for this, Mallorie." Bethanne looked around the table, checking on Donna and Scott. "Everything has its season, you know. We've been allowing more and more incursions into our psyches. It started with the Internet and has progressed through all our technology. Ever smaller, ever closer in, ever present... now implants. And look at computers: first, electric cells held humanity's intelligence, then we found out that light could hold a thousand times more. Now we have biological circuitry. Non-human, living intelligence. All of that has moved us along on a certain path. But something was developed earlier this week that created the exact environment necessary for the Rival to gain control. The Rival—that's my name, but he goes by many—has been waiting a long time, plotting, setting his own stage. Paul is a vehicle. The Rival has many allies besides Paul, but he has challengers, too, and I'm one of them. And I'm here to try to prevent his assent to the throne."

Donna reached over to place her hand on top of Bethanne's. "You're not alone. We're here." She paused to take a deep breath. "Jack's here, too." She smiled through the new tears flowing down her face.

Bethanne smiled and nodded. "So you know. I wondered how long it would take your brother to get through to you. He's learned a lot since he died."

Scott cleared his throat. "Mom, this is science fiction, right? You don't actually believe all this, do you? Dead relatives. Someone called the Rival plotting away to take over the world? This is crazy. Come on."

Bethanne looked him in the eye. "Scott, think about it. You've seen your dad since he died, right? Anyway, I'm going to have to ask you to trust me now. You're going to be needed. When Alek gets here, he might need a friend, someone closer to his own age, to bring him up to speed.

"Who's Alek?"

Bethanne stopped short. "Wow, I can't believe I missed that one—"

Donna interrupted, "Do you mean my nephew Alek?"

"Yes," Bethanne replied before turning back to Scott. "Donna's brother, Jack, the one who just died, had two sons, Alek and Matt. Matt is already with Claire, and they'll arrive shortly; we'll call

Alek to come too. So, I'm just asking if you'll agree to help him as Matt may be needed elsewhere."

Scott nodded, matching his mother's solemn expression. "Sure. Sure, I'll help, but how are Matt and Claire together?"

Bethanne took in the whole table again. "Let me explain." She looked first at Donna and Scott and then Mallorie. "Jack saw them reunite at Paul's speech this morning; he helped protect them from Paul's influence. They missed the speech. This was important. I allowed them to see Paul's effect without feeling it. Anyway, that's why Claire was so eager to get out on her own today, Mallorie. She wanted to meet up with Matt."

"What about Tess?" Donna asked.

"She's outside it; Jack hasn't been able to contact her at all. We'll leave her alone for now. Look, I don't know how this is all going to go down; my vision is obscured. I do know we are all in danger, but we have some protection, too. Before the hour is up, Paul will be aware of my presence here. I can't keep everything blocked any more. He's coming home early."

Mallorie leapt up from the table. Bethanne had gone too far. Bethanne reached out toward Mallorie. She had to keep her sister calm. Paul would be checking in. He needed to see that his wife was fine. Bethanne felt the room close in for a moment. The very atmosphere had changed. Nowhere to hide. What had she done? She backtracked and refocused on Mallorie. She penetrated though her sister's mind and found the thoughts of the last few minutes; she dispersed them. They dissolved. She interfered in a way that she abhorred, but she could see no alternative. Donna and Scott saw Mallorie's face settle into a serene composure. The moment endured unnaturally until Bethanne broke its hold by removing her phone from her pocket. She called Claire.

* * *

Saturday, 1:00 p.m. EDT

Jeff and Morgan were not talking. Morgan was navigating his way toward Delamater's house. The star, unwavering now, was locked into place there. *Damn. This woman had some serious energy.*

"We should call her," Morgan said.

"Oh, sure. What a great idea. 'Excuse me, I've just followed you all the way from Iowa City and was wondering if I could join you and your family.'"

"Exactly. What difference does it make? What have you got to lose?"

Jeff clenched his jaw. How the hell was he supposed to know what to do? He never knew what to do with people. People made him uncomfortable; they always had. And this was extreme. Bethanne was extreme. Not to mention Delamater. He leaned back into his seat and closed his eyes. He focused on his breathing until it regulated. *There. Now, how best to proceed?*

* * *

Saturday, 1:00 p.m. EDT

Paul stopped suddenly and looked up, startled. Something was going down at his house. He felt a massive rage out of nowhere. It was strong enough to clear his office. He took a deep breath. And another. And one more. Then he pressed the link to Mallorie.

She appeared immediately on the screen before him. "Hi, honey."

She seemed relaxed and normal. *What the hell?* "Hi, sweetheart. I had a sudden urge to call you. I'm surprised you're home. I thought you and Claire were going out to see the attractions, grab some lunch."

"Yeah, we were, but I got too tired. I guess it was all the

excitement this morning at City Hall. You were wonderful, by the way."

"Thanks, honey. You were, too. I'm so glad you were there with me." He paused to let his warm words sink in. "So, is Claire there, too?"

"No. She went out by herself—with our chauffeur, though. Hey, I've got some exciting news."

"You do? What's up?"

"Bethanne just arrived with Scott; you won't believe how big Scott is now."

Paul gripped the edge of his desk. He looked down at his fingers, white against the dark mahogany. *Bethanne? Here in the city? Shit.* He should have known. But then, just as suddenly as his anger had arrived, it left. And though it felt like he had regained his control, actually, he had lost it. *Paul, relax. This is perfect. We have her right where we want her.* Paul smiled into the vid. "No kidding? Well, there you go. Of course, they're staying with us, right?"

"Well, we haven't even talked about that yet. They just got here."

"Why didn't you call?"

"No, really, they just got here; that's why. So, what time do you think you'll be home?"

"I don't know. Maybe I'll come home early. Maybe I'll surprise you."

"That'd be great, honey. I'll see you when you get here."

"Good. See you then." Paul closed the link and walked over to the massive windows on his north facing wall. *Well, well, well. Bethanne. What do you know.* He had never liked her. Too goody-goody for him. And he hated the way she looked at him as though she could figure out what he was really thinking. *The eyes are the windows of the soul. Ha. That's rich.* She read what he wanted her to read. But he knew she didn't like him. Never had. And he knew that Mallorie would be listening to her now. Mallorie was vulnerable with that baby in her belly. He'd just have to set her straight once he dealt with Bethanne. Of course, that was going to be a bit tricky. *Now, how best to proceed?*

* * *

Saturday, 1:30 p.m. EDT

Bethanne held her hand up. Everyone stopped talking. Clatter in the hallway materialized into Claire and Matt. Bethanne rushed toward them and grabbed Claire up into her arms. Suddenly, Claire was crying. Matt stood a little behind her, ill at ease. He saw Mallorie, then Scott. He stopped at Donna.

"Hello, Matthew. It's been a long time." Donna moved forward and reached out her arms.

Matt allowed her to hug him a second before he pulled anxiously away. "Aunt Donna. I don't get it? What are you doing here? Did Mom call you? Did you hear about Dad?"

"Your mom didn't call, but I know your dad died, Matt. I'm so sorry. How are you? How is Alek taking it?"

"It's a big mess. I can't explain it. Nothing makes sense right now. So are you here because of Dad?"

"A lot is going on, Matt. I don't think I have any time to explain it right now, though."

Bethanne held her daughter's face in her hands, smoothing Claire's tears away with her thumbs. "Claire, I was so worried I wouldn't get here in time. And I didn't in some ways, but you managed without me."

"What are you talking about, Mom?"

"This morning, Paul gave his talk to as many teenagers your age as he could at one time without arousing suspicion. No one in that room was supposed to be immune to his influence. But you were. You had some help, though. Did you know what was happening?"

"No, I have no idea what you're talking about."

"You were in the room, but you weren't taken in by his speech, honey."

"Yeah. Well, before he even opened his mouth, I saw Matt and he saw me and that was the end of it. We just stared at each other the whole time. I didn't hear a word Uncle Paul said."

Claire looked at Matt. He nodded his head in agreement. "Nope. Me neither. Didn't hear a word."

"I can't believe you guys recognized each other from so long ago," Donna said, sidestepping the underlying confusion. "I'm assuming Claire's the girl in the pink dress, right? How long were you even together that day in Iowa, a couple hours? You were like ten or eleven, right?"

"It was love at first sight," Matt blurted. He blushed furiously as he looked helplessly down at his shoes. *Shit.*

"Yes, it was love at first sight," Claire agreed.

Matt looked up and met her eyes. *Really?*

"I see," Bethanne said. "Well, love's a force, that's for sure. And we're going to need lots of it. And we're going to have give it to Paul when he comes home. He's not going to want it, either."

"Yes he will," Mallorie disagreed. "He loves me, Bethanne. I know he seems a bit preoccupied, even cold, right now, but he does love me."

Bethanne decided to try again. "Paul loves you, darling. I believe that. But he's been disappearing for awhile now. He's given himself up to something else."

"I'm not following, Bethanne. What are you trying to say?"

"Remember when I told you the story of Faust? Well, it's like that in a way. Paul kind of made a deal with the devil, so to speak, but he wasn't really aware of it—not in the same way Faust was."

"Are you saying he's possessed by the devil? Are you insane?" Mallorie was angry now; she glared ferociously at Bethanne. "I know you've never liked Paul, but this is ridiculous. Paul may have his issues, but you, you're out of your mind."

"Mallorie, hold on. I'm not saying he's possessed—well, not in the way you mean it. But he is occupied—let's say influenced— heavily by someone who wants to harm us all. Paul's given this being some room to work. He didn't even know about it for a long time, but he's having to face it now.

"Don't you think I would have noticed if he was possessed, Bethanne?" Mallorie could barely stand to look at her.

"No, Mallorie, I don't think you would have noticed. You have to imagine an intelligence that surpasses any other on earth. Paul was already making room for the Rival when he first met you. In the beginning, Paul just wanted you for what you represented by being his. But he did learn to care about you—to love you. And that actually worked against the force that is trying to control him now. His love for you got in the way a bit. But, eventually, when things cooled down between you two, when you both grew used to each other, the Rival's influence over Paul could grow again. By the time he found out you were pregnant, Paul was almost helpless, though his joy at your condition presented another challenge to the Rival. If Paul hadn't given that speech to all the students, the Rival would have had to work harder than he did. That assembly washed Paul's last resistance away."

"Wait a second. Who's the Rival?" Matt asked.

"The Rival? Well, that's just my name for him."

Matt moved back toward Claire as Bethanne finished talking. It was too much. Claire looked at him and sensed his revulsion.

"Um, Mom. I don't mean to be disrespectful, but you must know how crazy this all sounds. I mean, well, I've had time to absorb some of this stuff, but really, this is too much. You sound like a paranoid crazy person."

Claire was right, of course. Bethanne looked around and saw that she'd gone way too far way too fast. "Okay. You're right. So, here's what I want you all to do for me." She looked around the room at each of them. "Indulge me. For the next few hours, just do as I ask. I won't ask you to do anything dangerous—but I need your help right now. If I'm wrong about everything, I promise I'll get some help, okay?"

The small group considered what she was saying; those closest to her considered Bethanne herself. She was the archetype of sensible, caring motherhood; she deserved a chance. And her ability to sense how crazy it all sounded gave Matt the reassurance he needed.

"Okay," Matt said. "What do you want us to do?"

"We need to shut down every piece of tech in the house. Especially all the AI stuff. And when you're done, Matt, I want you to find the central pod and disable it. No electricity, no wireless, nothing can be running through here; it's transport for the Rival."

"Gabrielle?" Claire asked.

"Gabrielle? Who's Gabrielle?" Bethanne asked.

"Gabrielle is the bot that helps Mallorie."

Bethanne stared at her daughter. Of course. She would have met her first human-looking bot. "Yes, even Gabrielle, honey."

Mallorie stared at her sister. This was insane. Insane. But as soon as she allowed herself to meet Bethanne's eyes, she let go of her anger and doubt and complied.

In seconds, Bethanne was alone in the kitchen. A melody came to her. *If you want it, here it is … an old movie, The Magic Christian. Strange.*

27

LAST FIRE

Saturday, 3:00 p.m. EDT

Delamater called Sgt. Baker to his office.

"Is everything all right then, sir?" Baker asked.

Delamater flashed him a look of disdain. "Like I'd tell you."

Baker's eyes widened, but he said nothing. Delamater had been unhinged all week.

Baker's look registered on Delamater, and he took a deep breath. "Sorry, my good man. It's been one helluva day. Now the wife's family is visiting… from Iowa. Jesus. Like I didn't have enough to do. I'm leaving early—now—to play host."

Baker's face revealed nothing. *God, this man was scary as hell.* He turned to look nearly but not directly at his boss. "No problem, chief. I'll handle whatever comes up. Let me know if you need me for anything."

Delamater looked out the window. Could he? No. If he used the police force now, he'd tip his hand. No, he'd have to handle this himself. It was all about timing. He walked out of the office and went down to the subway car he'd recalled from home.

Mallorie met him at the elevator. He covered his surprise and gave her his most charming smile. "Hey, sweetheart. You must be so excited to have your whole family here. What fun!"

Mallorie wavered for just a moment before walking into his arms. "Oh, Paul. It is wonderful. You know, they all just need to see you. Too much time has passed. We should have been going out to see them all along; then they'd know you better."

"I agree." Paul hugged her tightly. They parted and he placed his hand on her belly. "I bet as soon as Bethanne heard from Claire, she had to come out and see you for herself. Big sisters. Can anyone be more protective?"

Mallorie's mouth dropped open. "That's it! That's what's going on!"

Paul raised an eyebrow. "What are you talking about, honey?"

"It's been crazy ever since she got here. It's like she's nuts. Bethanne…"

"Bethanne what, baby?"

Mallorie looked away. She couldn't say it. She couldn't tell him. "It's nothing. Anyway, come on. Everyone's here."

"Everyone?"

"Yes. Bethanne and Scott, and Donna. And Claire just got back with Matt—that's Donna's nephew who lives here in the city. It's a full house."

"Really? What a coincidence." *What the hell is going on? Who the hell is Donna? And she has a nephew Claire knows? Here? How do I not know about this?*

Mallorie watched Paul closely, but in less than a second he had completed his mask. He looked at her affectionately, conspiratorially, and winked. "Well, let's get in there and start the party!" They walked hand in hand to the kitchen.

Paul noticed how unnaturally quiet it was. He looked at the kitchen screen and saw that it was off; all the tech was turned off. How pathetic. He laughed and turned his gaze on Bethanne. His eyes lasered into hers, malice sparking the air almost visibly.

Bethanne met his force complacently. She laughed, too, but hers was a different laugh. Merriment and warmth infused its airy tones. "Hi, Paul. My goodness, how you've changed."

Paul's jaw dropped. Was she out of her mind? He could kill her as easily as take another breath. Then he noticed that Mallorie had stepped away from him. He had to stay in control until he figured out what to do. "Yes. And you, too, have changed. Don't you think so, Mal?"

"Not really. What do you mean, Paul?"

Donna stepped in from the doorway behind them. "Hi."

Paul wheeled around, startled for a moment. This had to be his game not Bethanne's or anyone else's. No surprises except his. "You must be Donna."

"Yes. I've heard so much about you, Paul."

"From Bethanne?"

"Of course."

"Well, then I'm doomed." He laughed good-naturedly and continued. "Let's see how you feel about me once you get to know me yourself. You might be surprised."

Matt walked into the room with Claire. "Hello, sir," he said nodding to Paul.

"And you're the nephew," Paul said. "Nice to meet you, young man." He held out his hand.

Matt shook it and swallowed hard. Paul smiled. *That's right, boy. You have no idea what I can do.* But Matt didn't back away. Paul was furious. Who the hell did these people think they were?

"I saw you earlier today," Matt said quietly.

"You did? Where?"

"City Hall."

"You heard my speech?"

"I was in the front row."

Now Paul was uncertain. He didn't like confusion mixed up in his anger. How could this kid have been there and not belong to him? Had he been wrong about his effectiveness? But no. All those kids had been converted. He was sure of it. This kid was full of shit. *Wait. Of course.* This kid belonged to Bethanne; she'd been protecting him, and Claire too. They were the source of the disturbance at City Hall. *Well done, Bethanne... but now the ball's in my court. Game on.*

Suddenly, a wave of well-being swept over him. He took a deep breath and looking down, shook his head while a grin played at his lips. He looked up and smiled expansively at the whole room. "I have been so fortunate," Paul began. "Just think of it. I've got a beautiful wife who is blessing me with a child. I have the greatest job in the world—a job helping people feel safe and secure. I have friends and family like you to support Mallorie and me as we become new parents." He turned to Matt. "I'm glad you were at the meeting with all your peers; you, too, Claire. Together we can bring peace to the world. Who needs to wait for heaven; we will create heaven right here on earth." Paul's eyes brightened with unreleased tears.

Matt stood before him, utterly confused. Mallorie leaned against Paul, smiling. Claire stared at the happy couple and slipped her hand into Matt's. Look at these beautiful people. This is the pinnacle of success. She looked past them at Scott. He was smiling, too. He had always had a crush on Aunt Mallorie, so Paul had been someone he'd found easy to dislike. Now Scott was older. He saw that Paul was perfect for Mallorie and she for him.

Donna was smiling too, but her thoughts ricocheted back to Bethanne. Why did Bethanne hate Paul so much? Was she jealous because Mallorie had a husband and she didn't? It must be hard to be alone after being in love as much as Bethanne had been in love with David. She had heard that big sisters were often jealous of their little sisters. And who on earth wouldn't be jealous of Mallorie? And now Mallorie was pregnant, and her husband obviously loved her. Pity filled Donna's eyes as she looked at her best friend. *Poor Bethanne.*

Meanwhile, Bethanne stayed calm and focused. She felt herself filled with a profound purpose. She smiled to herself. He was good—very good—but then she'd known he would be. Her strict ethical code demanded that she honor the free will of every person; every transgression this past week had caused her great pain. Paul, however, didn't honor anyone's free will; trespassing was his modus operandi; another reason his power was so great in these times. No rules. No morality. No restrictions. He could take over this small room with little effort at all.

Paul felt his moment. He caressed Mallorie's shoulder. She looked up at him. "I think your sister must be really tired, honey. Why don't you fix her some tea while I show her to one of the extra rooms so she can relax?"

"What a great idea, Paul. I think we're all a little tired," Mallorie agreed.

Donna went to Bethanne's side. "Come on, kiddo. Time to get some rest. I think I'll do the same once Matt and I have had a chance to get reacquainted. Go ahead with Paul; I'll check in on you in a little while."

Bethanne looked into Donna's eyes, but before she could establish a deeper contact, Donna looked away.

Mallorie moved to the stove, ready to start the tea; she laughed. "I forgot. We turned off the electricity. Nothing in here works. I'll just—"

"That's okay. I don't need any tea," Bethanne interrupted. "I'll be fine. I guess you're right, though. I could use a rest."

"We have the perfect room for you up on the fifth floor," Paul said leading the way toward the kitchen door. He turned back to Mallorie. "Honey, I could use a few of the bots. Where are they?

"Um, well, we shut them down. All of them."

Paul gave Bethanne a quick look before responding, "Hmm. That was an interesting choice, honey. Well, why don't you start them up first and then get the rest of the house turned back on."

"Of course; right away." She looked at her sister again. "Oh, Bethanne, I'm so glad you're here. I had no idea you'd be so concerned about Claire; I should have set up a constant vidfeed. Well, it doesn't matter now. You just get a good rest; I'll see you in a little while."

"Thank you, Mallorie." Bethanne glanced at each of them, smiling a quiet goodbye before following Paul to the elevator. They were all so perfect. So wonderful. She would miss being with them.

"So, now what?" Bethanne asked Paul as the button for the fifth floor lit up under his touch.

"You're done," Paul said immediately without looking her way. When the elevator door opened, he pointed her into the smaller of the two bedrooms off the fifth floor kitchen. "I don't want to hurt anyone down there, Bethanne, though Claire may develop into a problem. And I don't like her little boyfriend."

"Claire won't be your problem, Paul. I'm your problem."

"Right, Bethanne. Come on. You may be strong, but I've got the master—I am the master. The—what do you call him—oh yeah, the Rival—well he's within me." Paul stopped talking and cocked his head to the side. *What did that mean? Who's the Rival?* Bethanne was looking with great intensity into his eyes. *What the hell is going on?* Suddenly, he heard an inner voice urgently demanding his attention. He listened to persuasive encouragements streaming toward him, marshalling his resolve. Then just as suddenly, he registered a disturbance from without—someone was here. *Dammit.*

He began backing out of the room, annoyed. "You'll have to excuse me for a moment, my dear. *More bullshit to deal with.* I strongly encourage you to stay up here," he began as a knock on the door sounded far below. "Oh, and if you decide to leave the room, Scott's dead."

"There are worse things than death, Paul," she replied. Bethanne tried to get him to look into her eyes again, but Paul was already halfway out the door. He knew better than to engage her when he couldn't focus completely.

Mallorie answered the door herself since she'd had no time to reactivate the doorbot. Standing at the entrance were two men she'd never seen before.

The white one spoke. "Mrs. Delamater? Um, hi, sorry, I recognize you from the vids. Anyway, my name is Jeff Clark. You don't know me, but I work for your husband, well at least I used to—." Morgan nudged him. "Is he home?" Jeff finished.

"Why, yes, he is. Is he expecting you? He didn't say anything to me."

"I believe he is expecting me."

"Oh, fine, well, come in. Come in. Things are a bit crazy right now. We have lots of company today."

Jeff glanced at Morgan before entering. "Beautiful place you have here, Mrs. Delamater."

Morgan looked at Jeff like he was insane. For that matter, maybe they both were. Everything appeared normal inside. Whatever they had imagined they would find here, they could find no visual evidence of its existence.

"Let me go get Paul," Mallorie said. "You can have a seat right in here."

She pointed to the little sitting room off the entrance. The two men followed her gesture, but didn't get far. Paul came from the other direction into the foyer.

"Hello, gentlemen. How lovely that you could join our little party today. I was wondering if you'd show up."

The two men turned to face Delamater. He directed his dazzling smile at them; not the least bit of concern marred his countenance. He was utterly and without question in charge of the situation.

"Why don't we go up to my office?" He turned to Mallorie. "We won't be long, dear. Why don't you ask the others what they'd like to do this afternoon. I'm sure Scott would love to see some of the sights. Maybe we should take the boat out and cruise around the island. Call Hank when you get the tech up and see if he can prepare for a departure in a couple hours. Maybe we could get out in time to see the sunset from the river."

"Paul, you are amazing. What a perfect idea. I'll call Hank as soon as I can."

Delamater led Jeff and Morgan up the stairs as he talked about his boat and its captain. The two men, perplexed by Paul's good nature, walked right behind. They entered his office and sat in the two leather chairs Paul indicated as he strode around his desk to take the regal chair behind it. "So, you're Morgan. How nice to meet you at last." He turned to Jeff. "What can I do for you, Jeff? You know, for the life of me, I can't imagine any business you and I might have that couldn't be handled our usual way. In other words, what are you doing here?"

Though Delamater's tone had stayed friendly, Jeff's heart started beating rapidly and his swallowing mechanism erupted. His hair raised itself from his skin as he immediately recognized the same impersonal malice issuing from Delamater's eyes that he'd seen in the cat's as it stood over Linux. *What the hell?* But the recognition was real and compelling. Paul was the most dangerous thing he'd ever confronted. Jeff's rational mind disappeared as he tried to figure out an escape route. Then he remembered Morgan. He had brought Morgan straight into this nightmare. Morgan had been right all along...

A knock issued from the front door again. Delamater's head whipped up. He looked to his screen, but it was blank. *What in god's name is taking so long with the tech?* He closed his eyes, while Morgan leaned forward to get Jeff's attention.

Jeff looked up at his friend then took a deep breath. *Calm down.* "Do you need to get that?" he asked.

Paul opened his eyes and refocused on Jeff. "No, *I* do not need to get that. So, I ask you again, what are you doing here?"

"I think you must know why I'm here, Delamater, but I'll play this out. In trying to come up with the new tech, I found a curious anomaly as the tech expanded outward. The people exhibiting this anomaly piqued my interest, so I decided to visit a few of them. Anyway, that's what I was doing down in Los Angeles, and we both know what happened to that old couple. Then I became invisible. You obviously breached my defenses because the next anomaly I visited got blown up too. So, no coincidence. Everyone with an anomaly that I investigated in person had a lethal electrical, um, accident. I followed the last anomaly straight to your door."

Delamater's face revealed something that Jeff had not been expecting. Delamater's eyes, in the blink of a second, showed confusion and fear, and his confident smile disappeared. If Jeff hadn't been watching carefully, he would have missed it because in a flash, Delamater recovered. "Well, well. A very interesting story," Delamater said. "However, I haven't the slightest idea what you're talking about. Perhaps you'd care to elaborate," he said.

Jeff exchanged glances with Morgan again. Was it possible that Delamater didn't understand what had happened? He cleared his throat. "Back in Los Angeles, I talked to a man by the name of Stuart Thompson. He had an EMF, an electromagnetic field, that was way outside the statistical norm, an anomaly if you will. Well, as you know, that night, Thompson's house blew up—some kind of electrical explosion. Both he and his wife were killed."

Delamater didn't respond; he stared into middle space. Jeff cleared his throat again and went on. "Then I went to Colorado to meet with another anomaly. There was a fire. Another fatality. Now I'm here."

Delamater appeared to reach a decision. He looked straight at Jeff. "And you suspect me because—"

"I don't know. I just know it has to be you, and I want to know how you did it—and I want to know why."

Paul slumped back into his chair. He appeared lost in his thoughts before he shot up to his feet and pierced Jeff with a fierce glare. "I see. Well, we did enjoy your little game of hide and seek, though you were never out of our awareness, Jeff. We just left you alone while we attended to some more important things. Nevertheless, we do appreciate you setting all this up for us. We know how to find the anomalies on our own now; they can't hide anymore. Poor Jeff. You never did have the ability to see the big picture. You must understand that sometimes people have to make sacrifices in the name of progress. Stuart Thompson was one of those unfortunates; his wife was collateral damage as was dear Mrs. Simms."

Paul paused, attentively listening to an unheard voice before changing his tack. "Look, it is up to leaders like you, Jeff, and me, of course, to get the world going in the right direction. Let's be realistic. We need to be safe, secure, at peace. We can create a heaven on earth. For far too long, the common man has been enslaved by those who preach life everlasting in a perfect universe beyond our understanding. Bullshit. The time is now and the place is here. Paradise is at our fingertips. We thought you were part of the answer."

Jeff shook his head and tried to get his mind straight. Why was he suddenly so confused? Delamater wasn't making any sense. Though he hadn't answered Jeff's question, he acted as if he *had*. He hadn't. He'd avoided the question completely and then started blathering about heaven and life everlasting… *What the hell?* And who was Delamater working with? Who was *we*?

Morgan appeared to be half asleep. Jeff, on his own, felt ill equipped to handle the situation, but he wanted to protect Morgan from this crazy person. Suddenly, as though a projector had illuminated a screen in his mind, Jeff saw a tableau displaying the events of the last week. From this perspective, he could see the objective course of events, those that involved him personally and those that didn't. He perceived all the connections that had brought him to this house. He mentally traveled to the kitchen. He saw the people there. Besides Delamater's wife, he saw another woman about her same age and four teenagers, one who had just arrived. He saw that he would need to somehow protect them as well. Though the episode lasted only a second, when it was over, Delamater was raging.

"No!" he bellowed. His eyes wild and furious, he pushed his chair back and bounded out of the room. His roar, supernatural, shook the entire house. Jeff and Morgan leapt from their chairs and rushed after him as he bounded up the stairs toward Bethanne.

Mallorie, with Matt's help, had been about to get the tech back up when Alek arrived. Just a few minutes later, the room reverberated with Delamater's cry from above. They all moved at once toward the stairs but were repelled by an unseen force driving them backward. Donna's hands flew to the sides of her head as Bethanne's voice urgently demanded that she get the children to safety. Claire and Scott wildly searched each other's eyes as they heard their mother's voice directing them to go with Donna. Matt and Alek were listening to another voice—their father was shouting at them to go with Donna too. Donna bent down to Mallorie who lay unconscious on the floor. Matt, simultaneously seeing Mallorie, helped Donna move her to the divan in the room she had recently indicated to Jeff and Morgan. While the others followed them into the room, Donna covered Mallorie with a silk throw that had been stretched along the back of the divan.

Upstairs, in the fifth floor bedroom, Paul stood in the doorway locked in Bethanne's benevolent gaze. She stood in the middle of the room, her arms held out in a gesture of motherly comfort; a gesture Paul recognized from his childhood—one his own mother had offered when he'd been hurt and needed her consolation.

"Paul," Bethanne said. "Paul. Come in; let's talk."

Tears sprang to his eyes. *What have I done?* "Bethanne, I don't know what's happening to me ..." He was still standing in the doorway, but now he leaned toward her. "I…" His voice trailed off as he appeared to lose himself in his own thoughts.

"Paul," Bethanne said with urgency. "Paul, don't listen to—"

"Too late, darling," he said, smiling imperiously, "Did you honestly think it was going to be that easy? I gave you more credit than that." Paul left the doorway and approached Bethanne. "I have lots of work to do, and you could have been a part of it all. Now, instead, I'm going to have to get rid of you—and all the others like you. Now that my man Jeff created the tech, it'll be easy. You—what does he call you—anomalies—now you can't hide anymore. And because you've been such low-profile nobodies, the world will notice just enough to agree that we must stop all the violence. By the way, did you know that you were the best of that breed? The others are more of a nuisance; you are the big game. Soon, though, you'll all be gone and my victory will be complete."

"Paul," Bethanne intoned. "I love you."

"Stop saying my name," Paul sputtered.

"Paul, can you hear yourself? Did you know that you were going to be killing innocent people? Did you know that you aren't making the world safer at all; you're making it so much worse?"

"That's not a very sophisticated look at things. Think about every single cultural advance. Some people have had to be sacrificed for the greater good. The part you're missing is that when this is all over, no one will die at another's hand—ever. The world will be perfect."

"Perfect for who, Paul?"

"I said, stop saying my name. Goddamit, are you stupid? You're about to die."

"Paul, perfect for who? For Mallorie? For your baby?"

Paul waivered. *Mallorie. The baby.* His thoughts turned to them both, and, with Bethanne's help, he was filled with love and longing.

Bethanne moved fast. She grabbed him in her arms and

focused her entire energy into her embrace. She felt him go rigid as she entered in and swept through his being, filling every cell and every thought with her profound love.

Paul suddenly saw everything in perfect clarity. He saw with horror the Rival's countenance—his utter lack of warmth and joy. He looked into his eyes and saw the total condescension with which the Rival viewed humanity—viewed him. And then Paul chose love, and he was free. He collapsed to the floor, pulling Bethanne with him. The Rival, in a blast of pure rage, dove through Bethanne's defenses and punctured her beating heart.

The room became silent and peaceful, like the room of a sleeping newborn. Like heaven.

Downstairs, in the little room, the same unnatural silence and peace descended upon the others. *What's going on?* Matt's eyes asked Donna the question. She shook her head. *No idea.*

Matt put his hand on his aunt's shoulder. "Look," he said quietly, "I'm going upstairs to see what's going on. You guys stay here with Mrs. Delamater."

They all looked at him. Without saying a word, Claire turned and ran out of the room with Scott on her heels. Donna pulled away from Matt and ran out behind them.

"Don't go, Matt. I'm really scared," Alek pleaded.

"Yeah, me too, but I can't stay here; someone has to, though. Alek, it's got to be you. Mrs. Delamater shouldn't wake up alone, right?"

Alek looked at Mallorie's unconscious form and nodded.

Matt reached out and gave him a quick hug. "Good decision. I love you. I'll be back before you know it," he said racing out the door.

Scott and Claire were already out of sight on the staircase. The force that had blocked them previously was no longer working. Matt saw Donna round the corner; he bounded up the stairs after them.

On the fifth floor, the door to one of the bedrooms was ajar. Jeff and Morgan lay crumpled on the floor in front of it. Jeff moaned and opened his eyes; he turned his head to locate Morgan and watched as Morgan regained consciousness and met his gaze. "We're too late. We must be too late." Jeff groaned as he pushed himself to a sitting position against the wall.

Morgan turned his head away and lay still, looking up at the ceiling. He rose up on his elbows. "Too late for what? What the hell just happened?"

"I don't know."

"Where's Mom?" Claire screamed, gasping as she and Scott reached the top of the stairs. Two strange men lay on the floor outside the bedroom door.

Jeff struggled to his feet. "Wait a second. Stay back. I think your mom's probably in there... with Delamater, but we don't know what's happened. Let me go first."

Claire looked at him like he was insane and pitched herself into the room. Scott knocked Jeff's restraining arm aside to follow his sister.

"Mom!" Claire threw herself to the floor. "Mom! Mom! Oh my God! Someone, please help me."

Scott, now on his mother's other side, was yelling, shaking her. "Mom, are you ok? Mom, wake up! Answer me!"

Jeff pulled Morgan to his feet and they both stood, dazed, in the doorway taking in the scene before their eyes.

Donna squeezed around the two men and entered the room. She bent down over Bethanne and grasped her wrist. But she already knew. They all knew. Bethanne was dead.

"There're worse things than dying." Claire and Scott sat back on their heels; Donna dropped Bethanne's wrist. Bethanne was talking to them inside their heads, telling them not to worry, telling them she was going to be with David now. Asking them to be calm. Reassuring them that all was well and as it should be. Matt came into the room and lowered himself to the floor next to Claire.

He cocked his head sideways as he heard Bethanne's comforting words.

Nothing moved. Silence. Time stopped. The sun descended below the top of the western window and slanted a ray onto Bethanne's body. Morgan remembered Caravaggio's painting of Mary's death; he'd got it right. He and Jeff watched with heaviness, each of them amazed by the family's silent acceptance. They, too, heard Bethanne's words of comfort and promise. The veil between the worlds of the seen and the unseen had been lifted. Jeff looked down at Paul. Was he dead, too? He entered the room and crouched next to him. He lifted Paul's arm by the wrist. No pulse.

The afternoon sunlight brightened the room, getting the mood wrong, misapplying its joyful rays onto the room's occupants as they grappled with the complexities of what had happened. Then the light shifted and a different quality appeared. Bethanne and David joined together with Jack to lift the weight of the day's events from their children's shoulders. The room itself disappeared, lost in a haze of diffuse and warm brilliance, and they all were enveloped by the weightless grace that the three disembodied parents bestowed on them. Bethanne turned their attention to Paul, who had been callously abandoned by his benefactor. His death had been the gift Bethanne had hoped for; Paul was now safe.

Still nothing moved. And nothing recorded the lack of movement. Then, slowly, reality once again asserted itself. *The tech didn't get restored.* This was Jeff's first practical realization. This one vital fact would inform all that happened next.

A phone rang—Matt's. He fumbled to turn it off, but answered it when he saw the caller. It was Alek calling from downstairs. "Alek, hey. Listen, don't worry. We'll be down in just a minute. Sorry." He hung up.

Donna looked up. "Okay, so, um, hello," she said facing Jeff and Morgan. She focused on Morgan. "What happened in here?"

Morgan took a deep breath. "We don't know. Honestly. We

were knocked unconscious by something, some force, and we didn't even see inside the room. We came to just before the kids got here."

Donna looked cautiously into his eyes. "So you had nothing to do with this?"

"Hell no. No, we were meeting with Paul in his office when he suddenly yelled and rushed out of the room." He paused. "Who are you?"

Donna nodded. "Okay. God, this is so—I don't even know what to call it, but anyway, I'm Donna. I'm a friend of Bethanne's. I drove Bethanne here—from Iowa. We drove from Iowa. And now she's dead." She hesitated then added, "Oh, and this is Bethanne's son, Scott, and her daughter, Claire. And this is my nephew, Matt. And he has a brother, Alek."

Matt, nodded. "He's with Mrs. Delamater." He looked down at Paul. "Oh, shit—sorry—um, I've got to go. I've got to get back to Alek before she wakes up. What if she's already awake? What are we going to tell her?" he asked glancing down at Paul.

Jeff finally found his voice. "We have to figure that out; we have to figure out a lot of stuff." He looked at Donna. "It's nice to meet you," he said, awkward as ever. "I used to work for Delamater. My name's Jeff, and this is Morgan. We, uh, well, we actually followed you out here... it's a long story."

Donna eyed him carefully. *Friend or foe?* She felt an immediate and irresistible repulsion; something was off about this guy. "Wow, you followed us? All the way from Iowa? I'm definitely going to want to hear about that... Jeff.

"Right."

An embarrassed silence came between them, broken by Morgan clearing his throat. "Kids," he said looking at the three teenagers. "I think you should go downstairs and fill Alex in on everything. Let's hope Mrs. Delamater slept through it all. She must have or the two of them would be up here, right? Anyway, it's time for us adults to figure out what we're going to do about all this."

Claire and Scott stood up with Matt and looked one last time at Bethanne. "Don't worry, Mom," Claire said, "I've got this."

The others looked at her curiously. They weren't sure what she meant, but they saw that whatever it was she was agreeing to do, she seemed more than sufficiently equipped for it. Claire took Scott's hand in one of hers and Matt's in her other and squeezed them briefly before letting them go. She led them out of the room.

"So, you were following us?" Donna prodded after the kids were gone.

"Yeah. As I was saying, I worked for Mr. Delamater. I... well, I am the one who developed all the tech that keeps track of everybody."

"Hmm; nice work. Remind me not to thank you."

"Yeah, I know. It gets worse. A few days ago, I came up with something new—something that would eliminate the need for implants to keep track of people. It's because a guy died here in New York City; he was murdered, and Mr. Delamater demanded that I figure something out, and I just wanted to help keep that from happening again."

"That guy who died—he was my brother, Jack. He's fine, by the way. You know, there're worse things than death, Jeff. Like your tech, for example. Even though it might have worked, even though it might have kept people alive, the person who controls all the tech gets to decide who is dangerous—and that's a terrible responsibility for anyone. No way that won't eventually get abused... 'absolute power corrupts absolutely.'"

"'And great men are almost always bad men,'" Jeff added, finishing Lord Acton's famous quote.

Donna looked up and let her gaze hold Jeff's. She felt sorry for him in a way; he was too smart for his own good. All head, no heart: one of the recipes for unethical decisions. Science had been accelerating in this direction for a long time. "You have to make it right, Jeff," she said at last.

Jeff heard what she said, but he knew he couldn't make everything right. Too much had happened. The world was too reliant on tech. Too many big steps back would destroy countless lives. But too few would destroy the world. Jeff would be doing lots of unpaid labor now. Lots of daily undoing. Lots of tech diversions to deploy in front of those who wanted to keep track of everyone on the planet.

Donna glared at him, misunderstanding his silence. "Look, I know it's not possible to get rid of all the tech—"

Morgan interrupted. "But this new one, this new tech, Jeff, this one's got to go. Now."

Jeff answered without looking up. "Yeah. That'll go first. But it won't be the only thing to go, Donna." Now he glanced up at her, and saw her make an effort to hide the mistrust and contempt he inspired in her. His awkwardness intensified.

Morgan looked from one to the other. "Okay. That's all fine. We'll save the world one day, but, folks, I think we need to get out of here. Delamater is one of the most important people on earth— and he's dead. And his sister-in-law is also dead. What we have here are two dead bodies. What are we going to do?"

"And this, my friend, is *why* you're my friend. Keeping it real." Jeff reached into his pocket and turned on his computer. His first command, in less than a second, destroyed the tech that had identified the high-level EMF's, the so-called anomalies. It was that simple.

"You know," Jeff said, directing his thoughts toward Morgan. "I think it makes sense that we have another electrical event. Another fire. Derek Burns already suspects that Delamater was involved in the explosion on the west coast. Colorado is also in Burns' jurisdiction. He'll assume the obvious – that the two explosions—well, three if we go ahead with this—are connected somehow."

Ashes to ashes.

Jeff looked at Donna. "I'll explain all this later; then you'll understand why we were following you and Bethanne."

Donna stared at him for an intense second, then turned to say goodbye to the best friend she'd ever had.

Morgan joined the others standing at the bottom of the stairs outside the little room where Mallorie still lay unconscious. Claire put her hand on his arm. "We're going to take a private subway. Everyone needs to follow me."

"Will you help me get Mrs. Delamater?" Matt asked Morgan. "She's still on the sofa; she's been unconscious the whole time." Mallorie was breathing steadily, her face relaxed. What dreams were keeping her so completely at peace? Morgan lifted her up in his arms, and Claire led them all toward the elevator. "I'll be down in a second," she said after pushing the hidden button.

Jeff sat on the bottom step in the foyer aligning the house tech with his own. He looked up as Claire approached. "I know what you're going to do," she said matter-of-factly. "We can get out of here without anyone seeing us by using the subway. It will take us to City Hall. Go ahead and set things up; I'll wait." She sat down next to him and closed her eyes.

A devastating malfunction was about to take place. Jeff made sure that the explosion would be localized. Of course, the house had been fortified to repel an attack—it would now contain the explosion; no one in the neighborhood would be hurt.

Jeff took the necessary steps to overlay any record of their comings and goings. Claire's idea of taking the secret subway to City Hall was perfect. His tech—and his love of maps—had revealed a tunnel walkway that led to the R line, which they could take up to Union Square and then go wherever they decided to go. He reanimated two bots and had them deliver the Volvo and the r8 to a safe lot close by.

When they reached the subway car, Jeff smiled grimly at

Morgan. "Look at this."

Morgan looked down at Jeff's vid. A message from Simms. "Congratulations," it said.

"Who *is* this guy?"

"Damned if I know," Morgan replied. "He's good, though."

"Yeah, he's really good. I'd like to see him again; get to know him better."

"You should. I think he has a lot he'd like to tell you."

"You see me living in Colorado?" Jeff asked as they all settled into the car and it began to move forward. He had never thought of leaving his sanctuary on the west coast.

"Why not; I've heard that people who leave California always move to Colorado." They both grinned. Jeff remembered a sign: *Don't Californicate Colorado.*

"What about you?" Jeff was suddenly worried; he couldn't imagine his life without Morgan in it.

"You know, I think I might make it out to Colorado eventually. The girl of my dreams just lost her biggest job today—hounding Delamater about surveillance tech. Maybe she'll be ready to move on."

Girl of my dreams? Jeff looked in amazement at his friend. This was for real. It did not make him happy. Morgan smiled at him, but Jeff couldn't smile back. He felt betrayed. He looked at the others in the car, the strange group he'd been thrown in with, and realized that he had a sense of responsibility toward them—a sense he'd never employed before.

Morgan interrupted his reverie. "Jeff, hey, are you okay?" Jeff, grim, looked down at his computer. The car was speeding along now; they were safely away. Time to get serious. "Here goes," he intoned. He pushed a button and seconds later a muffled thud pulsed the windows.

Claire sat with Mallorie's head cradled in her lap. Mallorie would wake up soon; they'd have to tell her everything, and Claire's attention would, of necessity, focus on her aunt. She placed her hand on Mallorie's swollen belly and began her work with the baby. A girl. Alaina. A girl even stronger than Bethanne. Maybe even stronger than Claire herself. This girl would be needed, as all children are, to save the world.

ALAINA'S NOTE TO READER:

So now you know what really caused the explosion. You also know that Paul Delamater and Bethanne Amundson were not killed by the explosion; they were both already dead. Probably things could have been handled less destructively, but as you can see, Jeff and the others were reacting to an enormous amount of stress with no sleep…

ALAINA AMUNDSON

THE END

Acknowledgements

I would like to thank, first and foremost, my daughter, Kelly Grant, who is a writer of depth and eloquence, for her corrections, suggestions, and encouragement from the book's inception to its completion. Thank you to my early readers—and encouragers—Kerry Myers, Joan Newton, Carrie Ashby, Sophia Loosli, Mani Mekler-Baker and Paul Baker, Christopher K., Jamie Branker, Cindi Halverson, and my mom, Wanda Meyer. Thank you to Rebecca Varon for her encouragement to finally get the book out.

I want to especially acknowledge Marty Safir, who made the final edits and designed the book cover and the layout of the book, and performed all the tedious work of preparing it for publication. His belief in the book spurred me on in the final stretch.

A multitude of thanks to my many students for their insights and participation in the dystopian literature classes I've taught over the years.

This book would not have been possible without the love and support of my family—my children, Kelly and Connor, and especially my husband, Bill, who has always believed in me no matter what I've aimed for.